Highlander Entangled

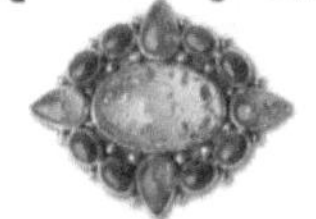

Stolen Highland Hearts
Book Two

JAYNE CASTEL

WINTER MIST
PRESS

All it takes is one careless encounter. She's lonely, he's reckless—it's a fatal combination. Passion and duty collide in Medieval Scotland.

Maggie Munro is widowed, barren, and a burden on her resentful uncle. Still grieving the man she loved and lost, she vows never to wed again. But then she meets a charming warrior at a king's council in Inverness.

Maggie doesn't realize it, but her life is about to get complicated.

Morgan Mackay—the younger brother of a Mackay chieftain—isn't looking for a wife. The Scottish parliament brings unpleasant surprises, yet amongst the turmoil, he finds himself irresistibly drawn to the lovely Maggie.

As the Scottish king deals out punishment to the warring northern clans, Maggie and Morgan throw caution to the wind for one steamy encounter ... but it has repercussions neither expect.

Steamy, emotional, and steeped in Scottish history, Jayne Castel's new series, set around the lives and loves of three Mackay siblings, will steal your heart.

Historical Romances by Jayne Castel

DARK AGES BRITAIN

The Kingdom of the East Angles series
Night Shadows (prequel novella)
Dark Under the Cover of Night (Book One)
Nightfall till Daybreak (Book Two)
The Deepening Night (Book Three)
*The Kingdom of the East Angles: The Complete
Series*

The Kingdom of Mercia series
The Breaking Dawn (Book One)
Darkest before Dawn (Book Two)
Dawn of Wolves (Book Three)
The Kingdom of Mercia: The Complete Series

The Kingdom of Northumbria series
The Whispering Wind (Book One)
Wind Song (Book Two)
Lord of the North Wind (Book Three)
The Kingdom of Northumbria: The Complete Series

DARK AGES SCOTLAND

The Warrior Brothers of Skye series
Blood Feud (Book One)
Barbarian Slave (Book Two)
Battle Eagle (Book Three)
The Warrior Brothers of Skye: The Complete Series

The Pict Wars series
Warrior's Heart (Book One)
Warrior's Secret (Book Two)
Warrior's Wrath (Book Three)
The Pict Wars: The Complete Series

Novellas
Winter's Promise

MEDIEVAL SCOTLAND

The Brides of Skye series
The Beast's Bride (Book One)
The Outlaw's Bride (Book Two)
The Rogue's Bride (Book Three)
The Brides of Skye: The Complete Series

The Sisters of Kilbride series
Unforgotten (Book One)
Awoken (Book Two)
Fallen (Book Three)
Claimed (Epilogue novella)

The Immortal Highland Centurions series
Maximus (Book One)
Cassian (Book Two)
Draco (Book Three)
The Laird's Return (Epilogue festive novella)

Stolen Highland Hearts series
Highlander Deceived (Book One)
Highlander Entangled (Book Two)
Highlander Forbidden (Book Three)

Epic Fantasy Romances by Jayne Castel

Light and Darkness series
Ruled by Shadows (Book One)
The Lost Swallow (Book Two)
Path of the Dark (Book Three)
Light and Darkness: The Complete Series

All characters and situations in this publication are fictitious, and any resemblance to living persons is purely coincidental.

Highlander Entangled, by Jayne Castel

ISBN: 978-0-473-56161-1 (paperback)

Published by Winter Mist Press

Edited by Tim Burton
Cover design by Winter Mist Press
Cover photography courtesy of www.shutterstock.com
Brooch image courtesy of www.pixabay.com

Highland Fairy Lullaby, adapted from
www.rampantscotland.com/songs/blsongs_lullaby.htm

Visit Jayne's website: www.jaynecastel.com

***

To Tim, my hero.

***

"You can only lose what you cling to."
—*Buddha*

1

I WILL WED NO ONE

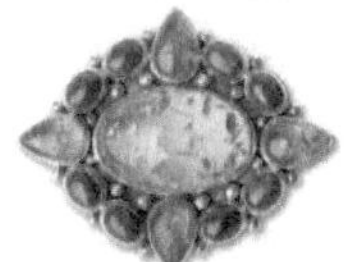

Caisteal Nan Corr
Strathnaver, Scotland

Spring, 1427

"YE ARE A burden to me, woman. I cannot wait to be rid of ye."

Maggie glanced up from spreading honey onto a wedge of bannock, her gaze alighting on her uncle's truculent face.

Indeed, Graeme Ross's expression across the table matched the bitterness of his words this morning.

He'd been reading a missive that had just been delivered by one of his men. Maggie thought him engrossed in it, so this outburst caught her by surprise.

However, his sentiment hadn't.

Her uncle made no secret that he didn't want her at Caisteal Nan Corr—a widower himself, he'd never shown any pity for the fact that she still mourned her husband.

Graeme's thick fingers clenched around the parchment he'd just rolled back up. Glaring, he picked up the scroll and waved it at her. "And finally, the moment has come. The king has called a council of the northern chiefs at Inverness. I'm going ... and so are ye. If I can't find a man who'll take ye off my hands there, I never will."

Cold washed over Maggie.

Slowly, deliberately, she lowered the knife she'd been using.

The news that King James was calling the Highland lairds to parliament wasn't surprising—the feuding had gotten out of control in the last few years—however, her uncle's callous words reminded her, yet again, of how little value she was to him.

"I don't wish to wed, uncle," she said, her voice cool and low. How many times had she told him this? And yet he refused to heed her. "And if my presence here offends ye so, I can go to Iona and take my vows."

This comment earned her a snort of derision. "Like yer fair sister?" His mouth twisted then. "Traitorous slut that she is!"

Maggie sucked in a deep breath. Her sister's behavior hadn't pleased her either, although his language was unnecessarily vulgar. Rhianna, who'd been an oblate at Iona nunnery, had run off with her lover. Even months later, the Highlands still whispered of the great scandal that the 'Jewel of the Highlands' had caused. Right now, Rhianna should have been wed to Connor Mackay of Farr—but instead, she'd worked a deception with a woman named Keira Gunn, who agreed to wed Mackay in her place.

And even more incredible, Keira Gunn was still wed to the chieftain. Her ruse had been exposed last autumn, at Samhuinn, yet Connor Mackay had surprised everyone by taking her home with him, and it was rumored she now carried his bairn.

Graeme Ross had raged about the outcome for weeks afterward. And even now, any mention of Rhianna—who was yet to be found—soured his mood.

"The nunnery is out of the question," her uncle continued, waggling that damn missive at her as if she were an errant bairn. "The prioress is a greedy woman and demands a 'gift' from me to the nunnery. Thanks to the actions of yer sister, the sum she requires is greater than that of *two* dowries." His gaze narrowed, boring into her, as he continued. "At Inverness, ye are to find yerself a husband from one of the allied clans ... a man of land and influence."

Maggie glared back at him. The chill that had settled in the pit of her belly now turned into a dull ache.

Her uncle spoke as if she had some value as a wife. But they both knew she didn't. Aye, she had a pretty face and a good figure—but she couldn't bear children. Not now.

"And will such a man want a woman who is barren?" she asked, her voice clipped.

Graeme Ross's meaty fist slammed down upon the table, causing the entire solar where they sat breaking their fast to shudder. "Ye will keep that detail to yerself, niece," he barked. "I will not have ye ruining this chance." He gestured to the doorway then. "Go on, get out of my sight. We leave at first light tomorrow, and I expect ye to pack yer prettiest kirtles." His gaze raked over her then. "Put away that crow's garb. I don't want to see ye wearing it again."

Of course, he was referring to the widow's black that Maggie had worn ever since her husband, Campbell, had died.

When Maggie didn't move, her uncle's face turned an ugly red. "Go ... now," he growled, "before I take ye by the ear and drag ye upstairs."

Jaw clenched, Maggie rose to her feet and walked stiffly from the solar. However, instead of going upstairs to her bed-chamber to begin packing, she picked up her skirts and fled from the tower house.

Ignoring the curious glances from the men who were shoeing horses in the bailey, Maggie ran across the cobbled space and through a wide stone arch out into the meadows beyond. The small, rectangular hold behind her sat upon an island surrounded by a swift river that flowed into a kyle to the east.

Breathing hard, Maggie took the path through the rippling grass and wildflowers to where a wood bridge spanned the River Corr. She halted in the middle of the bridge and leaned against the siding, her fingers curling around the rough wooden edge.

It was a glorious spring morning. The sun was warm upon her back, the sky above was robin's egg blue, and the air smelled sweet with the promise of the coming summer. Yet Maggie barely noticed it, such was her turmoil.

"Curse ye, uncle," she muttered to the croaking frogs, and to the dragonflies that flitted amongst the reeds beneath the bridge. "Ye will not marry me off like a fattened ewe." Her throat constricted then as thoughts of Campbell Munro surfaced.

Her breathing quickened.

Her husband had been gone two years now, killed in a skirmish against the Sutherlands—but she still missed him with a constant ache in her chest. She'd only just physically recovered from losing their bairn—and was still coming to terms with the devastating news that she could never bear another child—when he'd ridden out on that fateful day.

She'd never forget the last time she saw her husband. He'd turned in the saddle, the wind whipping the dark hair around his face, and smiled at her. Campbell had then raised a hand in farewell. A moment later, he'd been gone, the tattoo of his horse's hooves echoing through the crisp morning air.

Tears stung the back of Maggie's eyes at the image burned there. They weren't just tears of grief and regret—but of anger. She was tired of her uncle's callous treatment. She was tired of feeling as if she was an encumbrance. If Campbell's kin had welcomed her, she'd have stayed with the Munros. However, after his death, they'd asked her to leave.

And she'd found herself back here, the place where she'd grown up. A place full of memories of her parents and sister. All of them were gone now, and although her sister wasn't dead, she might as well have been. She'd never been close to Rhianna; the pair of them had always clashed, but after her escape from the nunnery, her sister was truly lost to her.

Maggie had never felt so alone. But even so, she wouldn't bend to Graeme Ross's bullying ways. He could shout, threaten, or even raise his fists to her, but it would make no difference.

"I will wed no one," she vowed aloud to the rushing waters beneath the bridge. "Uncle can drag me to Inverness and parade me before the chieftains, but he can't make me take another husband. I will not. I cannot."

2

A MEETING IN THE BAILEY

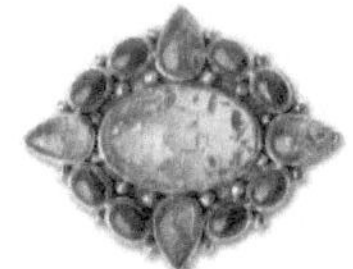

THE SIGHT OF the castle, its crenelated walls and towers outlined against the rose-pink sky, made a relieved smile curve Morgan Mackay's lips.

At last. The journey from Farr Castle in the far north-west of the Highlands to Inverness had taken longer than usual—for their party was a large one. Morgan was looking forward to a tankard of ale and a comfortable bed.

He slowed his courser to a walk and glanced down at where his wolfhound, Gritta, loped next to him. After a long day's travel, the dog's pink tongue lolled from its mouth. Just like him, the hound would be grateful to reach Inverness.

Morgan's gaze lifted once more to the fortress rising before him. Perched high above the eastern banks of the River Ness, just south of the cluster of peaked roofs that was Inverness town, the castle commanded a panoramic view. A flag—a white cross upon a blue background—fluttered from one of the towers in a gentle breeze. It was the flag of Saint Andrew, the patron saint of Scotland.

Morgan's smile faded a little at the sight of it. *Scotland.* Sometimes he felt as if this land were merely a colony of England. Over the last century, too many puppets had sat upon the Scottish throne. Their current ruler, James, wasn't one of those—as he was the rightful heir of the House of Stewart—but he'd lived for many years as an English hostage. James had only been permitted to take the throne once King Henry of England deigned to release him.

Morgan's brow furrowed. In truth, he had little loyalty to Scotland. It was his clan he cared about. The Mackays were everything to him. His allegiance to his clan-chief would always come first.

"I know that look." A voice drew him from his introspection. Morgan tore his attention from the castle to see his brother, Connor, watching him intently. "Ye are imagining stabbing yer dirk into George Gunn's belly, aren't ye?"

Morgan snorted. He hadn't been, although the thought certainly appealed. "I may not need to," he replied with a grin, "if the king deals that bastard out the punishment he deserves."

"Just as long as *we're* left alone," Connor said, his tone dry.

Morgan cocked an eyebrow. "The Mackays of Farr won't be dealt any harsh justice."

Connor held his gaze. "Why's that? We fought at Harpsdale like the others."

"Aye ... and we lost our laird," Morgan replied. His mood shadowed at these words. They were a reminder of that brutal day nearly a year ago now, when the Mackays and the Gunns had clashed—a vicious slaughter that had yielded no victor.

A slaughter that had taken their father.

"Aye, but will that be punishment enough for the king?" Connor asked, his voice suddenly subdued. He too would be remembering the sight of Rory Mackay screaming as he doubled over in agony. The memory would haunt Morgan till the end of his days.

He held his brother's gaze, troubled by the thought that Connor, as chieftain of the Mackays of Farr, might be punished for their family's role in the feuding with the Gunns. "It should be."

The brothers fell silent then, the 'clip-clop' of their horses' hooves the only sound upon the narrow road that ran alongside the sparkling waters of the Ness. They led a party of twenty, with a cart bringing up the rear.

Connor urged his roan stallion, Thunder, into a swift canter, leading the way toward the castle. Morgan followed upon his dapple-grey gelding, Archer. The party left Castle Road now, taking the steep path that led to the gatehouse above. The gates were open this evening and the portcullis raised, for they wouldn't be the only travelers arriving. The first session of parliament had been called for the following noon.

Clattering into the outer bailey—a wide, cobbled space flanked by low, thatched stone buildings—the Mackays drew up their lathered mounts. A number of men and horses already filled the bailey. The Mackays of Farr wouldn't be the only members of their clan in attendance either. Morgan wondered if their clan-chief had arrived yet from Castle Varrich.

"We should be just in time for supper," his cousin Kennan announced, swinging down from his horse.

"Always thinking of yer belly, husband," Kennan's wife chastised with an arch smile, as he helped her down from her palfrey.

"Aye, lass ... and of yers." Kennan cupped Cait's gently curving stomach. She was two moons gone with bairn, but unlike Connor's wife, Keira, who had made the journey in a cart at the back of the escort, Cait had insisted she could ride to Inverness. She'd spent the day traveling alongside Jaimee, Morgan's sister.

Connor dismounted his stallion and strode to the cart, helping his pregnant wife disembark. Keira was very evidently 'with bairn'. However, the babe wasn't due for another three months yet, and so Connor had allowed his wife to accompany them on this journey.

Still seated astride Archer, Morgan observed the tenderness and care his brother took with Keira. Her gaze gleamed as she wrapped her arms around Connor's waist and raised her face for a kiss. Smiling down at her, Connor reached out and brushed a lock of golden-brown hair off his wife's cheek.

The pair had been wedded around seven moons, yet the bond between them was something that made even Morgan take notice.

He'd never seen the like.

Morgan smiled at the irony of how things had turned out. He had no problem with Keira these days, although the ruse she'd woven in order to wed his brother had been difficult to pardon at first.

Keira was a Gunn, a member of one of the clans they'd been feuding with for years now. Not only that, she'd married Connor while pretending to be a woman named Rhianna Ross. The ruse had been exposed at Samhuinn, and the aftermath had shocked them all.

Connor had been supposed to deliver Keira back to her kin at Camster broch on Gunn lands. But upon meeting with the woman's awful parents, he'd changed his mind and taken her home to Farr Castle instead, where he'd eventually found it in his heart to forgive her.

Averting his gaze, as Connor and Keira kissed, Morgan's smile turned wistful. He didn't covet his brother's wife—and indeed didn't wish for a wife at all—but there was something about their happiness that made his carefree existence seem a little hollow.

Shrugging off the thought, Morgan loosed his feet from the stirrups and stroked Archer's sweaty neck. Wedded bliss be damned, what he needed at present was a tall tankard of ale and a plate of food. Kennan was right: they were in time for supper.

He was about to swing down from his horse and lead Archer into the stables, when barking erupted behind him.

Morgan tensed. *Gritta.*

Supper temporarily forgotten, he twisted in the saddle, his gaze traveling to the opposite side of the outer bailey.

Maggie didn't usually mind dogs. But this one was a huge beast, with a grizzled, grey coat and a snarl that turned her pony witless.

Tired after the long journey, she'd followed her uncle's party into the outer bailey and had been about to dismount when the hound appeared from nowhere.

The dog's barking echoed off the surrounding stone now as it bounded toward them. An instant later, Walnut, Maggie's sturdy garron, let out a shrill whinny and reared.

Cursing, Maggie threw herself forward, clutching at Walnut's coarse mane.

But it was too late.

Her placid Highland pony never reared, but today—in the face of the hell-wolf—he did.

The next thing Maggie knew, she was pitched backward, off the garron's back and into the air.

She hit the cobbles hard, falling on her side, and just missed being trodden on by one of Walnut's large feathered hooves. The garron danced sideways and kicked out at the wolfhound's snapping jaws.

Winded, pain-lancing down her right-side, Maggie lay there, while around her the outer bailey rang with angry male voices and the clatter of startled horses' hooves.

"Gritta!" A powerful male voice cut through the rest. "Stand down!"

Maggie watched dust-covered boots stride past her, and then the snarling subsided to a yelp. Clenching her jaw, she rolled onto her back to see a tall man with shaggy dark-blond hair haul the hound back from her pony and scruff it.

Submissive now, the beast cowered before he sent it scampering off across the bailey.

Only then did the dog's owner glance her way. Piercing green eyes, the color of a pine-thicket, met her gaze.

3

REMEMBERING

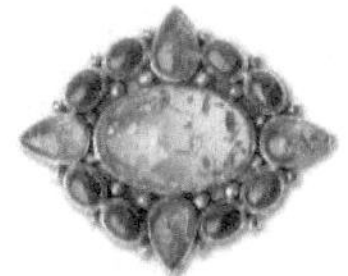

RECOGNITION FILTERED THROUGH Maggie as she stared up at the man.

I've seen him before.

"Are ye hurt?" the warrior asked, before she had the chance to place him. The anger had faded from his voice, concern replacing it. He crossed to Maggie then and hunkered down, his gaze sweeping along the length of her.

"What do ye think?" Pain and embarrassment turned her voice acerbic. The journey had wearied her, and she didn't want to be here anyway. This was the last thing she needed.

However, Maggie's snappish reply didn't disturb him. He merely cocked his head, those penetrating eyes never leaving hers as he waited for her to continue.

"My side hurts ... as does my wrist," Maggie muttered. That and her pride. The bailey was crammed full of newcomers this evening. Everyone had witnessed her tumble. "But I don't think anything's broken."

The warrior nodded. He was handsome, with a straight nose, high cheekbones, and a sensual mouth.

Again, a sense she'd already met him tickled her.

Where had she seen this man?

"I apologize for Gritta," he replied. "She doesn't usually behave like that."

Gritta. Maggie grimaced. The name meant 'strong'—an apt title indeed for such a fierce hound.

"Well, I suggest ye leave the hell-beast at home in future. My fall could've been a lot worse." Wincing, Maggie tried to push herself up.

The man flashed her a contrite smile. "Aye … maybe I should have." He then held out a hand to her. "Come on … let us see if ye can stand."

Maggie hesitated a moment.

This man's dog had caused this incident. She wasn't sure she wanted his help. However, it would appear churlish to refuse him, and so she reached out with her uninjured arm and took his hand.

And when she did, the feel of his fingers clasping hers, warm and strong, sent a flutter through her belly. It was a strange sensation, yet one Maggie recognized in an instant.

Attraction—it had been a while since she'd felt that pull.

Gently, he pulled Maggie to her feet.

Standing before him, she craned her neck up to meet his eye. The warrior, clad in chamois braies, hunting boots, and a loose brown lèine unlaced at the neck, towered over her—although that wasn't unusual. Most folk did. Unlike her tall, willowy younger sister, Maggie stood at only five feet.

It was then Maggie noted that he wore a clan sash across his chest. It was not the red and green of the Ross clan, but bands of emerald green and sea-blue.

This man was a Mackay.

Cold seeped over Maggie then, and she finally realized where she'd seen him.

Last year, at Samhuinn.

She and her uncle had traveled to Castle Varrich to see Rhianna and her new husband. But instead of spying her sister standing at the tall blond chieftain's side, Maggie had looked into the face of a stranger.

This man was brother to the chieftain of the Mackays of Farr. She remembered him standing nearby as Keira

Gunn's ruse was unmasked, a look of horror on his face that had mirrored her own.

They hadn't spoken that night, but she'd felt his gaze upon her later—after the Gunn interloper had been escorted into the castle by Connor Mackay. Morgan Mackay had actually moved in her direction later in the evening, but the clan-chief's brash son, Niel, had beaten him to it.

At the same moment that Maggie recognized him, realization also dawned in Morgan Mackay's eyes.

An uncomfortable pause stretched out between them, but then he inclined his head, a boyish—and devastating—smile stretching his beautifully molded lips. "It's Maggie, isn't it?"

"Niece!"

Graeme Ross's voice boomed across the bailey. Swiftly releasing Morgan's hand, for she realized then that she still held it, Maggie took a step back from him and twisted left.

Rubbing her injured wrist, her gaze settled upon her uncle. Still seated upon his heavy black courser, he'd witnessed the whole incident but hadn't made a move to assist her.

Her uncle's expression was thunderous. His dark brows had drawn into a single, disapproving line. "Ye do realize whom ye are talking to, woman?"

"Greetings, Ross," Morgan Mackay called out. Glancing back at him, Maggie noted the cool smile on the warrior's lips, the mocking glint in his eye. "Looking hale and hearty I see."

Graeme Ross curled his lip, not bothering to return the greeting. Instead, he kept his baleful stare upon Maggie. "Take yer garron into the stables."

Maggie didn't do as bid. Instead, she stared back at her uncle, resentment boiling in her belly. She wouldn't be ordered around like a cur. So she remained there, unmoving, as she continued to gently rub the arm she'd fallen on.

She'd have a mighty bruise there by the following day.

"Ross," Connor Mackay's voice intruded then. All gazes shifted to where the tall blond laird walked across the bailey toward them, although Maggie's attention quickly settled upon the regal brown-haired woman at his side.

Keira Gunn's belly hadn't been swollen the last time they'd met.

The rumors were indeed true. Not only had Connor Mackay kept this woman as his wife, but he'd also planted a seed in her womb.

And he'd brought her to Inverness.

Maggie couldn't help it; her gaze remained upon Keira's belly. A pain rose under her ribs then, a twisting sensation.

Once, she too had carried a bairn. Once, she too had hoped for a happy, contented life with a husband she adored. But then she'd lost everything.

Her uncle's muttered oath jolted Maggie from painful memories. "How dare ye bring that woman … that *deceiver* … here," he growled.

Keira halted at her husband's side, her cheeks flushing. Next to her, Connor Mackay's handsome face hardened.

"I dare because she is my *wife*," he replied coolly. "Insult her again, Ross, and I'll knock ye off yer horse."

Tension pulsed through the bailey at these words. Around them, the clamor of men, horses, and milling hounds quietened. Gazes, alive with curiosity, watched on.

With a sinking belly, Maggie realized that whispers of last year's scandal would follow them for the rest of their stay at Inverness thanks to this scene. She'd dared hope the matter would have been forgotten by now—but thanks to her uncle's belligerence, it wouldn't be.

Moments passed, and then Graeme Ross growled another curse, spat on the cobbles, and whirled his horse around, angling it toward the stables on the far side of the courtyard.

"Maggie," he barked. "Follow me. Now!"

Morgan watched the enraged Ross chieftain and his comely niece disappear inside the stables.

His gaze lingered on Lady Munro's small figure. Dressed in flowing blue, her dark hair braided in a long plait that fell between her shoulder blades, Morgan hadn't initially recognized the woman. Last time he'd seen her, months earlier, she'd caught his eye. But she'd been clad in widow's black then.

Watching her disappear through the stable door with her pony, Morgan's mouth lifted at the corners. Clearly, the mourning period was over—and the woman was even lovelier than he remembered.

Morgan's gaze traveled then to the shadow of the guard tower, where Gritta was hiding, and he frowned. Morgan never went anywhere without his faithful wolfhound. He'd raised Gritta from a tiny pup after her mother had rejected her. Now, five years later, man and beast had formed an unbreakable bond.

Yet he didn't know what had come over his wolfhound this evening. Gritta was used to being around horses and people. She hadn't attacked Maggie's garron, but she'd deliberately worried it. A fall on hard cobbles was painful. Despite the blistering tone she'd used with him, Morgan had seen the pain shadowing her sea-blue eyes.

"Maybe I shouldn't have come." Keira's voice intruded then.

Morgan turned to see his sister-by-marriage was also staring in the direction of the stables. A nerve flickered under one eye. "I thought Graeme Ross might have softened toward me ... but it appears he hasn't."

"It's not ye, lass," Morgan replied, flashing her a sympathetic smile. "The man is bitter over his niece running off and humiliating him. Ye are just a reminder."

Next to Keira, Connor was scowling. "I won't stand for his insults," he murmured. His brother's voice was soft, dangerous. "Graeme Ross needs to tread carefully over the next few days."

Morgan nodded. His attention shifted then to the stares from the warriors around them. All the northern clans were amassing here: Sutherland, More, Forbes, Ross, MacDonald, Leslie, Murray, Macmaken, Gunn, and Mackay, among others.

Of course, this was no summer gathering amongst friends. For the first time in years, feuding clans would be forced to eat, drink, sleep, and meet under the same roof—under the watchful eye of the king.

Tension filtered over him when his gaze settled upon plaids that he'd only ever seen on the battlefield.

If they didn't want fighting to erupt within the walls of Inverness Castle, they would *all* have to tread carefully indeed.

4

ACROSS THE HALL

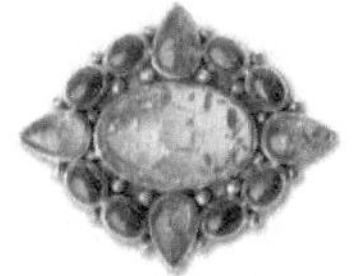

"LADY ROSS." ROBERT Mackay, the laird of Balnakeil broch, favored Maggie with a wink from across the table. The great hall of Inverness Castle vibrated with the boom of laughter and conversation, and so he had to raise his voice to be heard. "Ye are looking bonny indeed."

Maggie didn't smile in return. Instead, she cursed her uncle for insisting she make an effort with her appearance this evening. She'd donned her best plum-colored kirtle. Her maid, Aileana, had pulled her hair back from her face in an elaborate style that left curls spilling down her back.

It felt strange to be wearing such attire. After two years dressed in widow's black, Maggie was used to being invisible—and she'd preferred it that way. Having men comment on her appearance was tiresome indeed.

How weary she was of her uncle's meddling. Of course, he was desperate. Although they hadn't discussed it, they both knew that at twenty-six Maggie was heading toward the age where few men would want her.

This is his last chance to be rid of me, Maggie thought, her mouth thinning. *But if I can thwart him ... if I can get through this parliament without finding myself a husband ... he'll be stuck with me.* A little of the weariness that pressed down upon Maggie this evening eased as hope flickered in her breast. *Perhaps then, he'll pay the sum the priory demands.*

"Aye." Robert's younger brother, Duncan, grinned from next to him. "Good to see ye are done mourning yer husband."

This comment brought a snort from Robert, while Maggie tensed. Heat ignited in her belly.

They spoke as if Campbell Munro was an irrelevance, some incident from her past that was best forgotten. They didn't even refer to him by name. These were men who saw death regularly and had meted it out a number of times as well. The dead were ghosts to them, only the living mattered.

Drawing in a deep breath as she reined in her reaction, Maggie rubbed her left arm. It still ached after her tumble. She'd tried to use the accident to beg off dinner, but her uncle wouldn't hear of it. She needed to be visible.

As her temper cooled, weariness pressed down upon her once more. It was all too much. She longed to be alone in the sanctuary of her bed-chamber, not conversing with these men.

Swallowing hard, Maggie focused on the platters the servants had just set down upon the table. Despite her mood, a long day in the saddle had given her an appetite. But hungry or not, she hadn't wanted to join the clans for supper in the great hall.

"Pay those oafs no mind, Lady Munro." A smooth voice intruded then, and Maggie glanced up to see that Niel Mackay had taken his place upon the bench-seat beside her. "My clansmen have clearly forgotten their manners this eve."

Her uncle had ensured that Maggie was seated away from the Mackays of Farr—the family in question sat on the opposite side of the hall this evening—but he didn't have an issue with her talking to the other Mackays.

Niel held her gaze for a moment, a smile stretching his lips. He had penetrating blue eyes, chiseled good-looks, and short dark hair.

Aye, Niel Mackay was attractive—and yet there was a wolfishness to him that she didn't trust. All the same, he'd addressed her as 'Lady Munro', giving her more respect than the other men at the table had.

Maggie forced a tight smile. "Thank ye, Niel."

Niel's smile widened. "However, ye *are* looking comely this evening. Plum suits ye."

Maggie clenched her jaw. *Mother Mary, how will I weather this?*

"I take it ye aren't keen to be here?" Niel observed, his gaze never leaving her face.

Maggie frowned. "What gives ye that idea?"

"Yer expression says it all."

"I'm not a particularly social person," Maggie lied. Once, when Campbell had been alive, she had been. They'd often held feasts and dances for friends and family. "And I'm not fond of crowds."

Another falsehood. Before losing her husband, she'd loved attending clan gatherings and games with Campbell. She'd started to miss such events of late, although this parliament in Inverness was another matter entirely. She had no wish to be paraded before a host of unwed sons of clan-chiefs and chieftains.

"That's a pity, for it would be a shame for ye to lock yerself away," Niel replied. "Ye are still young enough to start again should ye wish to."

Maggie reached for her pewter goblet of wine. "I take it ye and yer kin are all in good health?" she asked, deliberately steering the topic of conversation away from herself. The delicious-looking meal suddenly lost its appeal, despite her growling belly.

"We are all well. Thank ye for asking." He flashed her a grin and helped himself to three large slices of venison.

"Is the clan-chief not a little nervous about this parliament?" she asked then, taking a sip of sloe wine.

Niel's smile slipped. "Why would he be?"

Maggie inclined her head. It always astounded her how little some men thought women knew about politics. On her visit to Castle Varrich the previous autumn, she'd noted how meek Niel's mother was; no doubt, she'd never offered an opinion in her life. But Maggie wasn't such a woman.

She had opinions, and she voiced them.

Maybe my mouth will keep my suitors at bay. She took another sip of wine, enjoying the warmth as it slid down her throat. It took the edge off things, just a little. "The king will want justice for Harpsdale," she continued. "Will he not?"

Niel's expression shuttered. "Aye," he replied warily. "From the Gunns."

"Does the king favor us Mackays then, Niel?" Robert Mackay asked, a goading tone to his voice. He now wore a sour expression, for Niel's presence at the table made it difficult for him to flirt with Maggie.

Niel picked up his goblet, holding it aloft in a mocking salute. "Of course ... why wouldn't he?"

Maggie helped herself to some food, ignoring the banter and boasts that crossed the table around her. She hoped that Niel would be taken up with other talk and leave her be for the moment. However, he soon turned his attention upon her once more.

"Have yer uncle's men tracked down yer sister yet?"

Maggie swallowed a mouthful of venison. She then shook her head. "She's hidden herself well it seems."

"So she is lost to ye?"

Maggie nodded. Her belly clenched. How had Niel managed to flip the conversation back to her so easily?

"I hear yer uncle still bears the Mackays of Farr a grudge over the whole incident," he continued. "Do ye resent them also?"

The question was a direct challenge.

Maggie glanced then, over at where the subject of their conversation sat. The Mackays of Farr were on the other side of the hall, although there was a gap between the tables that afforded her a direct view of them.

Connor Mackay sat with his wife, their heads bent together as they talked. Of course, Rhianna should have been sitting at Connor Mackay's side tonight, not Keira.

"I'll admit it was a shock to see them together," she murmured. "Yet they look so happy ... I can't be bitter about that."

She studied the laird and his wife a moment longer, before her attention settled upon Connor's younger brother.

Morgan Mackay. Owner of the hell-hound.

Maggie's mouth pursed. Her wrist ached dully now, a reminder of that incident. And yet, her gaze lingered on him all the same. The man was comely. His hair was a shade or two darker than his siblings', and unlike his brother, he didn't wear it long but cut in a disheveled style that kept falling over his eyes.

Sensing that he was being scrutinized, Morgan glanced up. Across the crowded great hall of Inverness Castle, their gazes met.

Met and held. And then, Morgan favored her with a lazy smile.

Irritated, Maggie broke the stare.

Arrogant churl. He clearly imagines himself as The Lord's gift to women. Now he'll think he has another admirer.

A man like Morgan would be used to drawing admiring looks from women, and would no doubt be preening after catching her looking his way.

Making a mental note to avoid Morgan Mackay during the rest of her stay in Inverness, Maggie turned back to Niel. Her heart jolted against her ribs when she realized he was watching her, his expression veiled. No doubt, he'd seen the direction of her stare and noted how his clansman had looked her way.

She expected a sardonic comment, yet he merely raised a questioning eyebrow and favored her with a smirk.

Grinding her teeth, Maggie stared down at her supper. Lord, how this all vexed and exhausted her. She longed to be upstairs, chatting to Aileana as her maid brushed out her hair. She wanted only solitude and peace—to climb into bed, pull up the covers, and pretend the rest of the world didn't exist for a short while.

She didn't want to be sitting in this den of wolves—and unwittingly encouraging some of them.

Patience, she counseled herself. *Just a few days and uncle will be forced to abandon this farce.*

But until then, she had to be on her guard.

5

GOOD NIGHT, MAGGIE

"MAGGIE ... WAIT," A male voice hailed Maggie as she hurried away from the great hall. Supper had seemed to go on for an age. At the first opportunity, as barrels of ale and mead were rolled out for a night of drinking, she'd risen from the table, bid Niel, Robert, and Duncan 'good night', and slipped out of the hall.

However, it appeared that someone had followed her.

Turning, Maggie tensed at the sight of Morgan Mackay approaching. He was smiling, and walked toward her with a long, loose-limbed stride.

Maggie sighed. This man was the last person she wanted to see at present. She'd planned on actively avoiding him, but here he was following her.

Couldn't he at least have the manners to address her formally, as Niel had? His familiarity rankled. "It's 'Lady Munro'," she reminded him coolly. "What do ye want?"

His smile slipped, just a little, and he came to a halt a few feet distant. "Apologies ... Lady Munro ... I don't wish to disturb ye." He spread his hands in a placating gesture. "But I didn't get a chance earlier ... to apologize properly. Ye could have split yer head open on the cobbles."

"Aye, I could have."

His brow furrowed. "Yer arm ... have ye had it tended to?"

Maggie shook her head. "There's no need. There'll be bruising … nothing more." To illustrate her point, she drew up the bell-sleeve of her kirtle and held out her forearm so he could see the mottled skin that had come up.

His frown deepened. Two strides brought him up close to her, and an instant later, he gently took hold of her wrist and raised her arm further so he could examine it.

His fingers were pleasantly warm and strong around her wrist, although Maggie fought the urge to yank her arm away. This was far too bold of him. To mask her discomfort, she scowled. "What are ye doing?"

He glanced up, his gaze snaring hers. "Ye really should get this seen to."

Maggie huffed. "I shall ask my maid to rub a salve on it before bed."

"See that ye do." The moment lengthened between them, before his mouth quirked. "As I said, I am sorry for Gritta's behavior. She never disgraces herself like that."

"And where is the beast now?" Maggie disengaged her wrist from his gentle grasp and stepped back. She'd encountered his type before. Morgan Mackay wielded boyish charm like a dirk-blade, but she had no time for it. The man was a nuisance.

His mouth curved into another affable smile. "Locked in my bed-chamber … out of mischief."

"That's a relief to hear," she replied, her tone dry now. She took another step back, widening the distance between them.

Morgan inclined his head. "So, my hound and I are forgiven then?"

Maggie drew in a deep, steadying breath, in an attempt to settle her rising irritation. "Aye," she replied, her tone clipped.

They lapsed into silence then. It was late. Night had long since fallen outdoors, and the sconces upon the walls cast long shadows across the hallway. Any moment now, others would emerge from the great hall and spy the two of them alone.

Maggie didn't want anyone to think Morgan was courting her.

"Will that be all, Mackay?" she asked, folding her arms across her chest. "It has been a long day."

He nodded, his mouth curving once more.

Maggie clenched her jaw. The man was insufferable—and she had almost reached the limits of her patience this evening. "Good night, then," she said, her tone clipped.

His gaze remained upon her, his green eyes dark in the hallowed light of the hallway. "Good night, Maggie. Sleep well."

Maggie let herself into her bed-chamber and closed the door firmly.

Good night, Maggie. Sleep well.

The words had been innocently spoken, and yet the man had virtually purred them. Aye, he was a seducer all right.

And he was wasting his time.

Maggie muttered a curse under her breath. She doubted Morgan Mackay had any interest in her as a potential wife; he was just a flirt. Even so, he was a reminder of how wary she had to be here.

She couldn't give any man the slightest encouragement.

"Maggie?" A sleepy voice intruded. Maggie jumped. She'd been so lost in her thoughts she hadn't spied Aileana, her lady's maid, emerge from a small adjoining chamber. Although the lass was still dressed, her curly dark hair was mussed. She'd clearly fallen asleep while waiting for her mistress to return.

Aileana halted, her brow furrowing as she studied Maggie's face. "Is something amiss? Does yer arm still pain ye?"

Maggie shook her head. "No, all is well." She then waved her maid away. "Ye go back to bed, lass. I can undress myself tonight."

Aileana's grey-blue eyes widened. "I don't mind."

"I know ye don't … off ye go."

Aileana did as bid, although not without a reproachful look, leaving Maggie alone in the chamber once more.

Aileana Munro had been with her ever since her marriage to Campbell six years earlier. After his death, she'd refused to be parted from Maggie—even if the rest of the Munros didn't want her to remain with them—and traveled back to live at Caisteal Nan Corr with her mistress.

Usually, Maggie and Aileana would chat and go over the day's events together as the maid readied her for bed. Aileana would be curious about the supper no doubt, but she would have to wait till the following day to hear about it.

Maggie wasn't in the mood for chatter. Aileana would find her poor company.

Crossing to the small window, she opened the wooden shutters and breathed in the crisp night air. Enjoying the coolness upon her face, Maggie leaned against the window ledge. Outdoors, the world slumbered, save for the occasional wail of a bairn or a dog bark. Her gaze swept over the fires of Inverness, before she tilted up her chin to view the moon. It was on the wax and bathed the world in its hoary light, glinting off the waters of the River Ness and Moray Firth beyond.

All the northern clans were assembled in Inverness now, and tomorrow at noon King James would hold his first assembly.

Maggie released a long sigh, letting the evening's tension ebb from her. Weakness flooded through her limbs, and she leaned heavily on the window ledge.

How she wished Campbell was with her right now. She missed having his strength and warmth in her life. There were times when she ached just to have her husband enfold her in his arms once more, to lie her cheek against his chest and hear the thunder of his heart.

But Campbell Munro could no longer hold her. And worse still, she could no longer speak to him—couldn't put things right.

Staring up at the moon, she blinked rapidly as her vision blurred. *Ye were my one true love, Campbell.* Her chest started to ache then. *There will never be anyone else.*

Another heavy sigh escaped Maggie. Reaching up, she wiped at the tears that now trickled down her face.

"I made ye a promise, mo ghràdh," she whispered to the night, "and I will honor it."

Morgan returned to the apartments he shared with his kin and entered the small solar to find his brother seated by the fire. Keira sat next to him with her feet upon a settle. The couple were conversing quietly together, although they stopped talking when Morgan entered.

"Back so soon?" Connor greeted his brother. "I thought ye'd be drinking with the others for a wee while yet."

Morgan favored him with a tired smile, before giving a jaw-cracking yawn. "Tomorrow's an important day," he replied. "And as good as the wine was this eve, I'd rather not wake up with a sore head."

In truth, he'd seen Maggie Munro leave the great hall and had decided a proper apology was in order. He'd caught her looking his way earlier in the evening but noticed also just how quickly she averted her gaze afterward. She was a winsome woman, yet troubled. It shouldn't have surprised him that her greeting was frosty when he caught up with her.

It was evident that Maggie didn't want to be in Inverness. And yet, despite her abrupt manner, he found himself intrigued by her.

Oblivious to the direction of his brother's thoughts, Connor loosed a sigh. "They were all drinking and feasting like it's Yuletide ... I'd wager some of them won't be making so merry tomorrow eve."

"Aye, everyone thinks they'll be the one to escape punishment." Morgan crossed the solar and sank down into a high-backed chair opposite Connor and Keira. "We all think *we're* in the right."

Keira's mouth quirked. "And weren't ye?"

Morgan met his sister-by-marriage's eye and smiled. Despite that he liked Keira, he never forgot that she was a Gunn. Sometimes he wondered if she harbored a secret allegiance to her kin. After all, blood was blood.

"Of course," he answered, holding her gaze. "They provoked us. They *always* provoke us." He paused then, his gaze flicking between husband and wife. "Did ye see the Gunns this eve?"

Keira's mouth compressed, before she nodded.

"Aye," Connor murmured. "I tried to ignore them, but George Gunn and his first-born walked right by our table."

Morgan leaned forward, spearing his brother with his gaze. "We must have reckoning for Harpsdale. They cut down our father, and Alexander Gunn nearly killed *ye*."

It had been a strain to remain seated during supper, while the men they'd faced in battle under a year earlier sat just a few yards distant. Connor had slain the warrior responsible for Rory Mackay's death, but that didn't make the Gunns' presence any less galling.

Connor scowled. He likely didn't appreciate being reminded of the scar he still bore from the Gunn heir's dirk blade. "Aye," his brother answered, his tone wary. "But we aren't here for vengeance ... we all know where that leads."

Morgan flashed Connor a hard smile. His brother hated the Gunns as much as the rest of them did, but he had a Gunn wife now, with a bairn on the way—and that complicated things. Nonetheless, Connor Mackay would raise arms again against their enemies if need be. They all would.

"With any luck, we shall have the pleasure of seeing George Gunn kneeling before the chopping block in a day or two," Morgan replied.

His brother's sudden glower made Morgan's smile slip. He stilled then, his gaze shifting to his sister-by-marriage. Keira's shoulders had gone rigid, and her gaze was shadowed. Keira never spoke of her clan, yet her expression now said it all. Deep-down she was still a proud Gunn, and he'd offended her.

"I'm sorry, Keira," Morgan murmured. "That was a blood-thirsty thing to say."

She favored him with a tight smile. "Aye, it was … although I understand why ye feel as ye do." She glanced then at her husband, placing a hand upon Connor's thigh. "I can't change who I am … or who my kin is … but ye must know that my loyalty is to the Mackays now."

6

A FACE IN THE CROWD

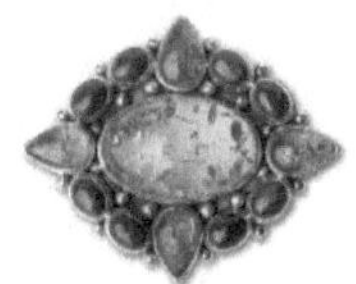

IT WAS A relief to step out of the castle and take a walk into town. The more time Maggie spent away from her uncle, the better. While they'd broken their fast together, he'd muttered something about introducing her to potential suitors afterward.

Maggie had decided then and there that she had to get away. The day was still new—noon and the king's audience were a few hours off—and as such, she'd donned a light woolen cloak and slipped out of the keep.

Usually, she took Aileana with her on her visits to market, but today Maggie wished to go alone. She'd spent a restless night and felt on edge this morning. Aileana's chatter would only fray her already brittle nerves.

It had been a few years since she'd last visited Inverness, yet she remembered that the town boasted a lively market every morning.

And it was a lovely morning to be out and about. The day was sunny with a pale blue sky above. A light breeze feathered in from the Firth, bringing with it the scent of brine and smoking herrings. The far-off shouts of men at the docks drifted across the water.

A faint smile curved Maggie's lips as she walked. The moment she'd stepped out of the castle, she'd felt lighter. This was exactly what she needed. She carried a wicker basket looped over one arm—just in case she found anything to tempt her—and her money purse, which nestled inside her cloak and contained a few silver pennies, clinked against her thigh as she walked. Her uncle gave her a tiny allowance. It wasn't much, but she was careful to save it for trips away from Caisteal Nan Corr.

A tightly-packed web of stone houses made up Inverness town. The dwellings on the outskirts were lower, with thatched roofs and gardens outdoors, but in the center of town, the buildings that surrounded the market square were grander, many of them two or three stories tall with slate roofs.

Covered stalls filled the cobbled market square this morning, the cries of hawkers echoing off the surrounding buildings. Maggie wandered amongst the other shoppers, enjoying the feel of being part of the crowd. She could be one of these housewives, off to buy fresh butter and salted pork for her family.

Maggie's step faltered at the thought, her hold on her basket tightening.

She would never have that—would never have the family she'd once dreamed of.

Bitterness soured her mouth. It seemed so unfair. Watching the ruddy faces of two local women who chatted together at the fishmonger's, bairns clinging to their skirts, she suddenly envied them. Her wants in life had been simple, and yet they'd been denied.

At least, once she escaped to Iona, she'd no longer have to endure reminders of what was lost to her.

Turning away, Maggie tried to focus on the present. She wanted to cheer herself up, not let memories shadow her day. Determined to enjoy the market, she wove her way through the crowd. She stopped off at a stall where a craftsman was showing off an array of leather satchels and pouches. Maggie's coin purse was getting a little worn these days so she bought another. After that, she passed stalls selling fruit and vegetables—where the first of the spring produce gleamed in the sun—before the aroma of baking enticed her.

Unable to resist, Maggie bought herself a hot pork pie. It was delicious, the pastry flaky and the filling juicy and well-seasoned. She was just brushing off the crumbs from her cloak, and wondering whether it would be greedy to retrace her steps and buy another, when a face across the crowd made her halt mid-stride.

A woman walked through the shoppers.

She was a beauty. Tall, with milky skin, golden-brown hair tumbled over her shoulders.

Maggie's breathing caught. *It can't be.*

But it was. She knew that face.

The second pie forgotten, Maggie took off now across the square. She caught up with the woman just as her quarry had almost reached a narrow side-street leading away from the market.

"Rhianna!"

The woman froze, her slender shoulders rounding. A heartbeat later, she swung around, revealing sea-blue eyes—the same shade as Maggie's own—wide upon a pale heart-shaped face.

"Maggie." Her name came out in a horrified gasp. An instant later though, Rhianna mastered her reaction. She managed a tight smile. "What a surprise."

Breathing hard, for she'd virtually flown across the market square to catch up with her sister, Maggie gasped, "A good one, I hope?"

Relief made her feel giddy, although she checked her enthusiasm. It had been a while since the pair of them had set eyes on each other—nearly four years to be exact. So much had happened in the meantime. When they'd last seen each other, Maggie had been happily wed to Campbell, while Rhianna had been disgruntled at being packed off to Iona nunnery, out of temptation's way. She knew that Maggie had lost her husband, for Maggie had sent word to Iona. However, Rhianna had never written back with her condolences.

When her sister didn't reply, Maggie stepped closer to her. "Rhianna?"

Rhianna's full lips compressed. "Of course I'm happy to see ye, Maggie." However, the words came out clipped.

Maggie swallowed. "I've been so worried. Uncle has had men out combing the Highlands for ye for months ... I never thought we'd find ye here."

Panic flared in Rhianna's eyes, dousing her reserve. "He can never know ye have seen me ... don't tell him, please."

Maggie's gaze narrowed. The euphoria of relief, of knowing that Rhianna was indeed alive and well was starting to fade. "Do ye realize that the man ye should have wed ... and the woman who helped ye fool him, are both here in Inverness? The game is up. Yer ruse was exposed at Samhuinn."

Rhianna's winsome face grew paler still. Throat bobbing, she looked south, to where the crenelated outline of the castle rose high against the pale sky. "They too must never learn I'm here."

Maggie's frown deepened. "Why *are* ye here? Ye could be anywhere in Scotland ... but Inverness?"

Rhianna dragged her attention back to her, and for an instant, Maggie witnessed uncertainty and worry in her eyes. However, it was fleeting, before Rhianna's expression turned obstinate—an expression that Maggie remembered well. "Callum needed work ... Inverness was the best place to look for it."

Did Maggie imagine it, or was there a note of bitterness in Rhianna's voice?

She realized then that Rhianna carried a basket before her, one that appeared full of dirty linen. She noted too that the kirtle her sister wore was of poor cloth and threadbare in places.

Aye, Rhianna's bearing was as queenly as ever, yet her face was thinner than Maggie remembered, and there were lines of tension around her mouth that hadn't been there years earlier.

"Do ye promise not to tell a soul that ye have seen me?" Rhianna's fingers clenched around the basket. Her once smooth hands were reddened and chapped. Again there was a brittleness to her tone. "My past life is dead to me now ... and I wish to keep it that way."

"But we are sisters!" Maggie's throat constricted as these words burst from her. Rhianna's gaze narrowed in response. They'd never been close, they both knew that—there was no point in pretending otherwise.

Nonetheless, Maggie had felt terribly alone of late. Losing Campbell and then being stuck at Caisteal Nan Corr with her uncle had isolated her from the world. Without Aileana's company, she'd have gone mad.

Having a sister in her life mattered more than it ever had before.

"We're very different women," Maggie admitted, embarrassed by her outburst. Rhianna's manner was off-putting, and yet Maggie longed to be open with her. "But we're bound by blood all the same." She paused then, her voice lowering. "I don't want to lose ye, Rhianna."

Silence fell between them. The sisters stared at each other for a long moment, and then Rhianna favored Maggie with a wary smile. "Very well. Let us start with a turn around the market square, shall we?"

Maggie's gaze fell to the basket of laundry. "Am I not keeping ye from something?"

Rhianna gave a soft laugh. "Oh, these sheets can wait. Come ... it is too fine a morning to worry about the washing."

The two women turned then. Together, they circled the crowded square. Rhianna seemed friendlier now, and Maggie wondered if she too had missed having family nearby. Maggie's belly knotted then. Maybe she should have made more of an effort to get on with her headstrong sister in the past. Perhaps she'd changed—or maybe they both had.

They stopped together at a cloth merchant's stall and examined the fine silks, rolls of cotton, and damasks on display. Afterward, the sisters moved past the bakery stall where Maggie had stopped earlier. The toothsome aroma of baking wafted over them.

Rhianna's belly gave a loud growl.

"Mother Mary!" Rhianna's cheeks reddened. "What a terrible noise ... I do apologize."

Maggie's gaze traveled over her sister once more. Indeed, Rhianna, who'd always been willowy, was looking even more slender these days. Was she not getting enough to eat?

"The pies there are scrumptious. I tried one earlier," Maggie admitted, "and was tempted to get another. Will ye join me?"

A smile bloomed across Rhianna's face. "Aye ... that is a fine idea."

Reaching into her cloak, Maggie retraced her steps. She then pulled out her change purse and handed over a small silver penny to the woman at the bakery stall.

Uncle has a fondness for pork pies, she thought. *Maybe I should get him and Aileana one too*. Perhaps the gesture would sweeten Graeme's attitude toward her a little.

Maggie handed Rhianna their pies while she dug back into her purse for another penny. "Another two please," she said with a smile. "And can ye wrap these up?"

"Of course, lass." The woman grinned. "Just a moment." She reached for a scrap of cloth and deftly wrapped up the remaining pies, before securing the package with a length of twine. "Here ye go."

"Thank ye." Maggie took the pies, popped them into her basket, and turned back to Rhianna "Let us find a place to sit and ..."

Her voice trailed off as she realized that Rhianna was no longer standing next to her.

Her sister was gone—only a basket of dirty washing remained.

Maggie looked for Rhianna everywhere in the square and the tangle of streets beyond, but she didn't find her.

Rhianna had disappeared into the shadows like a wraith.

Maggie returned to the market square once again, casting her gaze around the milling crowd. Hot, flustered, and oddly tearful, she felt like the world's greatest fool. She'd been so relieved to see her sister again, but Rhianna evidently hadn't felt the same way. As they'd explored the market together, hope had flowered within Maggie. She had lost her husband, yet regained her sister. But now that hope had turned out to be only a mirage.

The turn around the square had been a play for time. Rhianna was looking for an opportunity to slip away—and had taken it the moment one had presented itself.

Muttering a curse under her breath, Maggie glanced up at the sky. The sun was starting to climb high. Noon wasn't far off; she needed to return to the keep and ready herself for the king's assembly. Despite that it would be impossible for potential suitors to woo her during the councils, Maggie's uncle had insisted on his niece's attendance. He wanted her visible at all times.

Making her way across the square, Maggie vowed she wouldn't leave things with Rhianna there.

I'll find ye. Ye won't escape me that easily.

She'd just emerged onto the wide thoroughfare leading up to the castle, when a man's voice hailed her from behind.

"A fine morning to be alive, it is not, Maggie?"

7

KEEPING A SECRET

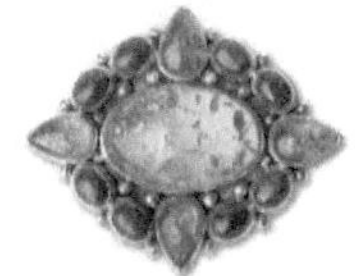

MAGGIE HALTED, TENSION rippling through her. Only one man besides her uncle had the presumption to call her by her first name—and she wasn't in the mood to bandy words with him.

Swiveling on her heel, her gaze fixed upon the tall warrior with wavy dark-blond hair who now strode toward her. Morgan Mackay wore a friendly smile as he raised a hand to greet her. His grey wolfhound padded along at his side, tongue lolling.

Maggie's body coiled at the sight of the hound. She didn't trust the dog any more than she did its owner.

Curse it, can't I go anywhere without crossing paths with this man?

Morgan's smile faded, his gaze flicking from Maggie to his dog. He halted a few feet away, and his hound sat obediently at his side. "All is well. Gritta means ye no harm." He then reached down and ruffled the beast's ears. "See ... as gentle as a lamb."

Maggie gave a snort, the kind her uncle would have glowered at her for making. Not a ladylike sound indeed. However, she didn't care. "It's 'Lady Munro'," she greeted him. "Do I have to keep reminding ye of that?"

He favored her with a boyish grin, not remotely chagrined. She noted that he had a deep dimple in his left cheek when he smiled. "Sorry, I keep forgetting." His attention then shifted to her basket. "Did ye enjoy the market?"

"Well enough." Maggie knew she was being rude, but Morgan Mackay and his flirtatious manner grated on her nerves. She didn't want to encourage him—she didn't want to encourage *any* man. Instead, she wanted to discover why her sister was in Inverness, dressed in threadbare clothes, hauling about baskets of dirty laundry. There was a tale behind all this.

Maggie had to find a way to track her sister down.

Morgan's gaze searched her face. "Is something amiss?" he asked. "Ye aren't truly afraid of Gritta, are ye? I swear she'll behave herself in the future."

Maggie scowled. "I hope so, Mackay." She paused then, letting out a deep sigh. "Although I admit I'm preoccupied."

He cocked an eyebrow, inviting her to continue.

Maggie ground her teeth. Why had she told him that?

"If something is worrying ye, perhaps I can help?"

Maggie raised her chin. She was tempted to tell him that she didn't need his assistance—in whatever form— yet something prevented her.

To consider telling this man about her sister was risky. Morgan Mackay had been there when Keira Gunn's ruse had been revealed, and would likely pass on news of Rhianna's presence in Inverness to his brother. Yet the need to speak to someone was strong.

She could tell Aileana, but although she was fond of her maid, she knew she had a tendency to gossip with the other servants. Plus, Aileana had formed an 'attachment' of late with Athol, Graeme Ross's manservant. Lovers often 'talked'—and Maggie didn't want her uncle to learn that Rhianna was here in Inverness.

She'd promised Rhianna not to tell anyone she was here, yet her sister had betrayed her by running off. And Maggie *did* require help if she was to track her down. As much as she hated to admit it—for she'd promised herself she'd avoid him—she needed to take this man into her confidence.

"I bumped into my sister earlier," she said finally, her tone wary. "I don't suppose ye could help me find her?"

For a moment, Morgan just looked back at her, a quizzical expression upon his face, and then realization dawned. "Rhianna Ross is here?"

Maggie nodded. "She fled before I could find out where she's living, but I have to locate her. I must speak to her again." Maggie shifted closer to Morgan then, craning her neck up to hold his gaze. God's teeth, the Mackay men were giants. She felt like a child standing before him. "Ye cannot say anything to yer brother or his wife about this. Please promise me ye won't."

Morgan's handsome face sobered. "Ye have my word. This is the last thing Connor or Keira needs to hear at present."

Relief filtered through Maggie, causing the knot of tension within her to loosen a little. The stern expression he now wore reassured her. He was protective of his brother.

"Are ye sure ye want to search for yer sister?" he asked after a pause. "Aye, I will help ye look for her, but it sounds like she doesn't want to be found."

Maggie considered his words. "Clearly ... since she ran off. But I need to find out if she is truly well."

He frowned. "What makes ye think she isn't?"

"She was thin and dressed poorly, with work-worn hands. She was also carrying a basket of washing. I think perhaps she may be working as a washerwoman."

Morgan inclined his head. "Well then, she shouldn't be that difficult to locate."

"Good," Maggie replied with a nod. "I intend to start looking for her tomorrow."

Morgan smiled. "Shall we meet in the afternoon once the morning audience with the king is over ... and go in search of her together?" He flashed her another smile, his cheek dimpling once more. "I can't have ye going door-to-door by yerself, Maggie ... it could be dangerous."

Maggie frowned, swallowing the urge to chastise him for being overly familiar once more, and for patronizing her. Of course she couldn't go in search of her sister alone. Why did he think she'd asked him for his assistance?

Heaving in a deep breath, she let her irritation settle. The man was an incorrigible flirt, yet there was sincerity in his gaze as he waited for her answer. She didn't sense anything wolfish or predatory about him. He genuinely wanted to help her.

"Aye, very well then, *Morgan*," she replied, using his first name boldly as well. "As soon as the noon meal is over with tomorrow, we shall meet at the gates."

Morgan entered the great hall behind Connor and Keira to find it differently arranged than the day before. Instead of long tables covering the wide floor, benches now lined either side of the cavernous rectangular space.

And upon the dais sat two thrones, one slightly larger than the other.

All of those amassed at the castle had taken their noon meals in their apartments today before descending to the great hall for the king's audience.

After lingering in town with the lovely widow, Morgan had gone upstairs to find his kin had nearly finished their meal.

"Ye'd better hurry." Kennan had thrown a bannock to him. "I hear the king despises latecomers."

The rumble of voices in the great hall was a lot more subdued than at supper of the eve before. It was becoming real now: the clan-chiefs and chieftains of the north were about to meet with the king—and James wasn't happy with them.

Morgan paused a moment, his gaze sweeping the lines of men and women who were taking their places upon the long benches. Halfway down the line on the right-hand side of the great hall, he spied Maggie.

Without hesitation, Morgan headed over to her.

The morning had indeed taken an interesting turn when he'd encountered the Munro widow in town. And now he'd learned that her sister was hiding somewhere in Inverness.

He hadn't lied to Maggie when he'd promised not to say a word to either Connor or Keira. The pair of them had been through much. Keira had played her role in the deception, but Rhianna had orchestrated it all. He didn't want to dredge it all up again—and neither, it seemed, did Maggie.

Morgan's gaze settled upon her now. She wore a blue kirtle that matched her eyes, her dark hair braided into a long plait that hung over one shoulder.

Maggie's eyes widened when she saw him approach.

"What are ye doing?" she hissed as he wedged himself in next to her, forcing Andrew More—a heavyset, sweaty man who'd been attempting to engage Maggie in conversation—aside. "My uncle will have a fit if he sees us seated together."

Morgan's gaze flicked to where Graeme Ross sat with the Ross clan-chief nearer the dais. The two men were deep in conversation. "I wouldn't worry about him." He leaned closer to her then, casting her a conspirator's smile, his voice dropping to a whisper. "Besides, I thought ye looked in need of rescuing." Morgan wasn't exaggerating—Andrew More was reputed to be the biggest bore in all the Highlands.

Maggie's mouth thinned. "Is that so?"

She looked as if she was about to say something else, but the bray of a Highland pipe interrupted them. The shrill noise reverberated through the hall, echoing up into the wooden rafters. All the attendees were seated now, and the rumble of voices died to a whisper.

An imposing man clad in flowing red strode into the great hall, with a fair-faced woman on his arm. A group of guards in chainmail rattled in after them.

Morgan observed King James with interest. The man was younger than he'd expected, in his early thirties at most, but then he'd only been crowned three years earlier. Thick auburn hair flowed over the shoulders of the rich crimson surcoat he wore. As he passed by, Morgan caught a glimpse of a boldly featured long face and a pointed chin covered in a neatly trimmed beard. The king had sharp brown eyes, a broad brow, and a mouth that was at present curved into a half-smile.

The slender woman on his arm would be Joan, Queen of Scotland. Elegant, the woman glided across the wooden floor like a swan, her dark-blonde hair piled high upon her head.

The wailing of the Highland pipe followed the king and queen to the dais, only ceasing when they had lowered themselves onto their thrones. The escort of guards, heavy claidheamh-mòrs hanging from their hips, took up their positions, flanking the royal couple.

As the last strains of the pipe died away, the king swept his gaze over the amassed men and women who flanked the sides of the great hall.

"Lords of the north ... I am pleased to see ye all here," he greeted them. He had a low, powerful voice that traveled to every corner of the chamber. "I realize this is short notice ... but such a parliament is long overdue." He paused then, his features hardening. "Order must be restored in the Highlands ... I will not have my chiefs brawling like misbehaving bairns."

A chill silence followed this rebuke.

Morgan stiffened, his gaze narrowing. The king wasn't one to bandy words it seemed. Morgan glanced then, across the hall at where his kin had taken seats directly opposite. Connor wore a shuttered expression, although his lips had compressed in a look Morgan knew well. He didn't appreciate the reproach.

Farther down the bench sat Angus-Dow Mackay and his son, Niel. The Mackay sat with his beefy arms crossed over his barrel chest, his heavy brow furrowed, while Niel's sharp-featured face was tense, watchful.

At the far end of the line—as far away from the Mackays as possible—sat the Gunns. George Gunn was scowling, as was his son Alexander.

The bastards look worried, Morgan thought grimly. *Good*. However, now that he sat in the great hall listening to King James, the confidence he'd felt upon his arrival in Inverness dimmed slightly. The king seemed angry at all of them.

"I will now explain how this council will be conducted," James continued. "Today I shall hear from each clan-chief in turn. In yer own words, ye are to give me a summary of the part ye have played in the hostilities between the clans." The king's broad brow furrowed. "I urge each of ye to consider yer words carefully, for ye shall be judged on them."

King James's announcement caused murmurs to ripple down the benches. Morgan shared a glance with Maggie. The king appeared generous in letting his clan-chiefs speak for themselves before he dealt out his punishment. However, some of the clan-chiefs were better orators than others. Some would state their position strongly, using well-chosen words, while others would likely blunder along, spewing out a list of injustices committed against them.

Morgan's belly tightened as he shifted his attention back to his own clan-chief.

Angus Mackay now wore a disgruntled expression. The man was a fighter, not a diplomat. Morgan hoped his mouth wouldn't get all of them into trouble.

"Let us start with Alexander MacDonald." King James spoke once more, his voice cutting through the murmuring. "Let the 'Lord of the Isles' say his piece." There was no mistaking the sarcasm in the king's voice, or the glint in his brown eyes.

Morgan tensed. Of course, *his* personal focus was on his clan's feud with the Gunns. Yet it was just one of the issues to be dealt with at this parliament.

The first of the clan-chiefs—the man who'd once been the king's greatest ally—would now defend himself. MacDonald had helped James rid himself of his enemies, but he was no longer a favorite of the king. Relations between them had soured of late, and rumors circulated that James wished to humble him.

The whispering died down, all gazes swiveling then to the tall, dark-haired man who rose from his seat at the far end of the great hall.

8

IN IRONS

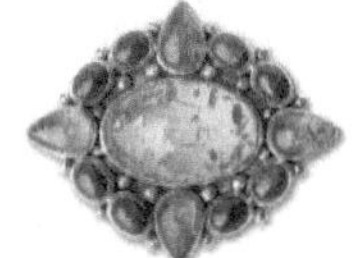

"ANGUS WILL HANG us all if he's not careful."

Morgan strode into the guest solar and headed straight for the jug of wine on the side-board. After the afternoon he'd just endured, he could easily scull the entire jug himself, leaving nothing for anyone else. His arse was numb from sitting on that hard bench for hours. Even being seated next to the lovely Maggie hadn't made the afternoon bearable. Like him, the widow had worn an exasperated expression as the audience wore on. Morgan's mood, which had been mellow when he'd entered the great hall, gradually soured.

Reaching for the jug, Morgan began pouring wine into cups. Halfway through the task, he glanced up and met his brother's eye.

Connor was scowling. "Aye, that's also my concern," he muttered.

The brother's gazes fused. Today had revealed that this parliament was going to be far more dramatic than either of them had anticipated. Real worry gnawed at Morgan now. If the council went ill for their clan, was Connor also at risk?

The whole situation was infuriating, and concerning.

"The devil take me, I never want to hear such shite again," Morgan growled. His head ached from listening to the rantings of bitter, hate-fueled men.

Connor nodded wearily. "I've never heard so many lies told in one afternoon. The way they talk, every one of them is an aingeal."

Morgan muttered a curse under his breath as he finished pouring the wine. He then passed cups to Kennan, Cait, Keira, and Jaimee as they too filed into the solar. Anger simmered in his belly. Surely the king would see George Gunn for the brute he was?

"I know we've all had our differences, but I had no idea there was so much loathing between the clans," Jaimee said. Her green eyes were wide as she took her cup from Morgan.

"Aye, lass," Connor replied with a shake of his head. "Ye think it's just the Mackays and the Gunns who hate each other, but that's only the tip of it. There was a bloody brawl in the stables this morning between the Leslies and the Forbes."

Morgan's gaze widened. He'd missed that. Nonetheless, the hostility between those two clans was well known. It had started thirty years earlier when Andrew Leslie ran off with John Forbes's betrothed—the 'Fair Maid of Kemnay'. Many a clan feud had ignited over a woman.

"Does the king really think he can restore order?" Keira asked. The long day had taken its toll on them all, and Connor's wife looked drawn and tired now.

"He hopes to, mo ghràdh," Connor replied with a sigh. "And if he deals out a harsh enough punishment, the northern chiefs will behave themselves for a while."

Across the solar, Kennan snorted. He sank down onto the window-seat next to his wife and turned toward Connor. "As yer brother pointed out, our clan-chief didn't do himself any favors today."

Morgan ground his teeth. Angus Mackay had lurched to his feet and lumbered to the center of the hall, before beginning an angry rant about what treacherous dogs the Gunns were. He'd even stabbed an accusing finger at George Gunn himself a few times—and when he had, the air in the great hall had grown heavy with menace.

The Gunn clan-chief had stared back at the Mackay, his grey eyes hard and predatory. But when it was his time to speak, George Gunn had surprised them all with his eloquence. Unlike the Mackay, he'd looked at the king and no one else. He'd kept his summary brief, factual, and emotionless.

Morgan had glared at the Gunn clan-chief throughout his entire speech, as he imagined sinking a dirk-blade into the liar's gut. However, there was no denying that George Gunn had made a better impression than Angus Mackay.

"So, what happens now?" Cait asked, breaking the brittle silence. She leaned against Kennan, wrapping an arm about his waist. "Do we have to listen to more of that tomorrow?"

Connor shook his head. "It's up to the king now. In the morning he will decide who will be punished ... and then in the coming days, he will choose what forms his punishment will take. All we can do is wait."

Everyone gathered early in the great hall. A subdued hush settled over the space, all eyes watching as the king and queen entered and made their way to the dais.

Maggie shifted on the hard bench-seat. She sat between her uncle and his manservant, Athol, this morning. The two men were both in surly moods, her uncle especially.

Worry knotted in Maggie's belly when her thoughts turned to the Ross clan-chief. She'd wed a Munro, yet her loyalty to the Ross clan remained. Things were looking ill-favored for John Ross. He'd given an account of his actions the day before, and although his excuses had sounded plausible to Maggie, she hadn't missed the thunderous look upon King James's face as he'd listened to the clan-chief.

John Ross's reputation as a trouble-maker had clearly gone before him.

Maggie frowned. She couldn't help but think her clan-chief was being maneuvered into position by his enemies and abandoned by his allies. He'd fought at Angus Mackay's side at the Battle of Harpsdale, but the Mackay clan-chief hadn't bothered to put in a good word for him during yesterday's summary. Likely, he was too concerned with his own fate.

Stifling a sigh, Maggie shifted her attention across the hall.

Morgan Mackay had just taken a seat with his kin opposite.

Her gaze lingered upon him a moment, misgiving feathering through her. Was she wise to have involved him? This afternoon, once the council was done with, they would meet once more and go in search of Rhianna together.

She'd had a restless night. It was difficult to sleep with so much on her mind. The parliament and her uncle's attempts at match-making aside, Rhianna's situation, and the way she'd run off, gnawed at Maggie.

But the fact she'd confided in one of the Mackays made her feel queasy.

Aye, she needed assistance, but her choice had likely been a poor one. Nonetheless, it was done now. Hopefully, they'd locate Rhianna without too much difficulty—and without her uncle discovering her sister was in Inverness.

The hush in the great hall grew deeper, the last of the whispering dying away. There was no screeching Highland pipe this morning, no fanfare. When the king eventually spoke he looked tired, as if he'd been up most of the night deliberating over what the clan-chiefs had presented to him the day before.

"This morning's council will be a short one." There was a harder edge to the James's voice this morning. "When I call yer name, stand up and walk to the center of the hall."

Maggie tensed, nerves twisting under her ribcage. The king's bluntness was putting her on edge. He was a popular king—as he'd done much for the administration of justice for the common people—and whenever he'd spoken the day before, she'd been struck by how clever he was, how cultured. But right now, she feared him.

The king plucked a rolled parchment from the sleeve of his blood-red surcoat and unfurled it. An instant later, he began to read. "Alexander MacDonald. Mary Ross. Kenneth More. Angus Macmaken. William Leslie." He read the names slowly, but with only the barest pause between them. "Angus Murray. John Ross. Angus-Dow Mackay."

At hearing her clan-chief's name, Maggie's heart started hammering against her ribs. It was as she'd feared. Her gaze cut to where the man himself sat farther down the bench. His face was impassive, giving nothing away. Beside him, the clan-chief's wife's face paled.

Those whose names had been called rose to their feet and moved to the center of the floor. There was one woman among them—Mary, Countess of Ross. Tall and proud, she stepped up next to her son, Alexander MacDonald.

The Mackay clan-chief joined the amassing group, while John Ross did the same. Angus Mackay wore an affronted, indignant expression.

Maggie's chest was beginning to ache, and she let out the breath she hadn't even realized she was holding. She glanced then across at where Morgan Mackay was also watching the proceedings.

She couldn't help it; she wanted to see his reaction.

Morgan's handsome face had gone hard. Like Maggie, he wouldn't have failed to note that George Gunn's name *hadn't* been called.

King James rose to his feet, his gaze sweeping over the amassed group. He looked every inch the king this morning. There wasn't a trace of good humor on his face.

"After much deliberation, I have decided that ye are all deserving of punishment." The king then gestured to the guards that flanked him. Maggie spied movement at the entrance to the great hall, where another group of chain-mailed and armed men had appeared. "Put each of them in irons and escort them back to their chambers." He paused then, his auburn brows drawing together. "Yer individual fates will be decided over the coming days. Until then, yer doors will be guarded at all times ... and none of yer followers, or kin, may speak to ye."

"We have to do something." Morgan's voice, rough with anger, echoed through the solar. "The king can't put our clan-chief in irons and *not* George Gunn."

He swiveled to where Niel Mackay stood next to the hearth. The clan-chief's son had barely uttered a word since leaving the great hall. His lean face was pale and all taut angles. "Gunn's a liar," he finally rasped.

Silence fell in the solar. Niel had joined Connor, Morgan, and Kennan when they'd returned to their lodgings.

"Unfortunately, Gunn put forward a strong argument yesterday," Connor ventured after a lengthy pause. "And unlike yer father, he didn't lose his temper."

Niel's mouth twisted. "Aye, he spun a tale instead."

Connor's expression turned pained. "Aye, he made much of the fact we made the first move at Harpsdale."

"Gunn took great pains to make us look like warmongers," Morgan added, his temper simmering. "He forgot to mention all the border raids. He left out the tales of our burned villages, razed crops, and stolen cattle."

"Of course he did," Connor replied, bitterness lacing his voice.

And if only our clan-chief had made more of that.

The words were unspoken, and yet the truth hung like a condemnation in the air.

Angus Mackay had been virtually incoherent in his vitriol the day before, as he'd ranted on about what honorless dogs the Gunns were. He hadn't helped his own case at all—and now the king had put him in irons.

He was locked away, and no one—not even his son or wife—was allowed to speak to him. If the king looked unfavorably on him, he risked losing his head.

Heaviness settled in Morgan's gut. His attention shifted back to Niel. The warrior, who'd been Connor and Morgan's friend since childhood, stood stiffly before the fireplace. Outrage vibrated off him, however, there was now a hunted look in his eyes. "My father isn't to blame for the feuding," he choked out the words. "I can't stand by and let him be punished for defending his lands. It's a Highlander's right."

"Ye won't," Morgan answered swiftly. His comment earned him a warning look from Connor, yet he ignored it. "If James deals yer father a harsh justice, we shall speak up. *All* of us."

"Careful, Morgan," Connor murmured, his voice a low rumble in the solar. "We're dancing on a knife-edge here. Loyalty is an admirable quality ... but if the king can imprison our clan-chief, he can do the same to all who follow him."

9

CHARITY

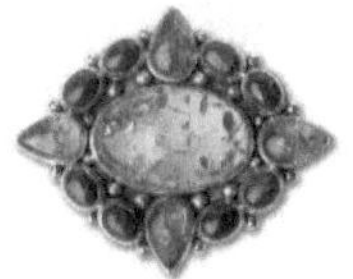

MORGAN MACKAY WAS frowning when he approached the gatehouse. As always, that dog of his padded at his side.

Watching him draw near, Maggie tensed. Had he changed his mind about accompanying her, about helping her? A chill washed over her. Had he betrayed her trust and told his brother that Rhianna was here?

It occurred to her then that she didn't know this man at all. He could have lied to her the day before. Not for the first time, she wished she'd exercised some prudence and not confided in him.

"Do ye go anywhere without that beast?" Maggie inwardly winced at the acerbic edge to her greeting. However, worry had set her nerves on edge.

Morgan's frown eased. "She doesn't follow me to the privy, if that's what ye are asking." His pine-green eyes twinkled then. "Or to bed."

The way he said those last words, the suggestive edge to them, caused Maggie to tense.

His charm was wasted upon her. Aye, he was attractive, and she'd felt the frisson of heat that had sparked between them when he'd taken her hand in the outer-bailey two days earlier. But Maggie was too practical to be taken in by melting looks.

"Are ye and yer hound ready to depart then?" she asked crisply. She'd managed to slip out while her uncle

~ 67 ~

was huddled with the other Ross chieftains after the audience.

"Aye … come on." Morgan glanced around him, his gaze keen. "It'll be a relief to escape the tension within these walls for a short while."

Maggie nodded. "With both our clan-chiefs in irons, things are indeed looking grim," she replied with a sigh. "My uncle's worried that the king will turn his eye to the chieftains who followed the arrested clan-chiefs. I'm sure that possibility hasn't escaped yer brother either?"

Morgan's lips thinned, his expression hardening once more. "No," he murmured. "It hasn't."

Without another word, the pair of them made their way out of the castle and down the incline into town. The day before had been bright and breezy, but today the sky was dull and grey, the air oppressively humid.

As they made their way along the thoroughfare toward the market square, Maggie shot Morgan a questioning glance. "Where should we start looking?"

"Yesterday ye described the possibility of her working as a washerwoman," he replied. "Let's begin our search by visiting all the washhouses in town."

Maggie frowned. "I don't think this is the life she was hoping for," she murmured. "My sister has always enjoyed finery and luxury."

Morgan snorted. "Aye, well she made a choice, didn't she?"

She had, although Maggie wouldn't have put things so bluntly. But then, Rhianna's choices had caused Morgan's elder brother a great deal of trouble, so she could hardly blame him for not sympathizing with her sister.

There were three washhouses in Inverness.

Leaving Morgan out on the street with his hound, with instructions to come looking for her if she didn't reappear shortly, Maggie entered the first washhouse on their list. She peered through the clouds of steam at the pink-cheeked women bent over wooden tubs, hoping to see her sister.

The first two stops were a disappointment. None of the women there knew of anyone called Rhianna, or of anyone matching her description. Granted, the washerwomen Maggie spoke to were reserved in their manner toward her, their gazes wary. High-born women didn't venture into washhouses. Her presence clearly made them suspicious of her.

Maggie had the sensation that even if they knew Rhianna well, they wouldn't tell her.

Finally, they reached the last of the washhouses, on the northern edge of town. Unlike the first two, which were enclosed, this washhouse consisted of a wide yard, covered with hide tarpaulins. Drying washing festooned the space like spider webs, and the sharp scent of lye and wet linen filled the air.

This time, Morgan followed Maggie inside, Gritta obedient at his heel.

And there, bent over a bench as she pummeled a wet lèine with a laundry bat, was Rhianna Ross.

Maggie stopped short, for a moment merely watching her sister.

The sleeves of Rhianna's kirtle were rolled up, exposing strong, sinewy arms. Her face was flushed, and her hair stuck in damp tendrils across her forehead as she worked.

But even in a washhouse, Rhianna's beauty shone like the sun.

Maggie heard the scuff of Morgan's boots as he stopped behind her. She imagined he was also staring at Rhianna. He wouldn't have met her before, but rumors of the 'Jewel of the Highlands' had traveled far and wide.

The sisters didn't look alike at all. Rhianna had taken after their father—a strikingly attractive man with golden-brown hair—while Maggie had inherited her mother's small frame and dark-hair.

Maggie cleared her throat.

Rhianna glanced up and froze.

For a long moment, the pair of them merely watched each other. And then Rhianna put down her laundry bat, a wide wooden paddle she was using to beat dirt out of the clothing. When she spoke, her voice was cool. "What are ye doing here?"

"We lost each other yesterday," Maggie replied evenly. Her sister's frosty tone cut her, although she tried not to show it. "I needed to make sure ye were well."

Rhianna scowled. "And as ye can see, I am."

Maggie drew closer, aware of the curious looks they were getting from the surrounding washerwomen. Some of them weren't staring at the two sisters though, but at the man standing behind Maggie.

Morgan Mackay also drew Rhianna's eye. She glanced beyond Maggie's shoulder, her gaze turning speculative. "Who's this? I told ye not to tell anyone I was here."

"He's a friend of mine."

"And does he have a name?"

"Morgan Mackay at yer service," Morgan introduced himself.

Rhianna's face went rigid, her eyes flying wide. "God's bones, Maggie," she hissed, leaning across the bench toward her. "Why would ye bring a Mackay here?"

"There's no need to worry, sister." Maggie raised her arms in a placating gesture, before she twisted and cut Morgan a sharp look. She really wished he'd kept his mouth shut. "Morgan is only here as my escort ... he won't say anything."

"Aye, my brother will never learn that the woman he was betrothed to for years is in Inverness," Morgan continued. His voice was silky, yet there was a hard undertone—and when Maggie glanced over her shoulder once more, she saw that Morgan was frowning.

"Ye need to go," Rhianna spoke between clenched teeth, her gaze shifting from Morgan back to Maggie. "*Both* of ye."

"Not yet." Maggie stepped closer. Stubbornness rose within her. Rhianna wouldn't tell her what to do. "I can't just leave ye here. Where's Callum? Why isn't he taking care of ye?"

The two sisters locked gazes for a long moment. Rhianna's willowy frame went rigid. She was as tense as a hind about to flee hunters. The wrong word, and she'd bolt. However, this time Maggie wouldn't lose her.

She folded her arms across her breasts and waited for her sister to respond.

"Callum has apprenticed at a local smithy," Rhianna admitted finally. Her voice was clipped, as if she was forcing the words out.

"And can't he support ye both?" Maggie's gaze dropped to Rhianna's reddened, chapped hands.

Seeing the direction of her look, Rhianna's mouth twisted. "Ye think I'm too good to be working here, do ye, Maggie?"

"No ... it's just that—"

"It's honest work."

Maggie drew in a deep breath, reining in her frustration. "I'm sure it is ... I'd just hoped that since ye decided to run away with Callum, that he would provide for ye."

Rhianna stared back at her, and then her blue eyes guttered. Her bow-shaped mouth trembled. "He did ... at first," she whispered. "But he has taken to dicing in taverns after work. If I hadn't found this job, we wouldn't be able to pay our rent."

The words, brutally honest, shocked Maggie into silence.

She remembered Callum well. He'd been one of her uncle's best warriors—arrogant and roguishly attractive. Rhianna had been smitten with him for years before their uncle had decided to send her away to protect her virtue.

The silence stretched out, punctuated by the swishing of hot, soapy water and the rhythmic 'thwack' of laundry bats at the benches around them. The sisters were keeping their voices low, yet Maggie sensed the women nearby were straining to hear what was passing between them.

Maggie stepped closer still, her gaze never leaving her sister's. "Ye don't need to stay here, Rhianna," she murmured, her voice turning urgent. "Come away with me."

Rhianna's gaze narrowed. "What? To Caisteal Nan Corr? I'm sure that would delight our dear uncle." Her mouth twisted then, and she leaned forward, so that their faces were only inches apart. "Ye always thought yerself cleverer than me, Maggie. Even now, ye talk to me as if I'm a halfwit." Her sister's gaze narrowed. "Even losing yer beloved husband hasn't humbled ye."

Maggie flinched. It was impossible not to. Her sister's words were intentionally cruel, and they cut deep. "Rhianna," she rasped. "That's not true. I've never—"

"Leave me, Maggie," Rhianna answered, her features tightening. "And take yer *friend* with ye."

Panic flared within Maggie, her heart beating a tattoo against her ribs. This wasn't how she'd envisaged this conversation going. She'd wanted to help her sister, wanted to rescue her.

But Rhianna clearly didn't want to be rescued.

She resented Maggie too much for that. And she had too much pride.

Maggie's throat tightened. She didn't want to weep, but she was on the verge of doing so. She hadn't realized Rhianna bore such a grudge against her. The way she remembered things, the pair of them had only clashed because of differing temperaments, not because she thought herself above Rhianna in any way.

However, underneath her upset, Maggie could feel her anger rising. It was a hot coal that pulsed just under her ribs. Whatever their differences, her sister was being unnecessarily rude.

Mastering her temper, Maggie dug into her cloak and retrieved her new change purse. She'd filled it with her carefully saved silver pennies before leaving her chamber earlier. She'd thought Rhianna might need her assistance.

"If ye won't come away with me, then at least accept this," she said, offering her sister the pouch. "It should help ease things for ye ... and Callum."

Rhianna stared at the pouch, and for an instant, Maggie saw relief flare in the depths of her sister's sea-blue eyes. But then anger doused it.

"We don't need yer charity," she growled. "Take yer coin and get out of here. I never wish to set eyes upon ye again."

Hot anger spiked through Maggie's belly. She'd had enough of her sister's rudeness. "It isn't charity," she snapped. With that, she slammed the purse down onto the bench between them. "Take it for yerself or throw it into the River Ness. I care not."

And with that, she turned, pushed past a stunned Morgan, and strode out into the street.

10

NOT THE MARRYING KIND

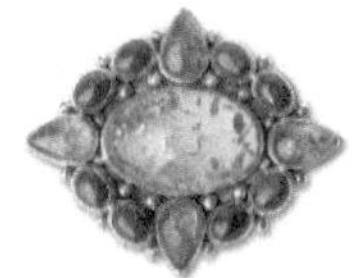

MAGGIE WAS HALFWAY down the street, heading back toward the center of town, when Morgan caught up with her.

"Wait up," he gasped, appearing at her side. "Hades … ye stride out like a warrior going into battle."

Maggie snorted, even as tears coursed down her cheeks. She tried to brush them away, yet now that she had begun to weep, she couldn't stop. Nearby, a group of women were beating out mats over a low wall. Abandoning their work, and their gossip, they turned to watch what they likely imagined was a lovers' quarrel. "Leave me be please," she choked. It was humiliating to let him see her this way, yet she couldn't hold back her grief. "I'm not fit company right at present."

She stumbled then, as a sob rose up within her. Suddenly, she couldn't go a step farther. Stopping in the middle of the cobbled way, she covered her face with her hands.

"Maggie." Morgan's voice was closer now, although the concern in it just made the sobs spiral up within her. She couldn't stand anyone being kind to her; it made her want to crumple to the ground and bawl like a bairn.

It was as if something had just broken inside her. Rhianna was the only true kin she had left, and her sister had just turned her back on her. Forever.

She'd wept herself ill after Campbell's death, had thought she hadn't any more tears to give. But as she stood in that lane weeping, Maggie realized that there was still a wide sea of regrets and disappointments beneath the grief at losing her husband.

Her relationship with her sister was one of them.

"She hates me," Maggie gasped. "I tried … but she would rather live in poverty than let me help her." It was impossible to speak then, as grief closed her throat.

An instant later, strong arms enfolded her, and she found her cheek pressed against Morgan's chest. It was a humid morning, and so he didn't wear a leather vest, just a loose lèine. As such, she could feel the heat of his body through the thin linen.

Maggie's body went rigid, yet Morgan held her there against him, his hand gently stroking her hair.

The fight went out of her then, and Maggie wept against his chest.

It was shameful. She'd never lost control like this in public before—even at Campbell's funeral she'd cried silently, head bowed, her face hidden by a veil.

But not so now.

It was all too much. The lingering grief. The regret that shadowed every waking breath. The loneliness she admitted to no one. And now her sister's scorn.

Morgan didn't say a word, he just let her cry.

Eventually, the tears spent themselves. Gasping, Maggie drew back and desperately tried to wipe down her face. What an awful fright she must look—her face blotchy, her nose running, and her eyes swollen. She noted then the damp patch across the front of Morgan's lèine.

"I've … I've made a mess of yer shirt," she mumbled, horror causing her to stumble over her words. How she wished she'd not agreed to allow Morgan to escort her today. Her sister's rejection—and her loss of control afterward—was bad enough as it was, without him bearing witness to it. At that moment, she just wanted to find a deep hole and crawl into it.

She glanced down and saw his wolfhound had joined them. It sat at its master's side, watching her with dark, soft eyes. And then, to her surprise, the beast got up and moved to Maggie, nuzzling its wet nose against the back of her hand.

The hound let out a low whine.

"Gritta sympathizes," Morgan murmured, "as do I Maggie ... and don't worry about my lèine. It'll dry."

"I'm sorry ye had to see all of that," Maggie replied with a sniff. Without realizing it, she reached out and stroked the dog's soft ears. The touch gave her comfort. Encouraged, Gritta pressed against her leg. "It was an ugly scene."

"Aye, but for what it's worth ... it wasn't ye who turned it ugly," Morgan replied.

Surprised, Maggie glanced up to find his gaze steady upon her. He wasn't smiling, and there was no trace of flirtation and teasing in his eyes. "Yer sister was unnecessarily cruel."

Maggie swallowed. "Maybe ... but she hates me all the same." Her throat constricted then, as more tears threatened. The saints preserve her, she needed to get a grip on herself. Morgan would think her hysterical if she dissolved into sobs again.

As if sensing her fragility, Morgan took hold of her arm, linking it through his. "Come, Maggie. I think ye could do with a tankard of ale to settle yer nerves. Let's find ourselves an alehouse."

Morgan ordered two ales and then took his seat at the booth, opposite Maggie. Meanwhile, Gritta had curled up under the table, at their feet. They'd entered the first alehouse they came across: *The Fox and Goose*, a small, smoky establishment just off the market square.

It was mid-afternoon—early for drinking—and so the interior of the alehouse was quiet. The air was heavy with peat-smoke blended with the sharp scent of hops.

Waiting for their ales to arrive, Morgan leaned against the leather back of the booth and regarded the woman opposite.

Maggie still looked upset. Her face was flushed, her eyes watery. Yet, there was something about seeing her like this that made her lovelier than ever. She'd been haughty and self-contained till now. But after she'd cried against his chest, she'd let him see the vulnerability that lay beneath.

Watching her, Morgan's breathing slowed.

There was nothing like a woman's tears to strip away a man's defenses. Maggie Munro drew him in, fascinated him.

Her sister had been churlish and nasty. Indeed, Rhianna was as bonny as the rumors reported. Even the humble setting couldn't diminish her beauty. But her loveliness had left Morgan cold.

Connor was lucky indeed to have escaped that fate. He was much better off with Keira.

Sharp tongue aside, Morgan hadn't liked the way Rhianna had insulted Maggie. Even though they barely knew each other, he'd felt a strange protectiveness as they'd stood in that washhouse.

"I must look a mess," Maggie mumbled, wiping at her still-damp cheeks.

"Ye look as bonny as ever," Morgan replied, his mouth quirking.

She huffed a weak laugh. "Liar."

"It's true," he insisted as the alehouse owner slammed two foaming tankards of ale in front of them. He hadn't lied; she really was comely. Her blue eyes were the color of the sea in high-summer. She had a heart-shaped face and lustrous dark hair. And that mouth—full and red, and bow-shaped—begged to be kissed.

Of course, he kept all of those thoughts to himself.

Maggie sniffed in response, before raising her tankard to her lips and taking a gulp.

Morgan followed suit. "I take it ye and yer sister's relationship in the past was ... strained?" Watching the pair of them interact had surprised him; how fortunate he was in his own siblings.

Maggie nodded and took another gulp of ale as if to fortify herself. "Aye ... we're only two years apart in age

... but it feels as if a decade separates us." She sighed then, her blue eyes shadowing. "Truthfully, I found her a selfish chit before our uncle sent her away to the nunnery ... and I'm not one to keep my opinions to myself."

Morgan smiled. He'd noticed her forthright manner, although he rather liked it. One always knew where one stood with a woman like Maggie. "So, she found ye bossy?" he teased gently.

Maggie pulled a face. "Aye, she was frustrated that I wouldn't do her bidding, although she locked horns with our uncle the most." She paused then. "I can't entirely blame her for that though ... ye have seen what kind of man he is."

Morgan had and didn't envy Maggie her living with that irascible old goat. "Maggie," he said after a brief pause, "why did ye return to Caisteal Nan Corr after yer husband died? Surely, ye would have been happier with the Munros?"

Her pretty features tensed, and Morgan immediately regretted the question. It was too direct. He wanted to understand this enigmatic widow a little better, yet he'd been too bold.

"I never got on with Campbell's family that well," she admitted, her gaze dropping to the tankard she'd wrapped her hands around. "His mother was a terrible scold, and following Campbell's funeral, before my tears had even dried, she asked me to leave Contullich Castle." Maggie heaved a sigh then. "Truthfully, I was happy to remove myself from her presence ... although I knew I wouldn't be any more welcome back at Caisteal Nan Corr. Ever since, uncle has been champing at the bit for me to emerge from mourning and find another husband."

"I'd noticed," Morgan replied, his tone dry. He took a sip of ale. It was excellent: bitter with a hoppy aftertaste. "And how do ye feel about the matter?"

She glanced up, those sharp blue eyes spearing him. "Is it not evident?"

His mouth curved. "Not entirely."

Her fingers tightened around the tankard. "I wish to remain a widow … and as long as I spurn any man my uncle pushes at me while this parliament lasts, I will." Her mouth twisted then. "Uncle knows I'm almost too old for the marriage market these days. This is his last opportunity to rid himself of me."

Morgan shook his head. They were of a similar age, yet no one pressured him to wed. However, it was different for men. "Even so," he replied, holding her gaze. "A husband would surely offer ye protection … and security for the future?"

Maggie's lips compressed. "I have little to offer a man," she replied crisply. "Not long before my husband left for battle the final time, I lost our bairn … the birth was difficult and the healer pronounced me barren." Maggie then heaved in a deep breath, as if those words had cost her.

Morgan went still. He felt the urge to reach out his hand to her but decided against it. The woman's candor caught him off-guard, and it was a few moments before he answered. "I wouldn't agree that ye have little to offer, Maggie," he replied gently. "However, I do think yer uncle should stop heckling ye."

"He's desperate … but sooner or later, he'll let me take my vows at Iona … even if it means he has to give the prioress a hefty donation."

"Ye don't seem like the kind of woman who'd take easily to a nun's life," Morgan replied with a smile. "If ye don't mind me saying so."

Maggie gave a cool laugh. "Ye are free with yer opinions today, Mackay."

"Am I wrong?"

"No … most likely not. But such a life is preferable to remaining at my uncle's holding." Maggie leaned back against the upholstered seat then. "Enough about me," she said, her mouth quirking. "What of *ye*, Morgan Mackay? Do ye have any plans to take a wife?"

There was a teasing edge to her voice, and Morgan found himself grinning in response before he shook his head. "No … I'm not the marrying kind."

11

RECKLESS

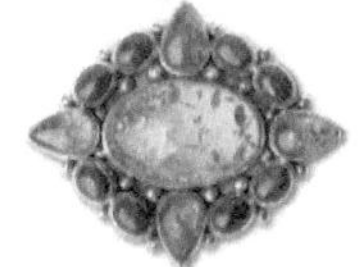

THE AFTERNOON WAS on the wane when the two of them finally emerged from *The Fox and Goose*. Rising to her feet, Maggie was disconcerted to find that the surrounding common room swayed.

"Heavens," she murmured, gripping the edge of the table to steady herself. "That ale was stronger than I thought."

How many tankards had she consumed? No more than three, surely? She'd been so engrossed in her verbal sparring with Morgan that she'd lost track of time and how much she'd drunk.

They hadn't eaten anything either, and so the ale had gone straight to her head.

"Aye." Morgan smiled at Maggie. "Here ... take my arm."

He stepped close, holding out his elbow for her to catch hold of. Aware of the heat and nearness of his body, Maggie slipped her arm through his, although she stumbled as she stepped away from the table.

Lord, I really have consumed too much ale.

How foolish of her. In the aftermath of the scene with her sister, she'd felt reckless. She hadn't wanted to return to the confines of the castle, to weather her uncle's nagging. Instead, she'd lingered here, in this smoky alehouse where no one could bother her—in the company of a man she barely knew.

After their brief exchange about her sister, and her widowhood, she and Morgan had kept the conversation light, playful.

She couldn't believe she'd revealed to him that she couldn't have bairns. The moment the words left her lips, she'd wanted to claw them back in. But Morgan's response had put her at ease.

And during the conversation that followed, Maggie forgot that she'd once vowed to avoid this man.

It felt liberating to be able to sit in an alehouse with a charming man. Morgan was a good listener too and appeared to be interested in Maggie's opinions—something she had sorely missed. Campbell had been her best friend, as well as her beloved husband. The lack of companionship, of having someone to confide in, had weighed heavily upon her.

Not that she'd confess her deepest thoughts to Morgan Mackay, mind. She'd already revealed far too much to him.

But all the same, the steadying strength of his arm felt good, and she leaned against him.

Calling a farewell to the proprietor, Morgan led them to the door. The alehouse was starting to fill up now, as the men who worked the docks, the smiths, and the workshops in town arrived.

On the way out, they passed a table of men dicing.

Maggie's gaze lingered on them, and she remembered her sister's revelation about Callum. He'd promised to protect Rhianna, to take her away to a better life, but only half a year later, he was already letting her down.

Men. Maggie's mouth thinned. It seemed she had wed the only good one.

Out on the narrow street, Maggie was surprised to see it was now raining. The grey clouds had lowered, and a fine mist drifted down over Inverness. Despite that dusk was still some way off, the torch-lighters had been out already. Golden light reflected off wet cobbles.

"Come on," Morgan said, casting her a grin. "It looks as if we are both about to get wet."

Still arm in arm, they made their way down the street, Gritta following silently behind, and emerged into the wide expanse of the market square. It seemed bigger at this hour, devoid of covered stalls and milling crowds. The smoking torches around the edge of it illuminated the gloom. There wasn't a soul about, for the rain had driven everybody indoors.

"Uncle is going to chew my ear off for avoiding him all afternoon," Maggie muttered. She bowed her head against the rain. Although fine, it fell heavily, coating everything in a thick dew. "I'll never hear the end of it."

"It's probably best he doesn't see us together," Morgan advised. "I'll let ye go on ahead when we near the gates."

Maggie sighed. His advice was prudent, sane, but it was a reminder of the cage she lived in.

"I don't want to go back there," she announced. "If I could, I'd run away now and never look back."

She glanced up then, her gaze meeting Morgan's, to find him favoring her with a surprised smile. "Where would ye go?"

"I don't know," Maggie admitted with a sigh. The ale had given her a loose, reckless tongue, but she didn't care. Suddenly, she felt the need to express all the frustration within her. Skidding to a stop, and nearly slipping on the wet cobbles, she turned to face Morgan, extracting her arm from his. "Anywhere. If I could, I'd take a fast horse and ride south ... and I'd keep going till the sea prevented me from riding any farther."

Morgan held her gaze, before raising a hand and brushing a wet curl of hair off her cheek. Tendrils had come free from her braid. "Ye'd be in England then, Maggie," he reminded her. "A worse fate than remaining with yer uncle, surely?"

She huffed. The sound was indelicate, yet she didn't care. She didn't feel like a lady at present. She felt wild, angry, and desperate to rid herself of the shackles that bound her.

"I'd suffer living amongst the English, Morgan," she told him firmly. "If it meant I was free ... like ye are."

She paused then, aware that his smile had faded, and he was staring down at her with an intense look that made her knees unsteady.

It's just the ale.

But was it?

This afternoon, she'd stepped out of her stifling life, and momentarily had lived as someone else. Morgan had made her feel like another woman, and the way he was looking at her now made an ache rise under her ribcage.

She'd told herself she'd never again want another man, never again ache to be touched, to be kissed.

But she did right now.

Please kiss me.

Answering her silent plea, he lowered his head and claimed her mouth with his.

It was a gentle kiss, a teasing kiss. Reaching down, he cupped her cheeks with his palms, brushing his mouth over hers. And then his tongue eased her lips apart.

Maggie welcomed him.

Unbidden, a sigh escaped her. Going up on tip-toe, she leaned into Morgan, kissing him back hungrily.

The taste of his mouth, the slide of his tongue against hers, was unraveling her wits, removing everything except a rising hunger that demanded to be sated.

Morgan Mackay was exciting, delicious.

With a groan low in his throat, Morgan gathered her against him. His hands slid down to cup the back of her neck and shoulders. His kiss grew urgent, harder, and Maggie eagerly matched his fervor.

Her hands slid up, over his wet lèine, her fingers itching to caress naked skin. She pressed herself against him, molding herself to him, a moan rising from deep within her.

Morgan drew away first—something which surprised Maggie, as he'd been kissing her with a hunger that was causing any remaining threads of her good sense to unravel.

He whispered a curse, staring down at her. Unlike earlier, he wasn't smiling now. Instead, his handsome face was strained, his green eyes dark in the torchlight.

"Ye will make me forget myself, if ye aren't careful," he warned.

Wildness spiked within Maggie once more. Just for a moment, she wished they could both forget themselves.

She knew Morgan Mackay wasn't interested in courting her. And she was as resolute as ever in her decision never to take another husband.

But a lover was something else. A lover was safe.

Just for a few heady moments, his kiss had chased away reality. How she wanted that forgetfulness again.

As if sensing her need, Morgan's mouth lifted at the corners. However, his gaze was just as limpid, as hungry, as before. "Please don't keep looking at me like that, Maggie," he murmured. "Or I really will throw caution to the wind."

Swallowing, Maggie stepped back from him.

Suddenly, she was aware of just how public their kiss had been. They stood on the edge of the now-empty market square, but anyone from the surrounding buildings could have seen them. It mattered not, for she knew few folk in this town, and yet if any of her clansmen ventured out from the castle and saw her here, she would be in trouble indeed.

He was right. She had to pull herself together. The ale had turned her body languid and warm, and had made her quite unlike herself. Once she sobered up, she would likely regret this.

"Come then," she said, forcing a briskness into her voice she didn't feel, and looping her arm through his once more. "Let's get back before uncle sends his manservant out looking for me."

Halfway up the incline toward the gatehouse, Morgan released Maggie's arm and let her go on ahead.

She didn't look back, although he kept his gaze upon her small form, shrouded by mist and rain, until she disappeared from sight.

Heaving a deep breath, Morgan waited a little longer still.

The ale, although delicious, had been stronger than he was used to. He'd enjoyed Maggie's company, and had been wondering over the past hours what those soft red lips would be like to kiss.

And now he knew.

Morgan murmured another curse under his breath.

The woman was fire. She kissed with a knowingness, an abandon that assured him she would be a delight to bed.

The devil take him, he'd wanted nothing more than to drag her into a dark alley, lift her skirts, and plow her hard against a wall. The heat of her kiss, the way her tongue danced and dueled with his, had made desire arch like an overstressed bow-string in his gut.

Morgan Mackay enjoyed women, and he'd lain with a few over the years, but it was rare for him to teeter on the edge of control like that.

His hound pushed against his leg then, interrupting his lust-filled thoughts. Gritta gave a low whine, making it clear she wasn't well pleased with being ignored all afternoon. Reaching down, Morgan stroked her neck. "Sorry, lass," he murmured with a rueful smile. "I have neglected ye, haven't I. Fear not ... ye will always be my best girl."

And with that, he set off toward the gates, his dog loping at his side.

12

SIGNS AND SUSPICION

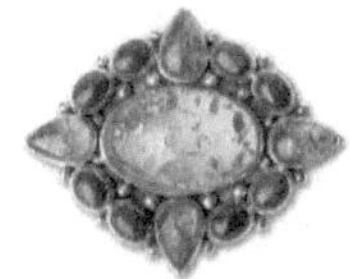

"HAVE YE BEEN drinking?"

Graeme Ross's growled question caught Maggie off-balance. Glancing up from where she was cutting up a piece of mutton before her, she turned to where her uncle sat beside her at the long table.

"Why do ye ask that?" she asked lightly, even if her heart sank.

She'd thought her gait steady, her speech unslurred.

"Yer cheeks are flushed," Graeme hissed.

Maggie went cold. They sat amongst a table of warriors. Niel Mackay sat directly opposite, his dark gaze lifting in curiosity at the muttered exchange between Graeme Ross and his niece.

"Ye have been elusive since we arrived. I couldn't find ye yesterday morning ... and I brought two prospective suitors up to our apartments earlier this afternoon to meet ye," her uncle continued, keeping his voice low, "but they got tired of waiting. Where have ye been hiding yerself away?"

"I went into town to do some shopping, uncle," she replied, forcing a light tone. "Surely, ye don't begrudge me that?"

His dark brows knitted together. "Ye went on yer own?"

"Aye, I didn't feel like company."

Her uncle's mouth pursed. "Widow or not, I don't want yer reputation tarnished. Next time, ye take Aileana or ye don't go at all."

Maggie clenched her jaw, her fingers tightening around her eating knife. How she grew tired of her uncle's boorish ways.

"Ye look as if ye got caught in the rain, Lady Munro," Niel spoke up then, drawing their attention. "Yer hair has a curl in it when damp."

Maggie straightened her spine and favored Niel with a tight smile. "Aye, I suppose it does."

She'd lingered in town too long, and upon returning to the keep hadn't had any time to change clothing or tidy herself up. She'd taken her hair out of its braid and hurriedly combed it through with her fingers, hoping that no one would notice her state of disarray. But Niel had—she wagered he was a man who missed little.

The moment her uncle had seen Maggie's bedraggled state at the entrance to the great hall, he'd glared at her.

He hadn't stopped glowering since.

"Mackay, ye will soon be wanting a wife," Graeme's voice cut across the table in an aggressive rumble. "My niece is a widow ... but she's still young enough ... and comely."

A cool smile stretched Niel Mackay's face, while Maggie fought the urge to cringe in her seat. Lord, how she wished her uncle wouldn't try to match-make. He had all the subtlety of a blunt ax.

Around them, some of the other warriors at the table—most of them unwed as well, Maggie noted—sniggered.

Cheeks blazing, Maggie stabbed at her mutton with her knife.

Curse ye, uncle.

"I seem to remember ye offering me yer niece last year," Niel drawled, "at Samhuinn."

"Aye ... and ye were evasive in yer response," Graeme challenged. "Do ye not find her bonny?"

Maggie glanced up to see that her uncle was leaning forward, his gaze holding the clan-chief son's.

Mortification, hot and prickly, rose within her. This was *awful*. Did Graeme Ross think he could bully men into showing interest in her?

Fortunately, Niel Mackay didn't look offended. Instead, he wore a veiled expression that was hard to read. Straightening up, he lifted a pewter goblet to his lips and took a sip of wine. "Yer niece is lovely indeed," he replied, glancing briefly in Maggie's direction. "I'm surprised nobody has sought her hand since then."

"Well, we've been cooped up for most of the winter, what with the bitter weather of late," Graeme muttered. "That is why I've brought her here."

Niel frowned. "This isn't the time or place for wooing," he replied, his tone cooling. "Especially after today's events."

Indeed, the mood inside the great hall was far different to the night of their arrival, Maggie noted. This evening, the air was subdued. There was no raucous laughter or singing. Most of the faces around her were tense and watchful. Everything would be decided over the next two days.

Graeme's mouth pursed at the chastisement, the florid color in his cheeks deepening. However, after a moment, her uncle dropped his gaze. "Aye," he huffed. "I suppose ye are right."

Niel shifted his attention to Maggie once more, his expression turning speculative. "All the same, I suppose I should start thinking about marriage one of these days."

Maggie stilled. She wasn't sure whether he was merely taking sport with her uncle, or whether he was actually serious.

Either way, she wasn't going to wed him.

She wasn't going to marry anyone.

"Well, my niece is a fine choice." Graeme puffed his barrel chest out. "Aye, she has a sharp tongue on her, but a firm hand will keep her in her place."

Maggie ground her teeth. Satan stick him with a pitch-fork, she wished her uncle would stop talking.

To her consternation, Niel Mackay merely smiled.

"I want ye to start following my niece."

Athol Ross glanced up from where he'd been pouring himself and his master cups of wine. They stood inside the chieftain's solar. The hour grew late, and Athol was restless. After the stress of the day, he longed to seek Aileana out and give her a tumble. They hadn't managed to lie together since their arrival in Inverness—something he intended to remedy tonight.

However, Graeme Ross had wanted to speak to him first.

"Follow her?" He didn't bother to hide the curiosity from his voice. "Really?"

His master scowled. "Aye ... the woman is up to something. She's disappeared into town twice since we arrived in Inverness, and this time returned home flushed with ale. I wouldn't be surprised if she's taken a lover."

Athol raised his brows, his interest piqued. "She's met someone here?" That was fast. They'd barely arrived, and Maggie didn't appear that sort of woman.

Ross's mouth flattened. "I don't know ... and that's why I need ye to track her whereabouts. Where she goes, ye follow ... until we leave Inverness."

"If she's found herself a lover, ye can just insist she weds him," Athol, ever-practical, pointed out. "Unless the man already has a wife."

The chieftain's expression darkened further at this last comment. "Lover or not, I don't want Maggie ruining her chances of finding a husband. This eve, Niel Mackay gave a sign that he may be interested in wedding her. One day that man will lead a clan ... such an alliance would benefit me greatly."

Athol swallowed the murmur of surprise that rose within him and carried the wine over to the high-backed chairs before the hearth. Ross was seated upon one of them, his thick legs upon a settle. The chieftain had been suffering from bouts of gout of late, the result of too much rich food and drink. The malady just soured his already irascible countenance further.

As such, Athol schooled his features into an interested expression, even if he found the comment ridiculous. Ross was letting desperation cloud his judgment. Niel Mackay was a clan-chief's son. He could have any woman he wanted, why would he want a widow?

A barren widow.

Aye, he knew the sorry tale. Aileana had whispered it to him one night, after a particularly energetic tumble.

"That is good news, indeed," Athol said, raising his goblet to the chieftain before taking a gulp of wine. "Let's hope Angus Mackay's fate tomorrow doesn't distract him then."

Graeme Ross's mouth pursed. Clearly, the thought hadn't escaped him either. "Aye," he muttered, "although if the Mackay was to be executed or imprisoned, Niel Mackay would need to take a wife, sooner rather than later."

13

A SON'S WRATH

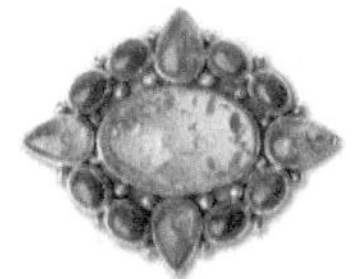

MAGGIE'S GAZE SETTLED upon the heavyset man who rose to his feet across the great hall. The chains he wore around his wrists clanked as he moved.

The time had come for Angus Mackay to hear his fate.

The clan-chief didn't hide his displeasure. His cheeks were flushed, his bearded jaw tense. However, unlike the day before, there was no belligerence in his blue eyes. Maggie fancied that she saw fear there instead.

She wasn't surprised. She barely knew him, yet her heart was pounding on his behalf, her palms sweaty.

Maggie wasn't the only one worried. She noted that the faces of the Mackays seated behind their clan-chief were all tense, their gazes troubled. After what they'd all just witnessed, they were right to be concerned about him.

Angus Mackay wasn't the first to be called before the king this morning. Alexander MacDonald and his mother, Mary, had both been sentenced to imprisonment, and after that three clan-chiefs had been condemned to a public beheading.

Maggie's throat constricted at the thought. One of the doomed men was John Ross. The king had sentenced the clan-chief for murdering the former 'Lord of the Isles', Alexander MacDonald's father.

On receiving his sentence, John Ross had swayed upon his feet, his face draining of color. And when the king's guards dragged him off to the dungeons, he'd begun muttering incoherently. His wife had then started weeping, her sobs ringing through the hall. Eventually, she'd had to be escorted from the hall.

Maggie had felt ill as she watched the poor woman go.

It was little wonder that Angus Mackay was visibly sweating as he moved to the center of the hall and faced the king.

James sat back on his throne, one leg crossing his knee at the ankle. As always, he was dressed in a fine scarlet surcoat, with velvet braies and high boots under it. His queen sat at his side. Joan's gaze gleamed with interest as she viewed the proceedings.

"Angus-Dow Mackay," James greeted him, his voice low and sure. "Ye stand before me, accused of many crimes ... the greatest of which is yer gathering of the armies of Strathnaver last summer to march upon the Gunns. Do ye deny this accusation?"

Mackay stared back at the king, his face sagging.

Pity stabbed Maggie under her ribs. The clan-chief looked defeated standing there, cowed by the dramatic sentencing earlier that morning.

The sour smell of sweat—the tang of fear—drifted across the great hall.

"No," Mackay finally replied, his voice gruff. "I do not, Yer Highness."

"So, ye freely admit that ye rallied a force of four thousand men from yer clan ... and from those allied to ye, and marched upon the Gunns?"

Angus Mackay's throat bobbed. "I do."

King James's face hardened. "I should take yer head for this, Mackay."

The clan-chief's face blanched, and the gasps of indrawn breaths followed. Maggie tore her attention from Angus Mackay, shifting it to the benches opposite, to Morgan. His face was grim, his gaze riveted upon the king. A few feet away, seated next to Connor Mackay, Niel Mackay wore a deep scowl.

Farther down the bench, George Gunn sat next to his son. The pair of them wore shuttered expressions, although Maggie imagined she glimpsed a gleam of victory in the Gunn clan-chief's eye. The man hadn't been held to account for anything during these councils. Now, his arch-nemesis risked losing his head.

Things couldn't have gone better for the Gunns.

The silence drew out, and when the king spoke once more, his voice held a challenge. "Tell me why ye shouldn't be executed for yer crimes, Mackay."

Angus Mackay swallowed hard. "What I did ... I did for my people," he rasped. "I was just protecting Strathnaver, as my forefathers before me have."

The king's mouth pursed. "Ye will need to do better than that, Mackay." His voice had chilled. "Or ye too will surely face the ax."

The Mackay clan-chief dropped his chin to his chest, his broad shoulders quivering.

Maggie's breathing caught at such a sight. The hulking, proud man looked broken.

"I apologize, Sire. I acted rashly ... arrogantly." He broke off there, remaining silent for a few moments as he seemed to focus his gaze upon a spot on the floor. "And as penance, I offer ye my son, Niel. Take him prisoner. Hold him as proof of my word that I will never again disobey ye."

Gasps reverberated through the great hall.

Like everyone else, Maggie looked to where the Mackays sat. All of them wore pole-axed expressions, but Niel's face had turned ashen. His blue eyes were wide as he stared at his father's back. A few feet away, his mother's mouth gaped. Estelle Mackay's expression was stricken.

"Ye'd offer up yer only son?" King James's voice cut through the murmurs that followed. "Just to save yer own neck?"

"Aye," Angus mumbled, still not raising his gaze. "I am the clan-chief. My people need me, Sire."

King James leaned forward then. "Niel Mackay ... what say ye to this arrangement?"

Niel didn't answer. Instead, his gaze glittered as it bored into his father.

Moments passed, and then Angus lifted his chin, straightened up, and turned to his son. His face was stony, his gaze veiled. "Ye must shoulder some of the blame, Niel," he rumbled. "Even after the king called for fighting to cease, ye led border raids. We … we stand in this together."

"Is that so?" The younger man's voice was flint-hard.

"Aye."

"Disloyal bastard!" Niel lunged at his father. One moment the warrior was seated with the rest of his clan, and the next he had his hands around Angus Mackay's neck.

A roar went up in the hall then. Estelle Mackay started shrieking. Warriors lurched to their feet, many of them urging Niel to throttle his father.

Maggie gasped, while next to her, Graeme Ross muttered an oath.

Across the hall, Connor and Morgan Mackay leaped up and rushed to where Angus and Niel wrestled. The clan-chief tried to fight his son off, yet it was impossible with his wrists in chains.

"Craven!" Niel tightened his grip. "Filthy fazart!"

Connor and Morgan gripped Niel by the shoulders and tried to haul him off his father. But such was his fury that he didn't even notice their efforts. Angus was going purple in the face now from lack of air.

"Guards!" The king's voice boomed through the din. "Break this rabble up!"

A swarm of warriors clad in mail and clinking armor descended upon the knot of struggling men. They tore Niel and Angus apart, knocking Connor and Morgan aside. However, neither brother returned to their seat. Instead, they flanked Niel protectively, while the soldiers formed a barrier between father and son. The clan-chief was wheezing and spluttering as he rubbed his injured neck.

Maggie watched, aghast. It was an ugly thing to witness—to see such a betrayal of trust between father and son.

Morgan Mackay stood at Niel's side, breathing hard. His handsome face was taut, his eyes a murderous shade of green; he looked just as angry as Niel himself.

"Niel Mackay." The king's gaze raked the clan-chief's son from head to foot. "I accept yer father's pledge of obedience and will indeed take ye as my prisoner." James paused there, letting his words sink in. "Henceforth ... ye will be imprisoned at Bass Rock, in the Firth of Forth. And there ye shall remain."

Morgan stormed down the hallway leading from the great hall, catching up with his brother. Connor and Keira had nearly reached the stairwell that led upstairs. "Ye can't let the Mackay get away with this," Morgan called out, his voice echoing down the corridor. "What he's done is an outrage."

Connor released Keira's arm and swiveled around. His brother's expression was thunderous, betraying that he too was fuming over what had just transpired inside the great hall. "What am I supposed to do, exactly?" Connor's voice was sharp. "The king has made his decision."

"But Angus just sacrificed his own son!"

"Aye, ye don't need to remind me of it," Connor bit back. "I was there. I witnessed the whole thing."

"He's sending Niel to Bass Rock," Keira reminded them. Her dark-blue gaze was troubled. "Few men ever leave that place." Like most folk, she would have heard the rumors of just how grim the prison was. Bass Rock, located off the North Berwick coast, was an isolated spot. It was said to be uninhabited, save for a colony of gannets and a lonely prison.

Niel had turned into a wild beast after the sentencing. His father had offered him up as a sacrifice, but he wasn't going to go quietly. His curses had rung high into the rafters as the guards subdued him, clamped his wrists in iron, and hauled him from the great hall.

It had pained Morgan that he hadn't been able to step up and help his friend. But despite the rage that pulsed within him, he'd known that to brawl with the guards would only turn the king's wrath on the Mackays of Farr. Morgan could be hot-headed, yet he wasn't a fool. Nonetheless, he wasn't about to let the matter drop.

"Gather the other chieftains," Morgan implored his brother. "We must go before the king in the morning ... ask him to reconsider."

Connor's jaw clenched. "And do what? Imprison Angus instead of Niel?"

"Aye ... after what that bastard just did to his son, he deserves it."

Connor muttered a curse and raked a hand through his hair.

Next to Connor, Keira chewed at her bottom lip. "Be careful, lads," she murmured. "The king is not pleased with the Mackays at present. Ye don't want to incur his wrath."

"Aye, love," Connor replied wearily. "But Morgan is right, we can't leave things as they are." He met Morgan's eye then. "Come on ... let's see if the other chieftains will stand with us tomorrow morning."

ENCOUNTERS IN THE GARDEN

MAGGIE HAD TO get out of the keep. She felt as if the walls were closing in on her.

Like the day before, this afternoon was gloomy. Yet although the drizzling hadn't ceased, Maggie ventured outdoors all the same.

After the morning's sentencing, the noon meal had been a somber affair. Most folk, the Ross clan included, had taken the meal in their quarters, rather than sit with the others in the great hall. Graeme had said nothing as he spooned boar stew into his mouth, and Maggie hadn't been inclined to chatter either.

Her uncle didn't nag her about meetings he might have organized with potential suitors over the meal. Nonetheless, Maggie was wary of lingering in his company.

Leaving Graeme to his brooding, she slipped out of their apartments.

The Mackay scandal aside, the news that John Ross would lose his head in two days' time had sent Clan Ross into a state of shock. The clan-chief's wife could be heard weeping, even from within the thick walls of her chamber.

Maggie's heart hurt at the raw sound. She didn't know the woman at all, had never even been introduced to her, otherwise she would have gone to comfort her.

Instead, she fled Lady Ross's sobbing and made her way to the walled garden within the keep's inner bailey.

She didn't go back into town. After her encounter with Rhianna, she wasn't in the mood to explore Inverness's cobbled streets anymore.

Maggie's thoughts were in turmoil. Life had suddenly turned complicated. The king's punishment had been far more severe than she'd anticipated—but just as disturbing was the afternoon she'd spent with Morgan Mackay the day before. She'd sat in an alehouse with a man she barely knew and downed drink like a slattern. And then she'd kissed him, or he'd kissed her. It didn't matter who'd started it; the fact remained that they'd embraced in broad daylight, where anyone might have seen them.

The memory of that heated kiss, of how good his body had felt pressed up against hers, stirred a restlessness within her that she didn't know how to deal with.

She hadn't kissed anyone since Campbell. Did her behavior make her disloyal?

Goose, she chided herself. *It was just a kiss. Ye aren't made of iron.*

Striding across the inner bailey, Maggie banished lingering thoughts of her encounter with the Mackay warrior. Perhaps a walk in the walled garden would help her regain her equilibrium. She'd heard it was a lovely spot, and with the persistent drizzle, there wasn't likely to be a soul about. She could get some much-needed solitude.

Entering the garden through a wide arch covered in roses that were just beginning to bud, Maggie viewed the space. She'd expected a courtyard-style garden, yet this one was laid out like a maze, with high yew hedges and trailing canopies of lilac, honeysuckle, and wisteria. The scents, brought out by the warm, damp air, were heady—more delicious than any perfume.

Maggie sucked the fragrance in and slowly felt the tension of the morning unravel.

King James had torn his way through the northern clan-chiefs. And when he'd finished dealing out his punishments, the king had risen to his feet, motioned to his wife, and waited while she linked her arm through his.

Then, without another word, the pair of them swept from the hall.

He still had one more audience to conduct the next day, but Maggie would feign a headache, a fever—anything really, to avoid going. She wouldn't attend the beheadings the following dawn either.

She'd seen enough of the king's justice.

Part of her knew he'd been left with no choice. He'd issued commands over the last two years, and none of the clan-chiefs had heeded him. However, his punishment had left them all reeling. It seemed so harsh.

Deep in thought, Maggie circuited the garden. Her boots crunched over small pebbles, while the rain continued to fall in a fine, silent veil.

It felt good to be on her own for a spell, to put her thoughts in order.

At least I won't have to worry about Niel Mackay wooing me now.

The uncharitable thought made her wince. The Mackay clan-chief's son wouldn't be taking a wife for a long while, if ever. And despite that she'd never warmed to Niel, Maggie felt for the man. His father had publicly betrayed him.

Rounding a corner, deep in thought, Maggie suddenly realized she wasn't the only one in the garden, as she'd believed.

A few yards away, a man and woman stood talking.

And the moment she saw them, Maggie knew she was intruding.

She halted, her feet making a loud 'crunch' on the pebbles. Nervously, she looked around, hoping to find an entrance to the heart of the maze. However, she'd just passed one.

It was too late anyway. They'd seen her.

Alexander Gunn and Jaimee Mackay.

Maggie's gaze widened. This was a pairing she'd never thought to bear witness to. After all, the Mackays and Gunns loathed each other, and Connor Mackay's recent marriage to Keira Gunn hadn't done anything to improve relations as far as Maggie could see.

And they were standing close. Barely a foot of air lay between them.

Yet, Maggie had to admit they made a striking couple. Alexander was tall, dark, and brawny, while Jaimee was willowy, her unbound red-gold hair curling in the drizzle.

They'd been staring at each other, gazes locked, but at Maggie's abrupt appearance, Alexander took a step back from Jaimee. Then, favoring both her and Maggie with a curt nod, he spun on his heel and stalked from the garden.

Cheeks warming, for it was obvious she'd interrupted an intense exchange, Maggie cleared her throat. "I'm sorry for the intrusion ... I didn't realize anyone else was in here."

Jaimee glanced Maggie's way, her pine-green eyes—the same hue as Morgan's, Maggie noted—narrowing. She then let out a gusting sigh. "Neither did I." Her attention flicked to where Alexander Gunn had just disappeared. "I certainly never expected to encounter *him* here."

Maggie inclined her head. So, this hadn't been a planned rendezvous. From their proximity to each other, and the intense way he'd been staring at the young woman, Maggie would have thought otherwise.

Mother Mary, ye are turning into a gossip, Maggie thought, aghast at the direction of her thoughts. She wasn't in a position to judge others at present, not after her heated kiss with Morgan Mackay the day before.

"Aye, yer clans aren't best of friends at present," Maggie said after an awkward pause. She burned to know why the Gunn clan-chief's son had sought out Jaimee here, for she hardly thought he'd decided to take a turn around the garden in the rain. However, she swallowed the question.

Jaimee laughed. "That's an understatement, Lady Munro," she murmured. "Although after this morning's mess, my clan are more focused on their own problems."

"How is the Mackay?" Maggie asked. "Has he offered any explanation to ye all, as to why he sacrificed his son?"

Jaimee's gaze shadowed, and she shook her head. "None of us have seen him. As soon as the sentencing ended, he disappeared into his apartments with his wife and hasn't yet emerged." Her expression hardened. "I'd wager he's too ashamed to face us."

Maggie nodded. The news didn't surprise her. In saving his own neck, Angus Mackay had likely driven a wedge between himself and his clan—one that would take some effort to remove.

Silence fell between the two women then. Uncomfortable, Maggie cleared her throat. She wasn't sure what to say to Jaimee Mackay.

"How are things at Farr Castle these days?" she finally asked in an attempt to fill the awkward pause. "Are yer brother and his wife happy together?"

Jaimee's expression turned guarded. "They are well-matched," she replied, her tone wary. "Maybe much more so than Connor and yer sister would have been."

There was no missing the edge to Jaimee's voice. She still harbored resentment toward Rhianna for the deception she had woven and the hurt her brother had suffered as a result.

"Aye, ye are right," Maggie admitted with a wry smile. "I've seen the way the pair of them look at each other. The laird is devoted to his wife."

Jaimee frowned. "Ye aren't angry?"

"No, why would I be?"

"Didn't ye want Connor to wed yer sister?"

Maggie gave a soft laugh. "My sister evidently didn't wish to become Lady Mackay of Farr. She took her fate into her own hands ... and in the end, things seem to have worked out for the best."

She thought then of Rhianna's life in Inverness, spending her days beating out soiled clothes in a washhouse while her man diced away their coin. Her sister had taken a great risk running away with her lover—and in fact things hadn't transpired as she'd hoped. Still, Maggie couldn't share the news with the woman before her.

"It was certainly bold ... what she did," Jaimee admitted.

Maggie exhaled sharply. "Aye, and selfish."

Jaimee nodded. "All the same, few women dare to go after what they want." Her gaze sharpened then. "I think widows have the best of things in many ways."

Maggie quirked an eyebrow. "Why would ye think that?"

"Well, ye have the 'respectability' of once having a husband, but the freedom to choose whether or not ye wed again."

"I wish ye'd tell my uncle that," Maggie grumbled. "The man dragged me to Inverness with the hope of finding me a husband."

Jaimee's green eyes widened. "What? Here, when men are being sentenced to death?"

"Aye, Graeme Ross's determination knows no bounds."

"No one can force ye to wed, if ye don't wish to," Jaimee informed Maggie then, her chin rising stubbornly. "I've already told Connor that."

Maggie raised an eyebrow. "So, ye wish to remain a spinster?"

"Aye."

"Will ye take the veil?"

The look of disgust on Jaimee's face made laughter bubble up inside Maggie. Her mouth twitched, although she managed to hold it back.

"I just wish for things to continue as they are at Farr Castle, but Connor brings up the subject of finding me a husband on a weekly basis now. He's started talking about holding a gathering in the summer so that suitors can court me."

"That sounds like a sensible idea."

Jaimee gave Maggie a withering look. "It would be, if I actually *wanted* a husband."

"Husbands aren't all that bad." Maggie gestured to the path behind her, suggesting that they both continue their walk. "I was once happily wed, and my match was an arranged one."

"Ye were one of the fortunate couples then," Jaimee replied as she fell in step with Maggie. The women began a slow circuit around the perimeter of the walled garden, retracing the path that Maggie had taken earlier.

Maggie favored the younger woman with a smile, although it was tinged with sadness. "Aye, I was."

A lone figure watched the two women emerge from the walled garden a short while later.

Hidden in the shadow of the granary, Athol Ross's gaze tracked Maggie and Jaimee as they made their way across the inner bailey toward the keep.

Frowning, Athol waited until they were well ahead of him before he pushed himself off the wall and followed.

Damn ye, Graeme Ross, he thought darkly. *I have better things to do with my time than dog the steps of yer niece.* Athol was manservant of the laird of Caisteal Nan Corr, not some lowlife who was happy to spend his days spying on others.

It wasn't as if the widow was interesting to follow. This enterprise might have been exciting if she'd indeed had a lover. Unlike his master, he doubted the woman was up to something. She'd been in mourning only a few days earlier after all.

So far, nothing Maggie had done had been suspicious. He'd seen Alexander Gunn emerge from the garden shortly after Maggie had entered it, which had piqued his interest. But when she'd left the garden with Jaimee Mackay, any suspicion that she'd gone into the garden for a tryst with the Gunn heir had vanished.

This is a waste of time.

Even so, Athol slipped into the keep in Maggie's wake.

15

STOLEN GLANCES

"WELL, THAT WENT well." The sarcasm in Connor's voice sliced through the damp air.

Striding next to him, as the brothers made their way across the outer-bailey toward the stables to check on their horses, Morgan scowled. "Aye, he barely listened to us."

"I did warn ye." Connor cast Morgan an exasperated look. "King James appears the affable sort, yet his mild manners hide a core of iron. Ye saw his face yesterday when he sentenced Niel. He enjoyed meting out justice to the Mackays."

Morgan ground his jaw, yet didn't argue with his brother. Curse him, Connor was right.

They'd managed to get all the Mackay chieftains in attendance—Robert Mackay of Balnakeil, Hugh Mackay of Loch Stach, and William Mackay of Dun Ugadale—to join them before they went in front of the king in his solar.

Each man had given a glowing account of Niel's character, before Connor had made a personal plea for clemency.

Morgan had joined the chieftains, standing behind them as they made their speeches, although his temper had quickened when he saw the boredom upon the king's face. They'd interrupted him breaking his fast. A table covered with platters of fresh bread and rounds of bannock; and pots of freshly churned butter, honey, porridge, and stewed fruit sat before the king and queen. Joan had sighed repeatedly as each Mackay chieftain said his piece.

The lack of respect toward his clansmen had rankled.

Connor had barely finished talking when the king had lifted a ring-encrusted hand and waved him away. "So, the four of ye are friends with the clan-chief's son," he drawled. "How does that make him worthy of releasing?"

"Yer Highness," Connor began, his voice roughening. "I can assure ye that—"

"Enough." The king gestured for the servants behind them to open the doors to the solar and usher his guests out. "Ye have all wasted my time long enough. Leave me to break my fast in peace."

Those words had infuriated Morgan. He'd wanted to grab the nearest object—a pot of congealing porridge— and empty it over the king's head.

The brothers now entered the stables. Connor went to check on Thunder, while Morgan ducked into Archer's stall. The gelding greeted him with a soft whicker. Morgan reached out and stroked the horse's neck.

"We can't give up," he said, knowing Connor could hear him in the next stall. "Maybe, if we can get a proper petition together, the king might listen."

Connor muttered something under his breath. "Didn't ye see how irritated he was? I think we should just drop it."

Morgan's mouth thinned, stubbornness rising within him. "I can't do that."

They needed Niel freed, his name cleared, or the likes of the Gunns and the Sutherlands would start circling like vultures. Angus Mackay had disgraced himself and dishonored his clan the day before. It was a scene that no one present in the great hall of Inverness would forget, least of all their enemies. Meanwhile, the other Mackay chieftains had lost faith in their clan-chief, and if nothing was done, a rot would likely soon set in.

"As ye can see, she has a bonny face and a fine figure." Graeme Ross's gravelly voice drifted across the table. "I know she's getting on a bit … but twenty-six isn't irredeemable. Maggie carries her years well."

Seated at the long table, Maggie tried to keep her temper under control.

However, as supper wore on, it was getting increasingly difficult to remain civil. Another long day of sentencing had passed, and with the dawn, three men would lose their heads. Even so, her uncle wouldn't leave things be. Maggie had spent the day hidden away in Inverness Castle's library. However, she'd been unable to escape this supper.

The great hall was half-empty this evening. Despite that they were encouraged to eat together, many of the clans had decided to take the meal in their apartments. Those who did dine in the hall wore somber expressions. Unlike the first supper in Inverness, conversation was a low, subdued rumble tonight.

A few male sniggers followed her uncle's comment, while heat bloomed across Maggie's cheeks.

Her fingers clenched around the knife she'd been using to fillet the trout on the plate before her. How she wished to use it on Graeme Ross.

"Aye, we all can see for ourselves that yer niece is comely." Robert Mackay's voice rumbled across the table. She glanced up to see the man was frowning. "But given Angus Mackay has recently made fools out of us— his own clansmen—I'm hardly in the mood to play suitor."

Graeme Ross's face turned red at this. "I am merely looking out for my niece," he growled.

No, ye are looking out for yerself, Maggie thought, dropping her gaze to the trout in front of her. She'd thought that, with the beheadings looming, he might have the decency to cease his quest to rid himself of her. But with the end of their stay at Inverness drawing near, it had only made him more aggressive, more desperate.

Robert Mackay said something else then, which made some of the other men snort with laughter, but Maggie wasn't listening. This supper had turned into an ordeal, and she no longer wanted to be part of it. Deliberately blocking out the surrounding conversation, she reached for her goblet and took a large gulp of sloe wine.

She wasn't given to consuming a lot of ale and wine, but this trip had taken its toll on her.

Just another day or two. Not long now, and she'd be free of the prospect of marriage forever.

Maggie glanced across the great hall at where the Mackays sat eating their supper. The clan-chief was nowhere in sight, but the Mackays of the various strongholds throughout the territory had all taken their places at a long table against the far wall. Like most folk in the hall, they weren't in high spirits. There were few smiles and no laughter.

Morgan was among them, seated between his brother and an auburn-haired warrior whose similar features marked him as kin.

Feeling her gaze upon him, Morgan glanced up, and for an instant, they stared at each other.

Heat suffused Maggie. They hadn't spoken since returning from town together two days earlier—not that there had been many opportunities to. Maggie had been absent during that afternoon's sentencing.

Morgan didn't smile as he locked gazes with her, and somehow his seriousness made her nervous.

Maggie's skin prickled, her breathing quickening.

"My niece is of course an accomplished woman." Graeme Ross's voice jerked her back to the conversation at her own table. She tore her gaze from Morgan's to see that her uncle hadn't yet finished making a fool of himself. "She knows how to organize servants, is a fine embroiderer, and has a pleasant singing voice. Isn't that right, Maggie? Go on, lass, give us a song."

Maggie glowered at her uncle, yet remained mutinously silent.

Seated next to his elder brother, Duncan Mackay smirked, before exchanging an amused look with Robert.

Maggie's shoulders rounded, and she dropped her gaze to her half-finished meal. She was beyond embarrassed now. There wasn't any point in wishing her uncle would shut his beak. He just couldn't seem to help himself.

But then, as Graeme Ross continued to drone on about all the reasons one of the men present should take an interest in his widowed niece, Maggie's thoughts drifted back to that afternoon after she and Morgan left *The Fox and Goose.*

For a short while, as they'd stood together in the rain, she'd come alive again. Now, curse him, she still craved his kisses, his touch.

Swallowing hard, Maggie fought the urge to reach up and rub the ache that had arisen under her breast bone. The Lord strike her down, how she wanted him. She'd thought her ability to feel lust had died with Campbell— yet Morgan had proved that it hadn't.

Maggie looked away. However, Morgan continued to watch her. She was a lone woman at a table of loud, opinionated men. He'd stolen glances her way earlier, noting her pained expression whenever her uncle spoke.

Graeme Ross wore a flustered expression now. Clearly, his attempts at match-making hadn't worked out. Morgan's mouth thinned. The man was an idiot to press the issue with the current mood inside Inverness Castle.

Even so, Morgan didn't like to see Maggie looking so uncomfortable. Her face was flushed, and her gaze hunted.

However, there was no mistaking the desire he'd seen when they'd locked gazes.

Heat had ignited in his belly as the stare drew out— and for a few brief moments, he'd forgotten the humiliating and worrying events of the past days. Instead, his world narrowed to the beautiful woman seated across the hall.

And as they'd stared at each other, he'd relived that kiss: the feel of her pliant, soft body pressed against his, the heat of her mouth, and the scent of lily that had enveloped him. Morgan's groin had started to ache, lust tightening his stomach muscles. He wanted so much more of Maggie Munro.

When she'd severed eye-contact, a strange sense of loss filtered over him. It was a discomforting sensation, not one he was used to.

Connor said something to him then, but Morgan merely nodded in response. He suddenly found it difficult to concentrate.

16

INSTINCT

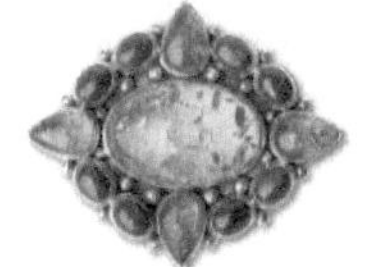

WHEN MORGAN LEFT the great hall, he glanced Maggie's way.

Their gazes locked once more, heat flaring in an instant.

Maggie's pulse started to race. His look was an open challenge, one so blatant that her mouth went dry.

Heart hammering, she glanced down at the empty goblet of wine she still clutched. It was getting late. She too should retire. Her uncle had already departed. Robert and Duncan Mackay's lack of interest in her as a potential wife had vexed him. He didn't seem to understand that most men of their rank could do much better than a twenty-six-year-old widow. As soon as servants cleared away the supper dishes, Graeme Ross had risen to his feet and stomped off.

Once the Mackays of Farr had all left, Maggie took her own leave. Murmuring a 'good night' to Robert and Duncan Mackay, she rose to her feet and exited from the hall.

Outside in the wide entranceway beyond, there wasn't a soul about.

Maggie paused a moment before she started to feel a bit foolish.

Loneliness and stress had clearly addled her wits. Had she truly expected Morgan to be waiting for her?

It was obvious she needed a good night's sleep. Perhaps she would ask Aileana to draw her a hot bath before she retired. It would soothe her nerves.

Maggie took the corridor away from the great hall. It was a wide, lofty hallway, framed by stone arches that led off to various chambers and service stairwells. Sconces illuminated the stone walls, highlighting the pink hue in the rock. The only sound was the scuff of Maggie's slippers on the pavers.

And then, when she neared the foot of the stairs, she spied a tall, lanky figure leaning against the wall. Morgan Mackay watched her approach under slightly lowered lids, his gaze tracking every movement.

Her gait slowed. Excitement fluttered in the pit of her belly.

"Hello, Maggie," he greeted her softly.

Maggie stopped before him. "Good eve, Morgan," she murmured. "Have ye had a pleasant evening?"

Goose! What a foolish thing to ask. Of course he hadn't. The Mackays were still reeling after the cowardly behavior of their clan-chief.

Morgan's mouth curved, his left cheek dimpling in a way that made her breathing quicken. "Well enough … it was better than yers I'd wager. I saw yer uncle was up to his old tricks."

Maggie cleared her throat. "Aye … the man never tires."

Silence fell between them then. Eventually, Morgan was the one to break it. "I enjoyed spending time with ye the other day."

Maggie swallowed, suddenly nervous. "Aye," she breathed. "Ye too are … good company."

Morgan pushed off the wall and stepped toward her.

She wet her lips, aware then that he was staring at her mouth. Things were moving quickly, and there was a part of her that quailed. However, fortune shone upon those who took life by the horns—or so folk said. Drawing in a steadying breath, she let her instincts rule.

Maggie took hold of Morgan's hand. A heartbeat passed, and then another.

Wordlessly, she led him toward an alcove. She'd
noted it as she'd approached the stairwell, a shadowy
space, where those traveling these corridors wouldn't see
them.

How can ye be this brazen? Her pulse now beat a
tattoo in her ears. She couldn't believe how bold she was
being. She'd never acted like this with Campbell. Even
after they'd been wed awhile, she'd always let him take
the lead. Being in Inverness had turned her into
someone she barely recognized.

Morgan didn't resist her. Still not speaking, they
crossed the hallway and stepped inside the alcove. It was
a surprisingly large space, filled with barrels of what
smelled like ale and mead. There weren't any torches or
sconces on the wall in here; the only light came from the
corridor beyond.

However, it was enough for Maggie to see the hunger
in Morgan Mackay's eyes.

As soon as they were out of sight of the hallways, he
stepped close, bent his head, and kissed her.

It was a hot and feverish embrace, hungrier than the
one he'd given her in the market square.

Since then, both of them had had time to think upon
the incident, and for desire to kindle and smolder.

And now that they were alone in this shadowed
alcove, passion ignited.

He kissed her wildly, and Maggie responded in kind.
Reaching up, she dug her fingers into his hair, reveling at
how silky it felt in her fingers. So different to the
hardness of his long body or the wet heat of his mouth.
He tasted faintly of the wine he'd drunk at supper. He
smelt of leather and the light scent of cloves from
whatever he'd used to recently bathe in. The rasp of his
stubbled jaw against her soft skin made Maggie gasp.

Groaning into her mouth, he pushed her hard up
against the rough stone wall. Grasping her wrists, he
lifted her arms high, pinning them against the wall above
her head with one hand while his lips grazed her jaw, his
tongue darting into the shell of her ear.

Maggie bit down on her bottom lip. She was trembling now. His lips left a wake of fire. Need clawed at her belly and made her breath come in ragged gasps.

His mouth traveled lower still, to the tender skin under her jaw. She arched against him, welcoming his touch. His free hand traveled down to the laces of her bodice.

In deft movements, he loosened them. The front of her kirtle gaped open. Underneath, Maggie wore a fine linen lèine. She glanced down, to see her breasts straining against the thin material, her nipples hard and dark.

Murmuring a curse under his breath, Morgan released her wrists and lowered himself before her.

His mouth fastened upon a nipple, and he suckled her hard through the material of her lèine. The sensation was so utterly delicious that Maggie had to clamp her jaw shut, to stifle the wanton moan that rose within her.

Even hidden away from the hallway, they couldn't make any noise in here.

He suckled her hard, teasing her nipple into a swollen bud, before shifting his attention to its twin. And all the while, Maggie writhed against him. She dug her fingers into his hair, urging him on.

Each suck, every time his teeth grazed the sensitive peak, the cradle of her hips turned molten. Pleasure pulsed through her, turning her breathing into urgent, panting gasps.

She couldn't bear it. She needed to have him inside her.

But Morgan was not yet done teasing her.

Cool air whispered against her bare legs as he drew up her skirts. Then, he lifted her left leg, placing it over his shoulder while he sank to his knees.

Maggie's breathing caught. *Lord, he's going to—*

Maggie clapped a hand over her mouth to stifle the mewling cry of pleasure that bubbled up inside her, at the feel of his finger sliding deep within her. She arched against him as his fingers, his lips, his tongue brought her to a shuddering peak.

She nearly forgot where they were, nearly cried out.

Pleasure shivered and throbbed through her, and she pressed herself against him, craving more.

And then he was no longer kneeling before her.

Morgan rose to his full height and lifted her against the wall once more, splaying her out like a butterfly while he pushed her skirts high around her waist. Unlacing his braies with one hand, his mouth captured hers once more.

The kiss was savage, demanding.

An instant later, he thrust inside her.

He was big, and the shock of penetration made Maggie gasp. Morgan stilled for a moment, letting her adjust, and then he ground his hips against hers in a slow, sensual dance that made Maggie groan into his mouth.

He filled her utterly. And the initial shock of having him buried deep inside her turned into something molten, something breathtaking.

Taking his lead, she moved her hips languorously against his. A thrill rippled through her when she heard the purely male growl low in his throat in response.

His tongue slid into her mouth, mimicking the movement of his hips as he began to move inside her. Maggie wrapped her legs around his hips, her heels digging into the hard muscles of his backside, urging him deeper still.

Maggie climaxed again, fast and hard, her cry muffled against his mouth. A heartbeat later, his lean body arched against hers, every muscle going rigid.

Breathing hard, they collapsed against the wall together.

Maggie buried her face in the curve of his neck, breathing him in. Morgan Mackay smelled better than any man had the right to. They clung together in the aftermath, and in those moments, Maggie forgot everything else.

"What. Is. This?"

In an instant, the languorous, boneless pleasure that suffused Maggie's body drained away.

Twisting her head, her gaze settled upon a familiar—and wholly unwelcome—figure.

Graeme Ross stood inside the entrance to the alcove, and his glare was fixed upon them both.

Maggie stared at her uncle, hardly able to believe he was actually standing there, witnessing this.

But he was.

The moment drew out, and although she didn't look his way, she sensed Morgan was also staring at Graeme Ross. A burly figure stepped up next to the chieftain.

Athol Ross was breathing hard, as if out of breath.

With a sinking feeling in her gut, Maggie understood.

Her sly uncle had bid his manservant to follow her. She'd thought she'd seen him that morning when she'd emerged from her chamber to take a quick walk before breaking her fast.

From the looks of things, Athol had seen her and Morgan disappear into the alcove before he'd sprinted up the stairs to fetch the chieftain.

Neither man averted his gaze. They didn't allow Morgan to withdraw from her and relace his braies, or for Maggie to do up the bodice of her kirtle. Instead, their presence invaded the alcove.

Morgan hadn't yet spoken a word.

"I think it's clear what they're doing," Athol replied to the chieftain's rhetorical question. His gaze glinted as it raked over them. "I bear witness to it, as do ye, Ross."

Maggie's throat tightened. The devil take Athol, she'd never liked the man and had wondered what Aileana saw in him. However, the pleasure he was taking in this made fury pulse in her belly, dousing the last of the languid pleasure of her coupling with Morgan.

"Yer parents would turn in their graves to see how low both their daughters have sunk." Maggie could have sworn she saw vindication flare in her uncle's dark eyes.

Maggie stared back at him. Like Morgan, she didn't speak. The shock of discovery had rendered her utterly mute for the moment.

"However, yer carelessness has given me the boon I've been seeking. I admit I was hoping for a better match—but after days of searching for a suitor, it seems nobody wants ye. At least this way, I am finally rid of ye," Graeme continued. His attention shifted to Morgan then. Maggie followed her uncle's gaze, looking at her lover for the first time since they'd been interrupted.

Morgan's handsome face was hard. There was no embarrassment, just simmering anger.

The two men locked gazes, and when her uncle spoke once more, there was a gloating edge to his voice. "Now ye must wed my niece, Mackay."

17

CAST OUT

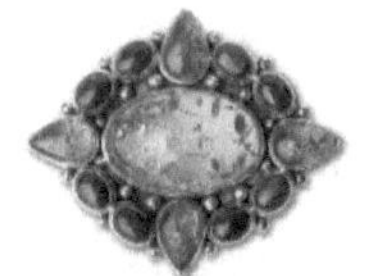

"I CAUGHT THEM, in the act … and my manservant also bore witness. There is no other choice. Yer brother has compromised my niece. They must be married at once."

Silence fell in the solar, a weighty pause that only served to stoke the ire simmering in Morgan's belly.

"Meddling bastard," he growled, his temper getting the better of him. He'd initially been taken by surprise in the alcove, but now that they'd all gone upstairs to his brother's solar, and dragged Connor and his wife from their bed, he was starting to feel truly vexed. "Were ye spying on us?"

"Aye," Graeme Ross shot back, his already high-colored cheeks reddening further. "And it's just as well too, for our Maggie was up to no good." His mouth twisted into a vicious smile as he shifted his attention to his niece.

Maggie glared back at him, her hands balling at her sides. She'd hardly uttered a word since her uncle had brought them up here. It felt crowded inside the solar. Connor and Keira stood near the glowing hearth, their eyes clouded with confusion, while Maggie and Morgan stood shoulder-to-shoulder in the center of the chamber, like two criminals about to be sentenced. The Ross chieftain faced them, while his man, Athol, stood by the door.

Morgan cast the manservant a jaundiced look. *Serpent.*

"Does Graeme Ross speak the truth, Morgan?" Connor asked finally. Glancing over at his brother, Morgan saw the lines of strain bracketing his brother's mouth, the wariness in his eyes. "Were ye caught swiving this woman?"

Mouth compressed, Morgan nodded. He could hardly deny it, could he? They'd been caught locked together, panting in the aftermath of their passion.

Whispering a curse, Connor dragged a hand through his hair.

Morgan drew in a deep breath to settle his rising temper. He could see the disappointment in Connor's eyes, the frustration, but the last thing he needed at present was a lecture from his elder brother.

Next to Connor, Keira looked on, silent and wide-eyed. Her gaze flicked from Maggie to Morgan, confused and questioning. She was likely wondering why the widow Munro would do something so foolish.

Morgan's belly clenched. He was responsible for this. They'd both been reckless, yet Maggie would never have thrown caution aside without his encouragement.

Connor's expression hardened then as he stared Morgan down. "Care to explain?" he demanded.

"I don't care who started it … or who's to blame," Graeme Ross interrupted, his tone belligerent. "The fact remains that my niece has been sullied. Yer brother must wed her."

"Must he?" Maggie shot back, rousing herself from the shock that settled over her after their discovery in the alcove. "Do I not have a say in things?"

"No, ye don't." The veins stood on out Graeme Ross's forehead as he took a threatening step toward Maggie.

Morgan tensed, readying himself to step between them if need be. He clenched his hands into fists. He'd take great pleasure in breaking the bastard's nose.

"Ye have been a boil on my arse for too long," Ross continued. "I have sheltered ye in my broch, have clothed and fed ye, and now I want rid of ye, woman."

"Ye can't force me to wed," she choked out. Maggie's face was a mask of fury as she glared back at her uncle, shoulders squared and fists clenched at her sides. Her blue eyes glittered.

"Enough!" Graeme Ross boomed. "I cast ye out! Go back to the Munros if they will have ye, but if ye ever darken my door, I will have ye stoned out of Caisteal Nan Corr."

The brutality of the man's words caused a shocked hush to settle over the solar.

Morgan stilled. He couldn't believe that Ross had disowned his niece, in front of them all.

Maggie's face had drained of color, except for two pink spots upon her cheekbones. Her horrified expression made something twist within Morgan's chest. How dare her uncle treat her so roughly?

"Have ye no honor, man?" he ground out. "Ye can't cast her out. This woman is yer blood."

Graeme Ross's mouth twisted. "Not anymore. She's *yer* problem now, Mackay."

"I can't go back to the Munros," Maggie whispered, the tremor in her voice betraying her shock. "Ye know they don't want me there."

"Well then." The triumph in Graeme Ross's voice made heat surge through Morgan's belly. The bastard was enjoying himself. "Ye have a predicament, niece." He turned then, flashing Connor a hard smile. "Ye'd better ensure yer brother makes an honest woman of her ... if ye Mackays have any honor, that is."

"Have ye lost yer wits, Ross?" Connor's voice was hard, his gaze wintry. "My brother's right. Ye can't turn yer back on yer own kin like this."

"Just watch me," Graeme Ross replied, his voice victorious. "From this moment forth, I wash my hands of the woman."

The chieftain then swiveled on his heel and strode from the solar without another word. His manservant, Athol, no longer looked so smug. Wearing a bewildered, slightly worried expression, he followed his master out of the room.

Silence settled over the chamber once they'd gone.

"I'm sorry." Maggie turned to Morgan, fixing him with an imploring look. Her eyes shimmered with tears. "I don't know what to do."

Keira stepped forward, her brow furrowed in concern. "Ye are better off free of that man," she offered, her voice soft yet sure.

Maggie's throat bobbed. "But he's the only kin I have left. I have no place else to go. She looked Keira directly in the eye then. "Without him, I'm completely alone in the world."

"No ye aren't," Morgan replied, waiting as Maggie shifted her gaze to him. His pulse was now galloping. He hadn't planned on taking a wife and certainly didn't want to propose under such circumstances. However, he couldn't let this farce continue, couldn't let Maggie fear for her future. He'd helped make this mess, and now he'd have to fix it. "For, if ye agree to it, I shall wed ye."

"I swear ye sometimes have the wits of a donkey. Why did ye do it? *Why*?"

Morgan had expected to weather his brother's fury, and Connor didn't disappoint him.

The moment they were alone in the solar—once Maggie and the others had retreated to their respective quarters—Connor turned on him.

Morgan met his brother's eye as he folded his arms across his chest. "The opportunity presented itself ... and it was something we *both* wanted."

"Ye may have already planted a bairn in her tonight," his brother countered. "Did ye think about that?"

Morgan didn't answer. Of course, Connor didn't know Maggie was unable to bear children—and Morgan certainly wasn't going to tell him.

Connor's green eyes narrowed, brows crashing together. A nerve ticked in his jaw, and his hands fisted at his sides. He was just moments away from lashing out at Morgan.

Tensing, Morgan dropped his arms to his sides, readying himself to respond. If his brother wanted a fight, he'd give him one.

They hadn't come to blows in earnest in many years, but in Morgan's current mood, he felt like a brawl. The frustration of the last few days—his anger at Angus Mackay, at the lying Gunns, and at the king simmered just beneath the surface.

As if sensing Morgan's belligerence, Connor's mouth thinned. "I warned ye something like this would happen one day. God's bones, Morgan. We should've left ye behind. We're here for serious matters … not for ye to swive yer way through Inverness Castle."

Morgan's mouth quirked into a humorless smile. "Really? Do ye think that's what I've been doing?"

Connor raked a hand through his hair. He'd done that so often since being torn from his bed that his hair was a tousled mess. "Graeme Ross's widowed niece?"

Morgan's mouth thinned. He wasn't going to dignify that comment with an answer. His choice in lovers was his own.

A weighty silence fell in the solar, broken only by the gentle crackling of the hearth behind them. Sinking down into a chair by the fire, Morgan dragged a hand down his face. "Maggie deserves better than this," he murmured finally. "Contrary to what ye believe, I *am* sorry for what happened. Truthfully, I don't wish to wed, but if I must, then I could do far worse than a woman like Maggie." Morgan glanced up then, meeting Connor's eye once more. "I won't see her mistreated."

Connor held his gaze, before huffing a deep sigh. "It's just as well ye feel that way," his brother replied, his voice dry. "Because this time tomorrow, she'll be yer wife."

18

A WIFE ONCE MORE

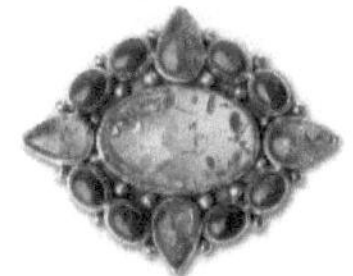

MAGGIE AND MORGAN wed in the doorway to Inverness kirk.

It was a grey, somber morning. There were few folk about, for most of the town had amassed in the market square for the public beheadings of those King James had convicted.

Maggie had no desire to attend the executions and had intended to hide away in her chamber while they took place. She had no wish to get married this morning either—yet here she was.

All ye had to do was make it through the stay in Inverness, and ye would have been free. Bitterness soured her mouth. Aye, she'd been so close to thwarting her uncle. So very close.

Standing there on the top step before the arched entrance to the kirk, Maggie's belly churned and cold sweat coated her skin.

It was to be a simple wedding. Apart from the ribbon of plaid Connor Mackay had given to the priest for the ceremony, there was no other ornamentation. Both Maggie and Morgan were dressed plainly. She wore a grey-blue kirtle, while he had chosen a dark-green lèine and buff-colored braies.

A small group had amassed to bear witness, looking on from the bottom of the steps. Graeme Ross was nowhere to be seen, although Connor Mackay and his wife had been joined by Jaimee, the auburn-haired warrior Morgan had introduced as his cousin, Kennan, and his wife, Cait.

All of them looked painfully serious this morning.

Morgan's face also bore lines of strain. He wore a solemn, determined expression, as if he were about to go to the healer for a tooth extraction. Maggie imagined she looked worse. She hadn't slept the night before.

The priest murmured the words that would join them as he wound a length of Mackay plaid around Maggie and Morgan's clasped hands.

Mother Mary, how did it come to this?

She'd taken a foolish risk, let her attraction to Morgan Mackay cloud her good sense. That was how. She should have realized that her uncle didn't trust her— especially when he'd questioned her about her visits into town.

Witless woman, this is yer own doing.

The admission made the boulder in her belly weigh all the heavier. Taking a husband was the last thing she wanted. Morgan was just as reluctant; hadn't he told her he wasn't the marrying kind?

Maggie's belly cramped. Of course, Morgan knew he was binding himself to a woman who could never bear him bairns. He'd been gallant, offering to wed her the night before. Maggie had thought Connor would force him to 'do the right thing', but the laird hadn't gotten the chance. Even so, Maggie wondered if Morgan now resented her, if he thought she'd somehow trapped him.

Once their hands were bound, the priest took Morgan through his vows, before turning his attention upon Maggie. "Please repeat the words after me," he intoned.

Dizziness swept over Maggie as she repeated the first line. "Ye are Blood of my Blood, and Bone of my Bone." Her voice sounded raspy, forced.

This was all wrong. She was still reeling from her uncle's words the night before. He'd washed his hands of her—his own kin. Family was everything to a Highlander; she couldn't believe he'd cast her out.

"I give ye my Body, that we Two might be One."

Her uncle didn't care if she starved on the streets. Ever since his brother's death, when he'd been saddled with two young nieces, Graeme Ross had resented Maggie and Rhianna. From the moment the girls had come of age, he'd itched to rid himself of them. And now he'd succeeded.

"I give ye my Spirit, 'til our Life shall be Done." Desperation clutched at Maggie's breast as she spoke those words. They were a lie. She couldn't give Morgan Mackay her spirit. Ever. That last sentence was a reminder of the vow she'd made to Campbell Munro after his death.

I will not wed again. Ever.

But here she was, breaking that promise. She'd betrayed her husband's memory. Tears prickled the back of her eyes. Blinking rapidly, she forced them back. She couldn't break down now, not in front of the priest.

What a curse it was to be born a woman. Maggie was dependent on her menfolk for survival. Rhianna's situation, in which her man had let her down, was a cautionary tale of what could happen when a woman lost the protection of her family, by choice or otherwise.

The vows concluded, the priest unwrapped the ribbon that bound them.

"Ye are now husband and wife." His voice carried through the damp air. "May yer union be blessed." The priest then nodded to Morgan, indicating that it was time to kiss his bride.

Maggie's body went rigid as Morgan stepped forward. They'd recently been as intimate as a man and woman could be, yet now his nearness felt strange. He wore a questioning expression that made her yearn to step away from him. However, her feet felt rooted to the spot. Bending close, Morgan brushed his lips over hers.

Maggie's breath gusted out of her, an ache rising deep in her chest.

It was done. Despite her wishes, she was now a wife once more.

An awkward silence filled the guest solar, while the Mackays of Farr took their noon meal together. They sat at a row of trestle tables the servants had carried in for them. After the wedding, Connor had decided that they wouldn't join the other clans in the great hall. Instead, they would share a quiet meal in private.

Even so, the lack of conversation was starting to put Morgan on edge.

He stole a glance at his wife next to him then. Maggie ate little, merely stirring her pottage with a wooden spoon. She'd been subdued ever since leaving the kirk.

Morgan's brow furrowed. He could hardly blame her for not looking ecstatic, although her glum expression dented his pride just a little. Surely being wed to him wasn't that depressing?

"We shall ride out tomorrow at first light," Connor announced finally, breaking the tense silence. He tore off a piece of bread and dipped it into the thick vegetable stew before him. "I see no reason to linger in Inverness now."

Morgan nodded his agreement. The sooner they departed this castle the better. This visit had left a sour taste in everyone's mouth.

"But before we do, we should say goodbye to Niel," Connor continued.

Morgan inclined his head. "Are they allowing him visitors?"

"Not many … but I've had a word with the dungeon master, and he's agreed to give ye and I a few moments with him." Connor paused there, a groove furrowing between his brows. "He'll be sent to Bass Rock the day after tomorrow."

Morgan swallowed a mouthful of stew and then took a gulp of wine from his goblet to wash it down. For a few moments, he pondered Niel's fate.

His looming incarceration aside, the man would be distraught. Morgan couldn't imagine what it was like to have one's father betray him. He knew that Niel could be ruthless and impetuous. Last Samhuinn, he'd drawn his dirk on Keira and accused her of being a Gunn spy. Nonetheless, Morgan had always respected him. Morgan and Connor had spent many a summer hawking and hunting with him.

Morgan wanted to see Niel, to assure him that his plight wouldn't be forgotten—and that they'd do their best to repair the damage the clan-chief had caused.

"We shall go down to the dungeons when we have finished eating," Connor concluded.

Across the table, Jaimee met Morgan's eye. Her gaze was searching, full of questions.

Morgan favored her with a reassuring smile in return. His kin were walking on eggshells around him today, as if they were worried he'd shatter. Aye, this marriage hadn't been planned, but he was sure he and Maggie would make the best of things.

He glanced then, once more, to his wife. Maggie didn't look up as she continued to play with her food. Her stillness, her inability to meet his gaze, caused worry to tighten Morgan's gut.

He intended to look after Maggie, to ensure that she was protected and happy at Farr. It was a shock to suddenly find himself with a wife, yet it surprised him how quickly he was adjusting to his new status.

However, as he observed Maggie's pale face, and her haunted expression, he realized she wouldn't recover so quickly.

"Come to bid me farewell?" Niel Mackay greeted Connor and Morgan, his voice flat.

He rose from the wooden pallet in the corner of the cell and moved across to the barred window. Reaching out, he gripped the iron bars with both hands.

The clan-chief's son wore a shuttered expression, although the deep groove between his dark brows and the lines that bracketed his mouth revealed the strain he was under.

"Aye." Connor stepped up close to the window. Behind him, four burly guards looked on. "Have ye seen yer father?"

Niel shook his head, his blue eyes hard. "The bastard can't face me."

"The Mackay chieftains went before the king yesterday," Connor replied. "We appealed on yer behalf, but he refused us."

Niel's mouth thinned. "Thank ye ... I appreciate that ye tried." There was a bleak edge to the warrior's voice that Morgan had never heard before. Usually, Niel was arrogantly sure of himself. "At least some of my clan are loyal to me."

"The king may soften with time," Morgan spoke up then, meeting Niel's eye. "When we return to Farr, I shall begin work on a proper petition. We will do all we can to free ye."

Niel's mouth curved, although his gaze remained bleak. "I'm grateful, Morgan." His attention then flicked between the two brothers. "We've known each other a long while, lads," he said softly. "And I will never forget our friendship." His gaze then rested upon the laird of Farr. "Things have been ... strained ... between us of late, Connor. I'm sorry for that."

A nerve flickered in Connor's cheek. Of course, Morgan knew he was referring to all the trouble with Keira. Niel's harshness toward her initially, his suspicion, had soured their relationship.

"I'll admit I was wrong about Keira Gunn." Niel's smile turned rueful. "And I'll also admit that I was a little envious of yer happiness."

Connor inclined his head. "Ye were?"

Niel's smile turned brittle. "Aye. Ye have something, Connor ... integrity, honor ... that draws good things to ye."

"Ye don't deserve this." Connor reached out then and clasped Niel's hand through the bars. "Yer father has made a grave error in sacrificing ye in his stead, and he will live to regret it."

"Aye," Morgan agreed, his voice roughening. "He risks the whole clan turning against him when they hear. We won't give up on ye, Niel. I give ye my word."

19

ALONE IN THE WORLD

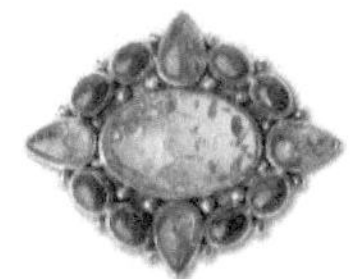

"YE ARE WED?" Aileana stared at Maggie, her face going slack with shock. "When?"

"This morning."

"But I thought ye were going off to watch the beheadings?"

"No … I got married instead." The urge to laugh bubbled up inside Maggie then—a hysteria was building within her, clawing to be let free. "That's why ye haven't seen me all day. Uncle caught me in an alcove with Morgan Mackay. I am now his wife … and we will depart for Farr Castle at dawn tomorrow."

Disbelief lit in Aileana's eyes. When she recovered, she managed to whisper, "And what about me?"

"Ye have two choices, lass," Maggie replied, forcing a briskness she didn't feel. "Ye can come with me … or ye can return to yer kin at Contullich Castle. Since uncle has washed his hands of me, ye likely won't be welcome back at Caisteal Nan Corr either."

A heartbeat passed before Aileana's grey-blue eyes filled with tears. And then her face crumpled.

Maggie's breathing caught. She'd been so caught up in her own turmoil, she'd forgotten about Aileana's lover. Her maid likely didn't want to be parted from Athol Ross.

"Oh Aileana," she murmured. "Ye haven't given yer heart to Athol, have ye?"

Her maid brushed at the tears that were now running down her cheeks. "Aye," she whispered.

Maggie drew in a steadying breath. Stepping close, she took the younger woman's hands. She was deeply in need of being comforted herself, but the bereft look on Aileana's face couldn't be borne. "I'm sorry, lass. I didn't want this either. But it is done now."

Aileana swallowed, her eyes still glistening with tears. Now that the news had sunk in, she regained control of herself. "If we are to leave so soon, I'd like to say goodbye to Athol," she replied huskily. "I must see him."

"Of course ye must." Maggie released her maid's hands and stepped back. "Go on … take the rest of the evening off."

Aileana's gaze widened. "But I need to help ye pack."

"I can get started on it alone. Go on."

Her maid looked undecided, but when Maggie waved toward the door, she gave a nod.

Maggie watched Aileana leave the chamber, listening as the door thudded shut and her maid's footfalls disappeared down the hallway beyond.

She felt for Aileana, she truly did—although she'd given her heart to a weasel.

Sighing, Maggie turned away, moving over to the window. She did need to start packing her things for their departure at dawn, yet all of a sudden, she couldn't summon the will.

Tearing open the shutters, which Aileana had closed for the evening, she perched on the window-ledge and stared out at the panorama that spread out below—as she had on her first evening in Inverness.

Then, she'd been resolute that her uncle wouldn't get his way. But he had.

Dusk, which came late this time of year, was settling in a soft mist over the rooftops of Inverness. Torches lit the town in a golden glow, the last of the grey day fading with the setting sun.

And somewhere out there was her sister.

Suddenly, Maggie wished she could rush to her, could cry upon her shoulder. However, that had never been the nature of their relationship. They were both too proud, too stubborn—perhaps that had been the problem between them.

Maggie's eyes burned, yet she couldn't weep. Instead, a heavy numbness had stolen over her. Shock.

I'm now Maggie Mackay.

Free will had been ripped from her. She was trapped.

There were worse fates than marriage to Morgan Mackay. He wasn't a bad man.

But she'd failed to keep her promise to Campbell, and on the morrow would ride off to make a life with her new husband—all because she'd given in to base lust.

Maggie let out a deep, shuddering sigh. This was her wedding night. By rights, it should have been a joyous eve. Under normal circumstances, their kin would have joined them at a wedding banquet and then man and wife would retire together to their marital chamber.

But Morgan and Maggie had already coupled. Did that mean the marriage vows were now sealed?

Her chest tightened then, panic rising. Dear Lord, she hoped Morgan wouldn't seek her out tonight.

Morgan retired early. He left his kin chatting in the solar and retreated to the solitude of his bed-chamber. Maggie hadn't joined them that evening, a clear sign that she too wished to be alone for a while.

Her absence didn't surprise Morgan. He'd seen the tension on her face, the pallor of her skin earlier. The woman hadn't met his eye squarely since the wedding ceremony. She was wed to him, yet she wasn't happy about it.

The situation with Niel, and the fact that Angus Mackay hadn't yet faced any of them to give an account of himself, had soured Morgan's mood anyway. But dwelling on his hasty marriage to a woman who didn't want to wed again made him feel a little depressed.

He wasn't sure what he'd gotten himself into, yet his gut warned him that a rocky road lay ahead.

Heaviness dogged his steps as he made his way down the hallway to his chamber. It was a relief to enter the small space and shut out the world for a short while.

Gritta was waiting for him.

Bounding forward, the wolfhound gave Morgan an enthusiastic welcome. She licked his hand and nudged hard against his leg.

"I know, I know," he murmured, leaning down to give the dog the attention she craved. "I've ignored ye today, lass." He patted her head then. "Fear not, we're going home tomorrow. What do ye think about that?"

The wolfhound stared up at him, her dark eyes filled with adoration.

With a sigh, Morgan moved over to the bed and sank down. Gritta followed him, before sitting at his feet and pushing against his thigh. He reached down and stroked her neck.

Gritta had become his closest companion of late. His brother and cousin often teased him about his love for the dog. "If we could find ye a woman ye could be so devoted to, all would be well," Connor had teased him at Yuletide.

Morgan had merely grinned back at his brother, as he fed the dog a choice morsel of venison under the table. Dogs were easier than people. They gave unconditional love and affection and demanded little in return.

Morgan liked that about Gritta.

"Well, lass ... I'm now a married man," he murmured, pushing his hair off his face with his free hand. "What do ye think about that?"

Gritta gave a low whine.

"Don't be like that ... ye have met Maggie. She's a good woman." Morgan frowned then. "Although ye are not to go frightening her pony again, do ye hear?"

The wolfhound nuzzled against him, oblivious to his words.

Morgan loosed a deep sigh, ruffling the dog's ears. "I've made a mess of things, haven't I?" he murmured.

Indeed, he had. Connor was right: his reckless ways had finally caught up with him—but he wasn't the only one to bear the consequences.

Morgan then recalled the awful scene with Graeme Ross the night before in the solar.

The hurt, the vulnerability, in Maggie's eyes had cut Morgan to the quick. Her uncle's cruelty had left her shaking, and he'd wanted to draw her into his arms and reassure her that he'd take care of her, that he'd shield her from harm.

That was why he'd proposed.

Maggie hadn't refused him, but since her uncle had disowned her, she'd been left with little choice but to wed him. Without Graeme Ross's protection, she was penniless, homeless.

Morgan's chest constricted. He felt as if he'd somehow forced her into this.

The urge to seek Maggie out rose within him. Her soft voice, her clever tongue, would be a welcome balm tonight. Yet he suppressed the impulse.

Maggie had been through a lot over the past day, and as such, he would give her the solitude she clearly wanted. However, with the dawn, they would ride out of Inverness together, and he would start to try and win her trust.

"God's bones." Morgan dragged a hand over his face. This was new territory to him. He didn't have any idea how to be a husband. He was used to entering into playful, light banter with women, but he sensed Maggie needed to be approached gently.

Her strong will and feisty nature hid much. Aye, she'd recently emerged from mourning, yet she likely still missed her dead husband. And now she'd lost her family as well. Both Maggie's sister and uncle had turned their backs on her.

She likely felt utterly alone in the world—but she wasn't.

Despite that Morgan wasn't ready to be shackled to a woman, he'd do his best to make Maggie happy, to make the shadows in her sea-blue eyes draw back.

The only problem was that he didn't know where to start.

20

THE MERCY OF STRANGERS

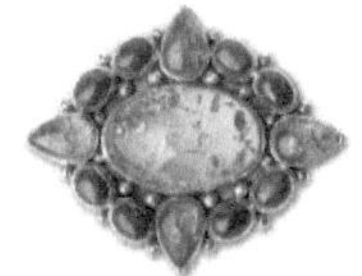

MAGGIE SWUNG UP onto the saddle and adjusted her skirts. Her garron snorted, impatient to be off. The gelding then angled its head left—casting a jaundiced eye upon a tall man mounting his dapple-grey courser and the leggy wolfhound standing at his side.

The Highland pony side-stepped, tossing its head. "Gritta is making Walnut nervous." Maggie leaned forward and stroked the pony's furry neck. "Will the hound behave itself?"

"She will, if she knows what's good for her," Morgan replied, casting a warning look down at his dog. "Worry not, Walnut will travel unmolested."

Morgan glanced up then, and their gazes met squarely for the first time since the wedding ceremony. A smile curved his lips. "How are ye faring this morning, Maggie?"

"Well enough," she replied stiffly. Lord, how uncomfortable this was. She couldn't believe this man was actually her husband. She couldn't insist he call her 'Lady Munro' now.

This whole situation felt surreal.

Maggie broke off eye contact, fiddling with Walnut's reins instead.

Around them, the rest of their party were readying themselves to leave. Both Keira and Cait were traveling in the wagon. Although Cait wasn't as heavily pregnant as Lady Mackay, she wished to keep Keira company. Aileana, red-eyed and withdrawn, had joined the two pregnant women, as had Keira and Jaimee's maids.

As such, the only women on horseback this morning were Maggie and Jaimee.

Connor led the way out of the outer bailey, just as the first rays of sun crested the eastern curtain wall. Morgan and Kennan followed, with Maggie and Jaimee right behind. Half of the Mackay escort rode at their heels, while the others followed behind the wagon.

But as Maggie rode out of Inverness Castle, she met a grisly sight beyond.

Three pikes had been driven into the ground to the left of the gates, and a severed head sat upon each one.

Maggie's gaze swept over the heads, her breath catching in her throat when she recognized John Ross. The Ross clan-chief's face was frozen in a stunned expression, his mouth gaping, his gaze empty.

Maggie stared, unable to quite believe this same man had been alive just a day earlier. John Ross had been a bluff, loud warrior, yet now his spirit had fled, leaving an empty, waxen likeness. It had been like that with Campbell. When they'd brought his corpse back, it didn't seem like him.

Nausea swept over Maggie, while next to her, Jaimee breathed a curse.

"It looks as if James wants to send all of us a clear message." Connor's face was grim as he surveyed the three gruesome heads. "This is what happens when we disobey the king."

"He won't silence us though," Morgan replied. Maggie dragged her gaze from John Ross's severed head to see that her new husband wore a hard expression, his eyes narrowed. "An injustice has been committed against Niel Mackay," he continued, his voice clipped, "and I intend to see it mended."

Silence followed his words. Connor shifted in the saddle, his attention swiveling to his younger brother. The laird's gaze shadowed then. He even opened his mouth, as if to caution Morgan, before checking himself.

Maggie frowned. She'd heard of the failed appeal by the Mackay chieftains to free Niel. The whole keep was abuzz with gossip about the Mackays. Folk whispered that Angus Mackay was no longer fit to rule his clan.

However, it surprised her that Morgan wasn't prepared to let the matter drop.

Maggie studied her husband's face; it was as if she were looking upon him for the first time. He'd married her to save her from a life on the streets, and yet she hardly knew the man at all. Most of the conversation that had passed between them until now had been light-hearted.

It shouldn't have surprised her that Morgan Mackay was a proud Highlander and fiercely loyal to his clan.

Maggie's throat started to ache then, and she swallowed to ease the uncomfortable sensation. Damn him, she didn't want to like Morgan as much as she did. Did he have to be so honorable?

How was she going to cope with being married to him?

The Mackay party left Inverness at their backs and rode west for a spell. They then took the northern highway into the heart of the Highlands. The road was a long one, hugging the eastern coast for a while before they'd strike out north-west.

Maggie knew the journey, for she'd made a similar one in coming here.

After days of low cloud and drizzle, the sky finally cleared and the sun bathed the earth. It warmed Maggie's face, but not the rest of her. A lump of ice had settled in her belly, and her hands and feet felt clammy and nerveless this morning. She kept her light woolen cloak on, even when others shed theirs and tied them behind their saddles.

Her anger at herself, her situation, and the sight outside the castle walls at dawn had drilled cold into her bones.

Uncle didn't even say goodbye.

After all those years, he'd just turned his back on her and left her to the mercy of strangers.

Maggie's gaze traveled ahead, to where the two brothers rode side-by-side. Kennan had fallen back to ride next to Jaimee, while Maggie now traveled alone, Walnut doggedly plodding after the leggier coursers.

Connor and Morgan conversed little during the course of the day, however, there remained a silent comradery between them. She'd noted the bond between the Mackay siblings back in Inverness, had secretly envied this family its closeness—and now she was part of it.

The bitter irony of it all wasn't lost on her.

The Mackays of Farr had little reason to bear her family any goodwill—after Rhianna's trickery—and yet they'd taken her in without complaint.

Even so, Morgan hadn't wanted to wed her. But he had a strong sense of justice, and he'd done what was right.

The day's end brought them to the village of Kildary. The hamlet, which sat near the shores of the glittering Gromarty Firth, was little more than a scattering of thatched-roofed stone cottages around a wide dirt square. But the village was big enough to house an inn.

Uneasiness stirred in Maggie's belly as she rode into Kildary. They were in the middle of Ross lands here, for the clan's seat, Balnagown Castle, was just out of sight of the village. Indeed, the Balnagown River flowed through the center of the hamlet.

John Ross would never return home to his castle. Instead, his wife was widowed and one of his sons would take his place as clan-chief.

It was a dark time for the Ross clan, and she wondered if news of the clan-chief's execution had reached Balnagown yet.

They stabled their horses behind the inn as the setting sun blazed to the west. It had been a fair day of travel, and they'd made good time. Maggie unsaddled Walnut in silence, paying little attention to her companions as her thoughts turned inward. One of the Mackay men offered to rub her pony down for her, but she brushed aside his offer.

Walnut was her responsibility. Apart from Aileana, he was her last link with her old life.

Maggie's maid was waiting for her in the courtyard between the stables and the inn when Maggie emerged. Aileana looked wan, her gaze forlorn. Maggie wasn't sure how the farewell with Athol had gone, but it was clear that her maid wasn't taking their new circumstances well.

"Aileana." Maggie stopped before the maid, her gaze taking in the strained lines of her face. "I know this must be difficult for ye, lass."

Aileana sniffed, blinking rapidly as her eyes filled with tears. "I'll be all right ... in a day or two," she replied bravely.

Maggie linked her arm through Aileana's, steering her toward the inn. "That's the spirit," she said, offering the younger woman a tense smile. "Come on, let's see what they're putting on for supper."

Truthfully, Maggie's appetite was poor this evening. She'd eaten little more than a few mouthfuls of bread and cheese all day and just wanted to retreat to her room. However, the whole Mackay party now filled the common room, the rumble of conversation washing over Maggie in a wave.

With a sinking heart, she saw that a space had been left free next to Morgan. Her husband wasn't looking her way. Instead, he was talking to his sister, who was seated across from him.

Jaimee glanced in Maggie's direction as she approached and favored her with a warm smile. Morgan turned, and also smiled, beckoning for her to join him.

Maggie's pulse quickened.

These people were her family now.

Aileana joined the two other maids farther down the table, while Maggie sat down next to Morgan.

As usual, Gritta had joined them. The hound had curled on the rush-strewn floor under the table, waiting for morsels of supper to be dropped for her. Gritta pushed a cold, wet nose against Maggie's hand, welcoming her. Maggie stroked the dog's head, taking solace from its affection. She looked ferocious, but the hound was actually sweet-natured.

Serving lasses appeared, bearing tankards of foaming ale that they placed before the hungry and thirsty travelers. As the lasses departed to fetch supper, Morgan leaned in. "We've hardly spoken all day," he said, his gaze searching Maggie's face. "How are ye bearing up?"

The kindness in his voice, the concern in his eyes, made her throat constrict. She'd feared he'd resent her for trapping him in this marriage, yet there was no trace of any such suspicion on Morgan's face this evening.

"I'm fine," Maggie replied, forcing a smile. "Thank ye for asking." Tearing her gaze from his, she wrapped her hands around the tankard before her and lifted it to her lips. The ale was strong, and she took a large gulp.

Plates of roast mutton and long loaves of oaten bread arrived then, interrupting them, and the rumble of conversation inside the common room died down.

Maggie's stomach had closed, yet she forced herself to eat. The mutton had been roasted slowly and was tender, and the bread was crusty and fresh.

Morgan attempted to draw her into conversation again, yet she answered him in short sentences, meeting his eye only when absolutely necessary. Eventually, he gave up trying and chatted instead to his cousin, Kennan.

Relieved to be left alone, Maggie pushed the remains of her supper around her dish. When a second round of ale was ordered after supper, she excused herself from the table and went upstairs.

In the cramped chamber where she and Morgan would spend the night, Maggie sat upon a stool, dressed in a lèine, while Aileana combed out her hair.

The women spoke little this evening, both lost in their own thoughts and worries. Once Aileana left the chamber, retiring to the room she would share with the other maids, Maggie let out a heavy sigh.

Her gaze then shifted to the bed. *It's hardly big enough for a couple.* Maggie had hoped Morgan might allow her another night alone, but the inn was cramped and there were barely enough rooms to accommodate the Mackay party as it was. Of course they had to share the same chamber.

Rising to her feet, Maggie glanced down at the ankle-length tunic she wore. She usually slept naked, but she wouldn't tonight. Still wearing her lèine, she pulled back the covers and slid into bed.

And then she lay there, staring up at the low beams overhead, waiting for her husband's arrival.

21

A MARRIAGE OF CONVENIENCE

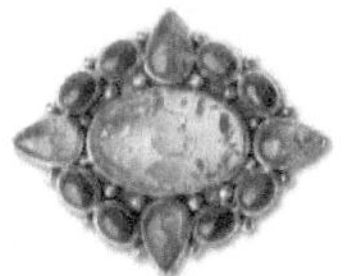

MORGAN PUT OFF going to bed. Connor and Keira had retired early. His sister-by-marriage's belly seemed to swell more with each passing day, and the journey was wearying for her. Kennan and Cait went upstairs shortly after, leaving Morgan alone with the Mackay warriors.

Dicing and games of knucklebones were in play down the table now, but Morgan didn't join in.

Eventually though, as the men around him got drunker, and Morgan toyed with his second tankard of ale, he decided he'd given Maggie enough time alone.

They needed to speak frankly.

Rising from the table, Morgan grimaced. He wasn't looking forward to this; Maggie had been withdrawn and uncommunicative during supper. He realized that all of this was difficult for her, yet he couldn't help her if she shut him out.

Taking the rickety wooden stairs up to the first floor, Morgan made his way to the last door on the right, Gritta padding along behind him.

Morgan reached for the door handle and glanced down at his hound. Usually, when he shared a bed-chamber for the night with a woman, he left Gritta outside, guarding the door. But it wasn't necessary tonight.

He didn't imagine this was to be a night of hot, sweaty passion—not when his wife could barely meet his eye.

Letting himself and Gritta into the bed-chamber, he noted that a small fire still glowed in the hearth, casting a dull-red glow over the room. Gritta walked to the hearth and curled up before it.

Morgan's gaze shifted to the bed, and he spied a tousled dark head of hair peeking up above the blankets.

Stilling a moment, he listened for her breathing. It was slow and even. Had she fallen asleep? He didn't want to wake her. Maybe this conversation could wait till the morning.

Maggie tried to keep her breathing slow and deep, feigning sleep, but it was hard.

The moment she heard the door handle turn, followed by Morgan's tread and the click of Gritta's paws on the wooden floor, she started to sweat.

Peeking out from under the covers, she watched him turn away from her. The fire still threw out enough light for her to see his tall frame.

Her breathing quickened when he stripped off his lèine, revealing broad shoulders and a long, muscular back. And when he pushed down his braies, her heart leaped against her ribs.

The columns of muscle on either side of his spine tapered down to a narrow waist and hips. Her gaze lingered on his tight buttocks before she admired his long legs.

She'd wanted to see him naked, that evening in the alcove, but their coupling had been too urgent, too frenzied.

Maggie twisted away and squeezed her eyes shut. She had to before Morgan turned around and she saw the rest of him—before he caught her looking at him.

She should have realized he'd sleep naked. Most folk did.

She'd edged up as far as she could to the far side of the bed. Even so, when the mattress dipped, she felt herself slide toward him.

The bed really was too small for the pair of them to share comfortably.

It was impossible to pretend she was still asleep now.

Feigning a sleepy moan, Maggie blinked her eyes open. She then rolled over toward him.

"Sorry, Maggie." Morgan's voice rumbled across the bed. "Did I wake ye?"

To her consternation, he too had rolled on his side. He now watched her.

"Aye," she lied. Curse the man, but the heat of his body warmed her like a glowing ember. She was sweating heavily now.

He held her gaze for a long moment, and then his mouth quirked. "This is ... awkward ... isn't it?"

Maggie huffed. "Ye think?"

"It all feels a bit ... strange."

Maggie swallowed. "Aye, well." She cleared her throat. "We should have been more careful ... if we had, ye could have been spared this."

Morgan's gaze shadowed. "I don't resent ye ... or regret what happened between us," he said softly. "But do ye blame me?"

Maggie stared back at him. The directness of his question threw her.

Morgan's brow furrowed. "Ye do."

"No," she replied, choking the word out. "It's just that ye didn't think things over before ye offered to wed me, Morgan ... and ye should have." She broke off, wishing her voice didn't sound so shrill. "I told ye I can never bear another bairn. Why would ye shackle yerself to a barren woman?"

Morgan's frown deepened. "There's more to yer worth than yer ability to give me children," he murmured.

Maggie's belly knotted. Why did he have to be so kind, so understanding? "But ye told me ye weren't the marrying kind." She was desperate for him to say something callous, something thoughtless—something that would make it easy to harden her heart against him.

Morgan's mouth lifted at the corners. "Aye … and I meant those words at the time." He paused then, before shaking his head. "But fate clearly had other plans for me."

"But aren't ye angry?" She was incredulous now. He was handling this situation much better than she would have in his place.

Morgan's eyes glinted. "Many things vex me at the moment, Maggie … but *ye* aren't one of them."

Silence fell then, and they stared at each other.

Maggie drew in a deep breath. This conversation was getting out of control. Morgan was looking at her as if he wanted to pull her into his arms and kiss her. She remembered well just how much she'd enjoyed being touched by him. It would be so easy to give herself to him again, yet she couldn't—not without making things clear.

They were wed now, and she wouldn't deny him his rights as her husband. However, she needed to be blunt with him, before they reached Farr Castle and started a life together.

"Morgan," she said softly, holding his gaze. "Ye did a noble thing, wedding me to give me yer protection … and I'm grateful."

He cocked an eyebrow. "But?"

Maggie heaved in a breath. "I'm yer wife, and I will act as such. I will lie with ye, obey ye, and give ye companionship … but I can never give ye my heart."

Morgan's expression didn't change, although his gaze narrowed just a fraction. "Ye won't?" His voice was quiet, questioning.

"Ye know I didn't wish to wed again," she replied, dogged now that she'd steered their conversation in this direction. "For I have known for a while now that I will never love another man."

Morgan's mouth curved into a rueful smile. "Ye must have loved yer husband very much … for that to be the case."

"I did." Maggie locked gazes with Morgan then, her jaw firming. "I'm sorry, but this is a marriage of convenience ... nothing more."

A marriage of convenience.

Morgan lay on his back, staring up at the rafters. Aye, he knew that—he just hadn't expected Maggie to spell out her terms so baldly to him.

He'd never met a woman so guarded, so intent on keeping him at arm's length. He was used to women fawning over him, vying for his attention. This was a new sensation, and not one he liked much.

If he was honest, her insistence had dented his pride.

Morgan glanced right, at where Maggie had turned over. She now lay with her back to him once more. Unlike Morgan, she hadn't gone to bed naked. But that aside, it was clear she didn't want him to touch her tonight.

He could hardly blame her.

Morgan shifted his attention back to the rafters, frowning.

He'd never been in love; he didn't even know if he was capable of going calf-eyed over a woman. He'd watched Kennan and Connor's smitten behavior with a veiled sense of superiority. *He* wouldn't ever make such a fool of himself. But not falling in love with his wife was one thing, being told she could never love him was another.

And, if he was honest with himself, it disturbed him.

22

ASK ME A QUESTION

THE SIGHT OF Farr Castle, rising against the northern sky, made Maggie catch her breath. She'd never visited the Mackays of Farr before but had heard that their stronghold perched high upon green cliffs, looking out to sea.

It was a fine spring day. A warm wind gusted in from the south, pushing fluffy clouds across a cerulean sky. The air smelled sweet, of earth and lush grass, and Maggie's mouth curved into a smile as they drew nearer to the castle.

Maybe life here wouldn't be so difficult.

She cast a glance over at her husband then, and her smile faded. Morgan rode beside her, his gaze trained on the horizon. She'd thought things would be strained the morning following their conversation in bed, yet Morgan had taken her revelation surprisingly well. Too well. The subject hadn't come up again, and his manner toward her hadn't altered. He was still affable and engaging, and when they retired for the night, their exchanges were light and easy.

Maggie tore her gaze from him, uneasiness filtering over her. They'd not yet lain together as man and wife. Morgan was giving her time to get used to her new situation. He was being considerate, kind.

She should have been grateful, for when he eventually bedded her, she wanted to make sure her emotions were locked down. Instead, his behavior toward her made Maggie nervous.

Morgan Mackay was easy to like, but she couldn't let herself love him.

Ever.

She'd failed to avoid another marriage, but she could keep her promise to Campbell if her heart remained walled off. The anxiety that had been clutching at her breast all day eased a little then. All of a sudden, she felt back in control.

Maggie shifted her attention up ahead, to where Cait and Kennan rode side-by-side. She was teasing him about something, and he threw back his head and laughed, the merry sound traveling over the emerald-green headland.

They passed a village on the road into the castle, a huddle of stone cottages with a kirk on the eastern edge. Maggie couldn't help but notice that the graveyard was a large one as they rode by, with several fresh headstones.

Just like her own kin, the Mackays of Farr hadn't been untouched by the years of Highland feuding.

The company left the village behind and approached the high ramparts that shielded the landward side of the castle. This close to the edge of the headland, Maggie had a panoramic view in every direction. The sea was a deep blue this afternoon, and gulls wheeled overhead, welcoming the Mackays home.

Inside the landward bailey, Connor Mackay swung down from his horse and went straight to his wife.

Perched atop Walnut, Maggie observed them. There was something about the way Connor and Keira interacted that captivated her.

The laird favored his wife with a soft smile, before taking hold of her hand and helping her down from the wagon. He then enfolded Keira in his arms, his mouth slanting across hers.

Realizing that she was staring, Maggie hurriedly averted her gaze.

The woman's husky voice echoed through the great hall, blending with the mournful strains of a harp. It was a song that Maggie knew well, one her mother had once sung to her at bedtime years earlier—a cautionary fairy lullaby.

> *I left my baby lying here,*
> *Lying here, lying here*
> *I left my baby lying here*
> *To go and gather blaeberries.*
>
> *I found the wee brown otter's track*
> *Otter's track, otter's track*
> *I found the wee brown otter's track*
> *But never a trace of my baby!*
>
> *I found the track of the swan on the lake*
> *Swan on the lake, swan on the lake*
> *I found the track of the swan on the lake*
> *But not the track of my baby!*
>
> *I found the trail of the mountain mist*
> *Mountain mist, mountain mist*
> *I found the trail of the mountain mist*
> *But never a trace of my baby!*

Memories drifted back to Maggie as she listened. The singer this eve had a lovely voice, but it didn't surpass that of Maggie's mother. Every night, she'd sung for her daughters. Wistfulness settled over Maggie. Her mother had been gone many years now, but the song made the years roll back.

Sipping at her wine, she glanced over at where Morgan sat. He leaned back in his chair, gently stroking his hound's ears while he too listened to the song. He wore a pensive expression as if the music also transported him to the past.

Music had that ability.

Supper had come and gone, and many folk had drifted out of the great hall to complete their end-of-day chores. However, those seated at the chieftain's table at the far end of the hall remained.

Taking another sip, Maggie watched a serving lass cross the hall toward them. Blonde and pretty, her ringlets framing a winsome face, the young woman carried a wooden tray.

She stepped upon the dais and started clearing up empty cups and goblets.

But as she neared Morgan, the lass's face tensed, a frown furrowing her previously flawless brow.

Mouth pursed, she cleared up the cups before Morgan. Then, casting him a scowl, the woman turned, and, balancing the tray against her hip, strode stiff-backed from the great hall.

Maggie's gaze tracked her, before she glanced back at Morgan.

He was frowning.

"A past dalliance, I take it?" she asked. It was a direct, bold question, although her tone was mild. She wasn't jealous—she had no right to be. She'd been trying to remain aloof with her husband, yet the bramble wine she'd drunk with supper lowered her guard. She was curious about the man she'd wed, for he'd spoken little about his past.

Next to Morgan, Kennan snorted, although his cousin ignored him. Instead, he met Maggie's eye, his expression shuttered. "Aye, Chrissa and I … spent time together last year."

Maggie arched an eyebrow, her mouth quirking.

A line furrowed between Morgan's brows. "Does that amuse ye?"

Maggie sobered. "No, husband."

"Then why were ye smirking?"

"I wasn't." Maggie raised a hand to hide another smile that tugged at her lips. There was something about

Morgan when he was affronted that made her want to laugh. "It just made me realize how little we know about each other."

His gaze snared hers. "All ye have to do is ask, Maggie … and I will tell ye everything there is to know."

"Don't do that, lass," Kennan quipped, grinning. "The rest of us aren't interested in hearing about his conquests."

Maggie's eyes widened in mock surprise. "*Conquests*?"

Morgan muttered a curse, casting his cousin a dark look. "Mind yer own business, Ken," he growled. "This is a private conversation."

He then turned so he faced Maggie squarely. Was it a challenge she spied in his eyes? "Go on … ask me something."

Maggie held his gaze. Kennan was wrong, she wasn't interested in asking him about his past affairs with women. There were plenty of things about Morgan that she found more intriguing.

"How old were ye when ye fought yer first battle?" she asked after a pause.

"Thirteen and a half winters."

"And how many fights have ye lost?"

"None."

Maggie fought the urge to roll her eyes. The man's arrogance knew no bounds.

She paused to think then, before lifting her chin to look him squarely in the eye. "Tell me then … what do ye fear?"

Morgan inclined his head. The harpist had struck another, livelier tune, one that many in the hall were now singing too. Few folk could overhear them now.

A lazy smile stretched his mouth. "Nothing."

Maggie snorted, irritation spiking through her. She found his glib responses slightly mocking. "Liar. We're all afraid of something."

Their gazes held, and slowly Morgan's smile faded. It seemed to occur to him then that she wasn't going to let him dissemble. Moments passed, and his eyes darkened.

"Very well," he replied, his voice low. "I fear for the future of my clan ... I fear that there will come a time when our enemies will circle us like wolves, and the name 'Mackay' will be lost forever."

23

KEEPING BUSY

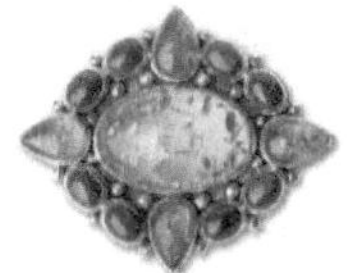

THE BEST WAY to avoid dwelling on one's worries was to keep busy.

The first morning that Maggie awoke in her new home, she excused herself early from the solar—where she'd joined Morgan and his family to break their fast with fresh bannocks, butter, and honey—and went down to the kitchens.

"Good morning," she greeted the cooks.

Three flushed faces glanced up from where they were bent over, kneading bread. One of them, a rawboned woman with frizzy red hair, frowned. "And ye are?"

"Maggie, Morgan Mackay's wife. And ye?"

The woman's cheeks grew pinker still as she straightened up and wiped her hands upon her apron. "I'm Elsa ... the castle's head cook." She dipped her head then. "Apologies, my lady. We didn't expect to see ye down here ... and so soon."

Maggie offered the flustered woman a smile. "Lady Mackay is feeling fatigued at present and has asked me to take over some of her duties." Her attention dropped to the nearby bench, where the carcasses of small plucked birds lay. "They look tasty. What have ye got planned for the noon meal?"

"We have grouse stew for today, served with oaten bread and braised kale."

Maggie nodded. "Excellent. Now, why don't ye show me the spence, Elsa? It seems as good a place as any to start."

The head cook's lips compressed at this request. "Aye, certainly … my lady." She nodded to the other women, making it clear that they should continue with their bread-making. Then the cook led the way through into the large space where the castle's food stores were kept.

Halting just inside the doorway, Maggie let her gaze travel over the store, before her brow furrowed.

The spence had an over-filled, shambolic look, as if the cooks merely came and went from it without taking time to put things in order. It badly needed tidying.

Maggie's frown deepened. She'd lost entire days in the larder at Caisteal Nan Corr. Sorting the spence was one of her least favorite chores.

This larder was nearly twice the size of that in her uncle's hold. Wooden shelving lined the walls, and a meat safe, which allowed cool air to circulate from outdoors into the store, had been carved into the exterior wall. Maggie inhaled the smells of the store—the musty, ripe scent of cured meats and cheese—before she studied the shelves more closely. Jumbled stacks of clay preserving jars and bottles weighed them down. Some of the shelves had cool stone slabs on them, where items such as freshly churned butter and bottles of milk sat.

Maggie turned to the cook. "I imagine an inventory hasn't been taken for a couple of weeks … what with Lady Mackay being away?"

Elsa's gaze flicked to the large leather-bound ledger that sat on a low table to the right of the doorway, before she frowned. "Aye." The woman was understandably wary of this stranger who'd appeared in her kitchen before asking very direct questions.

Maggie didn't blame her, although she wasn't criticizing. She wanted to help. However, her desire to assist wasn't an entirely selfless act. Tidying a messy spence was the perfect chore for a woman who'd let her dead husband down.

"Well, I'll just get stuck in then," Maggie replied briskly. "Ye can return to the kitchen now, Elsa. We can go over the meals ye have planned for the next week once I've finished here."

Elsa pressed her lips together once more, before reluctantly nodding.

A short while later, Maggie found herself alone in the space, a long, tedious task before her. Finally releasing a weary sigh, she picked up the ledger and moved over to the shelves. Aye, keeping busy was certainly a good idea. It would limit her time with Morgan and keep her mind off other matters.

Maggie frowned then.

However, it wasn't enough.

The evening before, after she'd challenged Morgan and he'd answered her, a sinking sensation had settled in the pit of Maggie's belly.

God's teeth, the man was hard to resist.

When he favored her with one of his direct, melting looks, her breathing came in short gasps and she felt all flustered. Worse still, she enjoyed his honesty and liked the sharp intelligence in his green eyes. The night before, he'd been respectful—and although they'd shared the same bed, he hadn't tried to tumble her.

If things continued in this vein, she would surely fall for him.

Maggie muttered a curse, her fingers clenching around the ledger. No—she couldn't let herself do that.

She'd wanted to leave Inverness without an offer of marriage, yet had somehow managed to find herself a husband. Even now, she could hardly believe what a mess she'd made of things. Circumstances might have forced her into this union, yet it was imperative she didn't fall in love with her new husband.

She'd been in shock after the wedding and had withdrawn from Morgan for a spell, but now they were at Farr Castle, she'd begun to warm to him once more.

Maggie lowered the ledger onto a shelf and stared sightlessly at the jars of salt she'd been about to count.

Then squeezing her eyes shut, she steeled herself for the decision she'd been avoiding since the night before.

Aye, she liked Morgan, but she couldn't be friends with him. It would only encourage him. Instead, she needed to push him away, to withdraw.

Maggie opened her eyes, swallowing as a sickly sensation crept over her. Cruelty didn't come easily to her. She'd never been a woman who enjoyed playing games with men. However, this wasn't a game. Her heart was in peril.

Her jaw clenched then, resolve stiffening her spine. No matter what happened, she would remain faithful to Campbell's memory.

"There ye are!" A relieved female voice intruded sometime later.

Maggie was crouched before the clay jars of preserves, brow furrowed as she counted them. She didn't look up at first.

"Maggie."

Halting her task, she sat back on her heels, irritation flooding through her. She'd lost count and would have to start again now.

Jaimee Mackay stood before her, hands on hips. "What are ye doing?"

"Just tidying up a bit."

"But Keira usually does that."

Maggie loosed an irritated sigh. "Aye, but she's asked me to take over now she's heavy with bairn."

Actually, when the two women had chatted the evening before, Maggie had *insisted* that Keira let her assume some of her responsibilities.

Jaimee's frown deepened. "Are ye usually like this?"

Maggie inclined her head. "Like what?"

"Don't get me wrong. I'm glad ye aren't an idler ... and I too like to keep busy ... but ye only just arrived here. No one expects ye to throw yerself into work." The younger woman paused then. "Besides, Morgan's been looking for ye all morning."

Maggie stilled, a cold lump settling in her belly. That was exactly the reason she'd hurried off to the kitchens first thing. "I'm sure Morgan has plenty to do without me getting under his feet," she replied with a strained smile.

Jaimee huffed. "Aye, but he'd have to find ye first."

"Maggie," Morgan's voice made Maggie glance up from where she was trying, in vain, to cinch Walnut's girth. "What are ye doing?"

"Isn't it obvious?" Maggie replied between gritted teeth. "This blasted thing won't do up. Surely, he hasn't put on that much weight since we arrived?"

"Here, let me help." Morgan stepped up next to her so that they stood shoulder-to-shoulder in the narrow stall. Maggie tensed, suppressing the urge to step away. She hated how 'aware' she was of him—how the heat of his body seemed to reach out and envelop her whenever he drew near.

She'd been at Farr just over three days, and Morgan had insisted he take her out for a ride and show her his brother's lands. Maggie had reluctantly agreed, although he'd had to drag her away from weeding the castle's courtyard garden to do so.

Morgan examined the girth, before letting out a laugh. "No wonder ye are having trouble ... this isn't Walnut's saddle. It's the one Cait uses for her palfrey. That girth was never going to fit around this fellow." Morgan gave Walnut an affectionate slap on the shoulder.

"Oh." Maggie's cheeks heated, as her gaze took in the saddle once more. He was right. It was much smaller and more delicately styled than the saddle she normally used. "Why didn't I notice that?"

"I don't know." Feeling his gaze upon her, Maggie glanced up and met his eye. Morgan was watching her, a speculative look upon his face. "Ye have been distracted ... withdrawn ... of late. Does something prey on yer mind, wife?"

Maggie swallowed, hurriedly averting her gaze once more. "No," she said, deliberately sharpening her tone. "I've been taken up with my new duties, that's all." With that, she reached forward, grasped the saddle, and hauled it off Walnut's back. "Come on ... we'll never get out of the castle at this rate."

They rode out of Farr Castle into a cool, slightly overcast spring morning. A nippy wind gusted in from the sea, and Maggie was glad she'd worn one of her heavier woolen kirtles and donned a fur-lined cloak. Winter was behind them now, yet the weather in the Highlands was notoriously fickle.

Firstly, Morgan took her to the village of Swordly, just north of Farr. The village sat on the edge of a sweeping bay. The sea was rough, an expanse of white-caps against the pale sky.

They approached Swordly in silence, and Maggie would have been happy to pass the entire journey that way. However, Morgan eventually spoke. "I'm off to gather support for the petition tomorrow," he offered.

Maggie didn't reply.

They passed through the village, heading toward the bare hills stretching north. Morgan's determination to see Niel Mackay freed impressed her, even if she'd noted that Connor had taken to scowling whenever Morgan attempted to raise the subject at mealtimes. The laird had been tense of late, and she wondered if the events at Inverness preyed on his mind.

Finally, Morgan cut her a concerned look. "Did ye hear me, Maggie?"

"Aye," she replied, affecting a slightly bored tone. "Whom will ye visit first?"

"I'll go north to the Sinclairs. Many of them are good friends of Niel's ... so I thought I'd start there."

"I thought ye would have started locally. Surely that's easier?"

"The Mackay chieftains will be the easiest to convince," he answered, "but we need the neighboring clans to back us, if Niel is to ever be freed."

Maggie shrugged before turning her attention to the wild landscape that surrounded them.

"Does yer new home please ye?" Morgan asked after a pause.

The hope in his voice made guilt clutch at Maggie's chest. Aye, she liked Farr Castle very much. However, she couldn't let Morgan know—not if she was going to keep him at arm's length.

"Well enough," she replied airily. "Although it's a bit too bare for my tastes."

He inclined his head. "That's part of its wild beauty, is it not?"

Maggie shrugged. "It's a pity it's so isolated … and small."

"Our territory is big enough. It extends as far as the River Naver to the south-west, and as far as Kirtomy Burn to the north." Morgan frowned then. "Although our southern and eastern borders with the Gunns are forever shifting."

"There are mountains between ye at least," Maggie pointed out with a snort. "Surely that keeps them at bay?"

Morgan's handsome face tensed, irritation flaring in his eyes. "Those mountains have several valleys and glens that make accessing our lands easier than ye'd think."

Maggie gave a disdainful laugh, even as she inwardly cringed. Lord, this was harder than she'd anticipated. She'd surely hate herself once she was done making Morgan dislike her. "It's ridiculous … ye worrying that the Gunns will bring the Mackays down. Ye fret unnecessarily."

A muscle bunched in Morgan's jaw. Good. She'd finally succeeded in angering him. "Is it?" he growled. "They'd love nothing more than to grind us into the dirt … to take our lands for themselves."

"I wouldn't focus so intently on yer enemies," Maggie drawled, deliberately not heeding the warning note in his voice. Now that she'd taken this road, she'd have to push on. "What about the Mackays themselves? I was there this morning in the solar, when yer brother read out that missive … it seems as though one of yer chieftains is brewing trouble."

Morgan scowled. Maggie noted the way his shoulders stiffened, and how his fingers clenched the reins. Of course, he didn't need reminding of the letter from Robert Mackay. Connor's expression had turned thunderous as he'd read it.

The laird of Balnakeil had stated that since all of them had lost confidence in Angus Mackay, they should meet to discuss the matter.

Connor had spat out an oath before tossing the missive upon the fire. "Somebody's getting too big for his braies," he'd growled. "I'll not have Robert Mackay make assumptions about where my loyalties lie."

A lengthy pause stretched out between Morgan and Maggie then, and not a companionable one. When Morgan spoke, his gaze was shuttered, guarded. "Aye, Robert is a stirrer all right, but my brother will deal with him."

24

HAVE YE FORGOTTEN?

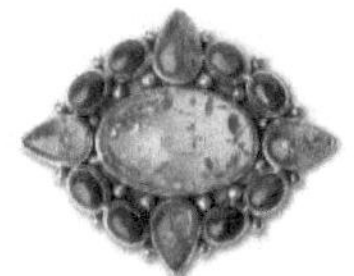

"HAVE YE FORGOTTEN, Morgan?"

Glancing up from where he'd been buttering his last piece of bannock, Morgan frowned. "Forgotten what?"

"Today is the twenty-fifth of April."

A chill settled over Morgan, his breathing slowing. "Is it a year already?"

"Aye," Jaimee replied, her eyes glittering now. "And it seems to have slipped both yer and Connor's minds that Ma died on this day."

The two siblings were seated in the laird's solar, lingering over their bannocks, butter, and honey. The others, including Maggie, had all departed. His wife had insisted on helping the servants do an inventory of the granary, in preparation for the harvests of oats and barley that would come later in the year. Maggie was keen to take on Keira's responsibilities—so keen in fact that he barely saw her. And when he did spend time with his wife, she had a tongue like an adder.

Morgan wasn't sure what had come over of her.

However, Morgan's attention wasn't currently on his aloof wife, but on Jaimee. His throat thickened. Damn it, his sister was right. Both brothers had forgotten.

Connor had spent the morning meal fussing over his wife. Keira was feeling fatigued, and Connor wanted Cullodina to look over her.

Morgan had insisted that he and Connor meet later in the day. They needed to discuss the petition he was preparing for Niel's release. Morgan had already visited the Sinclairs to gather letters and signatures—a trip that had been largely successful—but whenever he'd brought the subject up with his brother, Connor seemed reluctant to discuss it. He'd been preoccupied of late with how best to handle any rising dissension within the clan. Connor hadn't replied to Robert Mackay's letter, although he was now wary about what the man might do next.

Morgan wasn't going to let Connor ignore the petition though.

Aye, his brother was taken up with other matters, but that was no excuse.

Morgan reached out and placed a hand over his sister's. "I'm a dolt, Jaimee … as is Connor. Worry not, we shall hold a special supper in Ma's honor tonight."

Jaimee brushed away an errant tear that had escaped. Morgan started to feel like a beast. His sister wasn't a woman easily moved to tears. "I miss her," she whispered. "Not a day goes by when I don't wish she was still with us."

Morgan swallowed. "I too wish that," he said, his voice catching.

The loss of their mother had hit all of them hard. The stunned look on his father's face, the despair in his eyes when Cullodina had emerged from Rose's sickroom and announced the news of her passing, would haunt Morgan for the rest of his days.

Her illness had been so swift. None of them were prepared to lose her so suddenly.

And with Rose Mackay's death, laughter and joy had left Farr Castle for a time.

"Worry not, I will go and talk to Connor," Morgan assured his sister. "Despite all that's happened of late … this day must be marked."

Jaimee nodded, her eyes still glittering. "We haven't spoken much over the past days," she said, favoring him with a wan smile. "I've missed our chats."

Morgan smiled. "As have I. Things will get back to normal now we're home."

Silence fell between the siblings then, although eventually Jaimee broke it. "I like Maggie," she said softly. "I know ye weren't looking for a wife ... but ye could have done far worse."

Morgan cocked an eyebrow. "What's this? Has my sister decided that a wedded life might not be so bad after all?"

Jaimee snorted, even as her brow furrowed. "I think not, brother. It's different for men, as ye well know."

Indeed it was. Morgan's gaze traveled over his sister's face. He'd been distracted of late, but there was something different about her these days. Ever since they'd left Inverness, she'd been quieter than usual, her expression often introspective. His sister, usually so light-hearted, appeared troubled by something.

They'd settled back at Farr Castle now, yet her mood still hadn't righted itself.

Perhaps, Connor had been insisting too strongly that she take a husband. If that was the case, he'd talk to his brother and tell him to ease his nagging.

Jaimee would wed when she was ready. Marriage wasn't something anyone should be forced into.

Maggie strode along the cliff path. The afternoon sun warmed her face, yet she couldn't shake the low mood that had dogged her all day. She'd just taken a brisk walk to Swordly and was now on her way back to the castle. After helping Elsa and the other cooks prepare for the evening's feast, she'd needed some fresh air. The kitchen was hot and smoky, and Elsa was even crabbier than usual as the laird had only just informed them that he wanted a special supper to mark the first anniversary of Rose Mackay's death.

While at Swordly, Maggie had taken the opportunity to go foraging for herbs. The basket she carried under one arm was now filled with wild garlic and nettles, both of which were used for healing. Farr's healer, Cullodina, always needed ingredients for her potions and poultices.

Approaching the ramparts that protected the landward side of the castle, Maggie's gait slowed. Her gaze rested upon the square keep etched against the sky, tension filtering through her. Of course, once she re-entered the fortress, she risked bumping into her husband.

Treating Morgan with cool disdain was turning out to be harder than she'd anticipated. The man had a thick hide. Her stinging comments seemed to bounce off him. He'd been away for a few days, but every morning since his return, he greeted her with a smile and asked if she'd slept well. Maggie usually responded with a grunt or muttered comment, yet he merely teased her.

Maggie's brow furrowed. Although they had shared a bed since leaving Inverness, her husband still hadn't bedded her, and she wondered when that would change. Typically, she retired before him—exhaustion usually drove her to her bed early—and so she was often asleep by the time he joined her. However, that wouldn't put off most men.

Her belly fluttered as images of their stolen tryst in that alcove in Inverness Castle returned to her. Heat washed over her, and she scowled. There wasn't any point worrying over it. Her sharp tongue wouldn't keep Morgan at bay forever; they'd lie together sooner or later.

Maggie turned away from the castle. No, she most definitely wasn't ready to go back inside yet. She craved solitude this afternoon. Maybe she needed to walk a little farther.

Leaving the ramparts at her back, she walked back into Farr village. And without realizing it, her feet carried her toward the kirkyard.

Like the rest of the headland, it was a windswept spot, without a single tree to protect it. As such, some of the older headstones had listed right, as if pushed by the prevailing wind over the years.

Entering the yard, Maggie halted, tensing.

Morgan was there. Crouched before two gravestones, he had his back to her. The brisk afternoon breeze ruffled his dark-blond hair, and for a moment, Maggie merely stood there, not sure what to do.

She was intruding.

I should leave ... before he sees me.

Maggie spotted Gritta then, lazing in the shadow of a gravestone a few feet back from her master. The hound hadn't spied her yet, but she would soon.

Swiveling, Maggie made to retrace her steps. However, her boot crunched on the loose stones beneath her feet.

An instant later, Gritta raised her head and barked.

25

NEVER AN INTERRUPTION

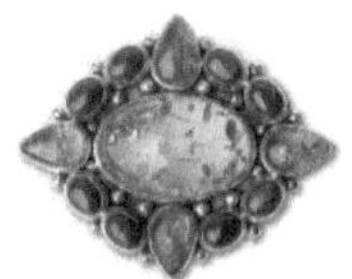

MORGAN GLANCED OVER his shoulder, his gaze settling upon Maggie.

He didn't smile, and Maggie's tension intensified. "Sorry," she muttered. "I was leaving."

"Ye don't have to do that," he replied.

"I do … I'm clearly interrupting."

He shook his head. "Ye are never an interruption, Maggie."

Warmth spread through her before she checked it. Curse him, why did he have to say such things? Frowning, Maggie took a step back. "All the same … I should leave ye be. I'll see ye back at the keep."

Gritta got up, tail wagging.

"Maggie, wait." Morgan rose to his feet, revealing the bunch of flowers that he'd placed at the foot of the grave. There were other bouquets, in clay pots, either side of the gravestone—most likely from Connor and Jaimee. "I meant it … please stay."

Wary, Maggie drew near, before her gaze dropped to the flowers he'd brought. Her lips curved. "Bluebells."

"Aye," he murmured. "They were Ma's favorite flowers. There's a dell in the hills, an hour's ride south of here, where they grow every spring."

Maggie looked up, studying his face. He'd made a special trip to gather flowers for his mother. "That was a lovely gesture," she replied, before she could prevent herself. She couldn't treat him with disdain—not when he was standing before his mother's grave. It was difficult enough to be cold with someone who didn't deserve such treatment, but she couldn't be so blatantly cruel.

Morgan grimaced. "Perhaps … although Jaimee would likely say it's the result of a guilty conscience." He paused there, raking a hand through his shaggy hair. "I completely forgot that today was the first anniversary of Ma's death."

Maggie glanced over at the twin gravestones. Husband and wife—buried side-by-side. "Ye have been … busy of late, Morgan," she replied. "I never met yer mother, but I think she'd forgive ye."

He gave a humorless laugh. "Connor forgot as well … Jaimee's quite rightly disgusted with us both."

Maggie shifted her attention back to Morgan, noting the tension around his mouth. "The dates on those stones are just months apart."

He nodded, his gaze shadowing. "Aye … Ma died in spring and Da at mid-summer."

Maggie stepped closer to the graves, studying them. "My parents were buried side-by-side outside Caisteal Nan Corr." A sigh rippled through Maggie then. She'd forgotten how kirkyards could make her melancholy. "My late husband, Campbell, is buried at Contullich Castle … I'm never likely to visit it again."

"Ye still grieve him." It wasn't a question but a fact.

"I suppose I do," Maggie admitted. "The first year was the worst." Her throat thickened then. "But it gets easier after that."

Pulling herself together, Maggie turned back to Morgan.

He was watching her with an odd look upon his face. "Ye have been unfriendly of late, Maggie," he said softly. "I'm beginning to think ye dislike me."

Maggie started to sweat. This was her chance to say something cutting or brush him off coldly. Yet the words stuck in her throat. "Don't be daft," she said, glancing away. "I'm just trying to adjust to my new life that's all ... it's difficult sometimes."

A pause drew out between them, before Morgan replied, "Ye don't have to keep yerself so busy." Maggie looked up to see his brow was furrowed. "Keira doesn't ask ye to exhaust yerself on her behalf ... and neither do I." He took a step closer, spearing her gaze with his. "Avoiding me isn't going to make settling in here any easier."

Maggie swallowed. "I know," she whispered. Panic grasped her by the throat. She needed to stop this conversation.

"Is there anything I can do ... to help?"

Heat flushed through Maggie. He was standing too close; his nearness was muddling her senses. Not trusting herself to speak, she merely shook her head.

Morgan was on edge when he returned to the keep. Making his way up to the chieftain's solar, he was relieved to find it empty for the moment. Usually, he would pour himself something to drink and sit by the fire, but since the early evening was bonny, he perched on the window-seat instead, his gaze traveling out to sea.

A stiff breeze rippled across the water. The sun sat low on the horizon now, glittering off the waves. The salty tang of the sea drifted in through the open window. Morgan breathed it in deeply, hoping that the familiar scent would settle him.

But it didn't.

He didn't understand Maggie at all. He hardly saw his wife these days, and when he did, she mystified him. One moment she treated him like something nasty she'd just scraped off her boot, and the next it seemed she could barely meet his eye. When he'd stepped close to her in the kirkyard, he'd seen Maggie's vulnerability—a fragility that warred with the tension vibrating from her body.

Something was definitely amiss with her, yet she wouldn't share her worries with him.

Morgan loosed a heavy sigh. Curse it all, Maggie had gotten under his skin. Despite her cool attitude toward him, he lived for the brief moments of the day when he saw her. He'd been away, but when he returned home, the first thing he'd done was seek her out. He didn't care that she greeted his smiles with a frown more often than not. Instead, he remembered the clever, compassionate woman he'd spent time with in Inverness; the one that teased him and smiled at his irreverent sense of humor.

Morgan's mouth thinned as frustration simmered within him. Aye, he yearned for his wife.

He'd asked her outright if she disliked him, and she'd denied it. That was a relief, at least. However, Morgan wasn't sure how to proceed. None of his affairs had lasted longer than a week or two at most. He wasn't used to being a husband, especially to a woman who hadn't wanted to wed again.

And yet, he wouldn't be deterred. He was determined to truly know her.

The whisper of the solar door opening drew Morgan's gaze from the view outside the window.

"There ye are." Connor halted. "We're opening a barrel of Ma's favorite sloe wine downstairs. Will ye join us?"

Morgan frowned. "I thought we were going to go over the petition before the feast?"

Connor heaved an irritated sigh. "Can't that wait till tomorrow?"

Morgan frowned. "Ye can't keep putting me off. We need to discuss this."

Connor's gaze narrowed. "Aye, and we will. *Tomorrow*. But today is a special occasion ... one ye and I forgot about." He motioned to the open door behind him. "Come on, Jaimee will have our guts if we're not downstairs soon."

Connor Mackay put on a fine feast to honor a year since his mother's passing. Maggie admired the garlands of wildflowers that hung from the heavy wooden beams overhead. It seemed that Morgan hadn't just collected enough bluebells to lie on his mother's grave. Vases of the vividly colored spring flowers lined the tables.

The harpist had returned, yet she didn't sing tonight. Instead, she played a series of soft instrumental tunes. The soulful music drifted through the hall, blending with the rumble of voices.

Spring lambs had been spit-roasted for the supper. Servants carried in the roasted carcasses before they proceeded to carve them at the foot of the dais.

After the food was served, the great hall of Farr Castle quieted. All gazes focused upon the laird as he rose to his feet.

Connor Mackay wore a grave expression as he prepared to address the hall. Maggie observed the laird with interest. His seriousness made him look older, even more imposing than usual. He wore a crisp white lèine with the Mackay sash across it, his golden-blond hair brushed out across his broad shoulders. Both the laird and lady Mackay wore matching green brooches upon their shoulders this eve.

"A year today, we lost Rose Mackay," Connor began, his voice carrying far across the hall. "My mother was taken from us suddenly ... and this keep hasn't been the same ever since. Her laugh will never again echo off the stone walls, and her kindness will never bring a smile to our faces." Connor paused then, his gaze swiveling to his kin. "But we have our memories to sustain us. And while Rose remains in our thoughts and hearts ... she will never truly be lost to us."

Maggie's chest constricted. Although she'd never met Rose, Connor's words had touched her.

The laird's gaze swept across the hall-full of Mackay warriors and their families. "I would like ye to raise yer cups now," he called to them, "and toast to her memory ... to Rose Mackay."

"To Rose Mackay." Voices echoed high into the rafters.

The feasting began.

As Maggie helped herself to a slice of lamb, her gaze traveled around the table. She was still a newcomer amongst the Mackays of Farr, but already she liked them far better than she had her Munro in-laws. Campbell's viperish mother had made life wearisome at Contullich. Here there was no mother-by-marriage, and the fact saddened her a little, for it sounded as if Rose Mackay had been a sweet soul.

Her offspring were a credit to her.

Chewing slowly, Maggie cast Morgan a sidelong glance.

She was wary of her husband this evening. And yet at the same time, she'd never been more aware of him. They sat side-by-side at the long table, close enough that she could feel the heat of his thigh near hers, could smell that familiar combination of virile male, leather, and the scent of clove he used for bathing.

She couldn't help herself; she breathed him in. His nearness made her feel a little giddy.

Maggie's fingers tightened around her eating knife before she forced herself to relax. There was nothing wrong with desiring her husband.

Lust wasn't *love*. It was much safer.

And yet, she needed to tread carefully now. Their conversation in the kirkyard had panicked her. She had to pull herself together, to rebuild her defenses.

But not this evening. At present, she couldn't seem to summon the will. Acting the shrew was wearisome indeed.

Sensing her gaze upon him, Morgan looked up. The serious expression he wore this evening suited him, she noted. He was a handsome man, but when he was pensive, his good-looks intensified. His pine-green eyes were usually bright or teasing, but not so tonight. They were darker than usual, solemn.

"Are ye enjoying the meal, Maggie?" Morgan asked.

Maggie swallowed, offering him a smile. "Aye ... it's delicious. Spring lamb is a treat indeed."

His mouth quirked. "It was my mother's favorite dish ... and it's also mine."

Their stare drew out, and suddenly it felt overly hot and airless inside the great hall of Farr Castle. Heat pooled low in Maggie's belly. Their gazes held, and in the depths of Morgan's eyes, she saw her own need reflected back at her. Need, and something else she couldn't quite identify.

The devil strike her down, when he looked at her like that, she struggled to draw breath.

The attraction between them was there—as strong as it had been in Inverness. And somehow, their meeting that afternoon had actually fanned the flames. It had been awkward, pained, and yet the intensity of his gaze, and the concern for her well-being she'd seen there, had made her want to throw herself into his arms.

They were wed now. They could share a bed without having to keep it secret. The trauma following their first coupling had made them keep their distance, but things were about to change.

Maggie knew with a certainty that made sweat bead across her body that they would lie together again tonight.

26

THE SCENT OF SEDUCTION

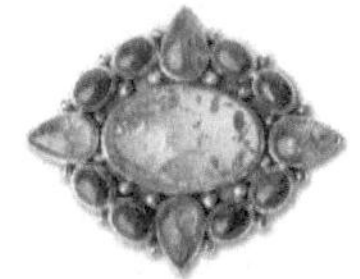

"SHALL I BRUSH some oil through yer hair? The one scented with lily?"

"Aye, thank ye, Aileana."

Seated before the hearth, perched on a stool, Maggie tried to calm the nerves dancing in her belly.

"I'm sure yer husband will like it," the maid continued. Aileana was in much brighter spirits these days. She'd been withdrawn initially, upon their arrival at Farr, but true to form, the lass had struck up friendships with the other servants. She'd certainly regained her former chattiness. "My Ma always said that lily is the scent of seduction."

Maggie gave an embarrassed laugh, shifting on her stool. "Did she?"

"Ye are fortunate, Maggie," Aileana continued with a wistful sigh. The floral scent enveloped them as she continued to brush her mistress's hair. "Morgan Mackay is a handsome man ... and a good one too."

Maggie tensed. Aye, that was the problem.

After Aileana left her, Maggie couldn't settle.

Removing the woolen robe she wore over her lèine, she started to pace before the fire. Aileana's chatter had distracted her for a short while, yet now she was alone once more, anxiety was getting the better of her.

She wasn't a virgin, and this wouldn't be the first time she'd been intimate with the man who was now her husband. Why then did her belly churn like that of a maiden on her wedding night?

Maggie halted her pacing, her heart lurching when she heard footfalls approaching the bed-chamber.

Hades, he's here!

Diving across the room, she landed on the edge of the bed.

Maggie was smoothing out the thin material of the lèine that covered her nakedness, when the door swung open and Morgan stepped inside.

Their gazes met across the chamber. Silently, his mouth curving at the corners, Morgan closed the door behind him. However, his gaze was as serious as it had been during supper.

There was an intensity to him, a focus, she'd not yet seen.

Maggie cleared her throat, trying to ignore the fact that her palms had started to sweat. "Where's yer friend?" she asked, cursing how high her voice was.

He offered her a proper smile. "Gritta is keeping watch outside tonight." Still observing her, Morgan heeled off his boots. His gaze then slid down from her face, over her body. The thin tunic was almost transparent in the firelight.

He could likely see her nipples through it.

Morgan then pulled off his lèine, and Maggie caught her breath.

His torso was leanly muscled and crisscrossed with several thin scars: a warrior's body.

Her breathing caught when he started to slowly unlace his braies.

However, Morgan was half-way through the process when he halted. He inclined his head, his brow furrowing. "Are ye sure ye are ready for this, Maggie?"

Lord, the way he said her name made her melt like butter on a hot griddle. Maggie licked her lips, her heart bucking against her breastbone. "Aye," she whispered.

Morgan pushed down his braies and stepped out of them. Then he walked toward the bed.

And all the while, his gaze never wavered from the comely figure perched upon the edge of it.

Did Maggie realize just how lovely she was, seated there in that filmy lèine, her dark hair spilling in heavy curls over her bare shoulders? The scent of lily drifted across the bed-chamber, and he breathed it in.

Just the sight of her made his chest ache with longing. Nervousness fluttered up under his ribs. Suddenly, he felt like a lad about to experience his first bedding. Maggie had that effect on him.

Her gaze took him in boldly, traveling down from his face to his chest, belly, and groin. There, it stayed. Maggie's lips parted, her blue eyes darkening. She stared at his arousal with an intensity that made his pulse start to hammer in his ears.

With just a look, this woman set him on fire.

When their gazes had locked during supper, he'd known that she wanted him. Even so, he'd had to ask— just to be sure she wasn't putting on a brave face.

He wanted her to know that he wouldn't force himself on her.

And yet her answer had made the tension in his gut unknot. Maggie stole far too many of his waking thoughts. She stoked a lust in him stronger than any he'd ever experienced, a desire that was starting to drive him mad.

Approaching the bed, he reached down and took her hands, drawing her to her feet. Maggie rose, her breathing catching when he took hold of her lèine and drew it over her head.

For the first time in their acquaintance, Morgan and Maggie stood before each other naked.

Stepping back from her, Morgan let his gaze devour Maggie's body. She was small yet strong, with high, firm breasts, and womanly hips. The darkness of her hair contrasted with the milky paleness of her skin, and when Morgan's gaze rested upon the thatch of soft hair between her thighs, the tattoo of his pulse quickened further still.

God's bones, he was hungry for her.

Stepping close, Morgan reached out, cupping Maggie's face with his hands, his mouth slanting over hers for a passionate kiss.

Maggie leaned toward him, her lips parting eagerly under his.

And in an instant, Morgan Mackay forgot himself.

He usually liked to take his time with a woman. They had the whole night ahead of them; there was no need to rush. But the hunger that grasped him in its clutches drove all thoughts of slowness from his head.

His mouth feasted on hers, and Maggie kissed him back with equal ferocity. Suddenly, his hands were everywhere—as were hers. He explored the smooth curve of her back, his breathing catching when his hands cupped her rounded buttocks. And then, when he bent his head and suckled her breasts, he was lost.

The next thing Morgan knew, he'd pushed Maggie back on the bed and spread her wide.

Her breathing came in ragged pants, the sound inflaming him.

There would be time to linger later. Right now, he had to have her.

Morgan slid deep inside Maggie, her heat enveloping him. Her sharply indrawn breath, followed by a sigh of pleasure, almost undid him.

Groaning a curse, Morgan arched back, his eyes fluttering shut. Being buried in her felt perfect.

He opened his eyes and gazed down at her flushed face, drinking her in. Lying back against the coverlet, her black hair spread out around her, Maggie stared up at him.

Morgan wasn't a pious man, but at that moment he felt like kneeling before the altar of this woman. If she were a religion, he'd be her supplicant. His heart was thundering so loudly against his ribs, it felt as if it would burst free.

Reaching out, he teased her nipples with his fingertips, tweaking them gently.

Maggie gasped, her gaze luminous. And then she lifted her hips toward him, rotating them in a sensual circle against him.

Morgan ground out another curse, before he started to take her in slow, even strokes. The effort it was taking him to temper his speed, when all he wanted was to plow her like a beast, caused his limbs to tremble. His self-control was on a tight, straining leash now. Sweat slicked his body, and hunger clawed at his gut.

Heedless to the war he was waging with himself, Maggie moaned and sighed beneath him. She raised her hips to meet each deep thrust.

A loud groan tore free from Morgan, reverberating through the chamber. Spreading her wider still, Morgan positioned himself over her, and he stared down at where their slick bodies met.

Breathing hard, Maggie's gaze followed his. She propped herself up on her elbows, watching the swollen length of his rod as it slid into her wetness.

It was the most erotic moment of Morgan's life. The excitement in her eyes, the way her breathing caught at the sight, made the leash snap.

He thrust into Maggie, pushing her along the coverlet. Then he held himself over her, capturing her mouth with his.

Morgan plowed her hard, without reserve, while she wrapped her limbs around him, drawing him deeper with each thrust.

And with each stroke, Morgan let himself fall. Each time he buried himself deep inside his wife, he came home. He couldn't be closer to anyone than this.

Something fractured within Morgan then, a reserve—one he hadn't even realized he'd been clinging to—gave way. He closed his eyes, squeezing them shut as tears threatened. His throat tightened as a wave of tenderness swamped him.

Maggie started to tremble under him, and when he ground his hips against hers, wet heat surged around

Morgan's shaft. His wife sobbed her pleasure, her head falling back to expose the long line of her neck.

Morgan's climax rose swiftly, snapping his back rigid. For a moment, the world went dark and hot, throbbing pleasure coursed through him. And then his ragged cry filled the chamber.

Coming back to earth afterward felt as if he'd just awoken from a fevered dream. Breathing hard, he propped himself up on his elbows. He was fearful of crushing Maggie, for he was a lot bigger than she was.

Instead, he gathered her trembling form in his arms and rolled onto his back, taking her with him.

For a time they lay like that, while their breathing steadied, the room stopped spinning, and the world returned to normal.

Morgan swallowed hard, blinking back tears. There were so many things he wanted to say, yet his tongue felt stuck to the roof of his mouth. He brushed a lock of dark hair off Maggie's face and met her sea-blue gaze.

Maggie stared back at him, and the moment drew out. "Morgan," she whispered finally, her voice catching. "I—"

He reached up, his thumb tracing her full lower-lip, halting her mid-sentence. His chest hurt with the emotions that now roiled there. He had to say something before his courage failed him.

"I'm glad ye are mine, Maggie," he rasped. "And I swear I'll spend the rest of my life treating ye like the queen ye are."

27

THE WAY IT IS

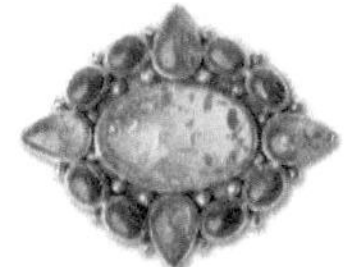

MAGGIE STARED DOWN at Morgan. Her heart was pounding so hard she was sure he could hear it. Her body, which had been languorous after their heated coupling, was now as tense as a bow-string.

"Morgan," she murmured warily. "I don't think—"

"I've fallen in love with ye, Maggie."

Maggie stilled. How she wished he hadn't spoken those words.

He looked at her with such a look of vulnerability upon his face that something deep within her twisted.

"Everything about ye calls my soul to yers," he continued, heedless of the panic that now bubbled up within her.

Maggie's breathing caught. She saw the sincerity, the longing in his eyes; he spoke the truth.

Her eyes closed. This was ill-news. Damn the man. Why had he fallen in love with her? Hadn't she done her best to discourage him?

"Maggie?" Concern edged his voice. "Is something wrong?"

Maggie opened her eyes, her gaze settling upon him. "Do ye not recall what I said to ye at Kildary?" she asked softly.

His handsome face stiffened. "Aye, but I thought—"

Maggie's jaw clenched. Like most men, he thought that a declaration of love would have a woman swooning at his feet. She hated the idea of hurting him, yet she couldn't let this go on a moment longer. "I can't love ye, Morgan. I just … can't."

Long moments passed, while Morgan stared up at her. When he finally spoke, there was a rough edge to his voice, even if his expression was now shuttered. "I don't understand. Is there something about me that offends ye?"

A lump rose in Maggie's throat. Why was he making this so hard? She didn't want to discuss the reasons why she couldn't love him. But there was a stubborn light in his eyes now. He wanted an answer from her. However, he wasn't going to get one that would satisfy him.

Maggie slid away from him and sat up. She then reached for a robe, pulling it around her nakedness. She needed a physical barrier between them when she said this.

"I made my position clear," she said, marveling at how cool and controlled her voice suddenly was, while her belly felt as if she were standing upon the deck of a pitching birlinn. She had her mask firmly in place once more. "And I now ask ye to respect it."

The hurt in Morgan's eyes cut her deep. He was the last person in the world she wanted to injure—for she genuinely liked him—and yet she had to keep him away.

"I'm sorry, Morgan, but that's the way it is."

A chill silence settled over the bed-chamber.

With just a handful of words, the mood had changed from warm and passionate to ice-cold.

A sickly sensation settled over Maggie. She looked away then, unable to meet his eye any longer. Instead, she studied the coverlet. The mattress shifted as he got up, but she didn't raise her gaze. She couldn't bear to look at him.

I should never have agreed to this marriage.

Morgan Mackay was a big-hearted man. He merited far better than this. He deserved a wife who was capable of loving him.

Maggie's vision blurred as she stared down at her hands, listening to the sounds of him dressing. She expected him to leave then, without another word, yet he didn't. She felt the weight of his stare upon her. He wanted her to look at him.

Slowly, Maggie lifted her chin, clenching her jaw as she braced for the impact.

Morgan's face was stony, his gaze veiled. "It's I who should apologize, Maggie," he murmured. The formality of his tone, especially after the passion they'd just shared, was like a physical blow. However, she'd expected no different. "There are some folk who love only once in a lifetime, and ye are one of them. Clearly, yer heart was buried with yer husband. I was an idiot not to see it."

Maggie stared back at him. "I can't change how I feel, Morgan," she replied, her voice husky now. "I can give ye my body, my loyalty, and companionship ... just not my heart."

Morgan's mouth compressed at that, yet he didn't utter another word. Instead, he turned away from her and left the bed-chamber, the door thudding gently shut behind him.

Alone on the bed, Maggie stared after him.

Ye have done the right thing. Her conscience whispered to her. *Ye can't let him love ye.*

A tear slid down Maggie's cheek. Aye, that was true enough. Why then did she feel like a beast?

Morgan went downstairs, Gritta padding after him. He didn't go to the chieftain's solar, as the room adjoined Connor and Keira's bed-chamber, and he didn't want to disturb them.

He couldn't weather talking to anyone else tonight. Not when he'd just made a gigantic fool of himself.

Humiliation burned like a coal in his belly as he entered the kitchens. He'd once watched Connor with bemusement, wondering at why his brother had made himself so miserable over Keira. But now he understood.

The kitchens were empty at this hour, and so Morgan helped himself to a pitcher of ale and a cup and carried them through to the great hall. His limbs felt heavy, as if he dragged rocks behind him. Everything seemed so hard these days. The petition was a huge task, one his brother didn't seem to want to help with. And now his wife had spurned him. If she'd actually punched him in the face, it would have hurt less. He'd hoped she'd warm to him with time, yet that seemed impossible now.

There wasn't a soul about, for it was past the witching hour now. The large bricks of peat in the hearth had burned low and were just glowing embers.

Morgan drew up a chair close to the fire and poured himself a cup of ale.

Sensing his grim mood, Gritta pushed against his leg with her nose, gazing up at him with adoring eyes.

"Aye, I know ye love me, lass," he murmured, ruffling the dog's ears. "At least someone does." His mouth twisted. "Lord, how pathetic I sound." He lifted his cup to his lips and took a long pull. The ale tasted a bit flat, with a bitter aftertaste. Wrinkling his face, he set the cup aside. It seemed he couldn't even drown his sorrows tonight. Instead, he would have to sit here sober and relive the humiliation.

He didn't want to think about what had transpired upstairs, yet he couldn't stop himself.

The memory of how Maggie had withdrawn from him, the things she'd said, and the cool and calm way she'd uttered them, wrenched like a dirk-blade to the belly.

She'd cut him down like he was some witless knave.

Morgan had lived a charmed life where women were concerned. Kennan had ribbed him over it many times. None of his lovers had made life difficult for him, and he'd always been the one to end their dalliances. Until now, he'd managed to avoid any entanglements.

Kennan's wife, Cait, had once teased him that life caught up with men like him eventually. "When ye fall, it'll be hard, Morgan," she'd told him with a knowing twinkle in her eye. "Mark my words."

At the time, he'd laughed the comment off.

But he wasn't laughing now.

He was in love with his wife. The signs had been there right from the beginning. He'd been drawn to the Maggie from the day Gritta had disgraced herself in the outer bailey and he'd come to Maggie's aid.

He'd initially dismissed his interest in her as merely lustful. He'd already noted how comely she was the previous Samhuinn, although with Niel Mackay sniffing around her—and with his brother's heart in tatters—Morgan had kept his distance.

Morgan stared at the glowing embers of the hearth, heaviness pressing down upon his shoulders.

I should have stayed away from her in Inverness.

Aye, hindsight was a fine thing. Yet it was too late for such thoughts. He shouldn't have helped Maggie search for her sister. He shouldn't have taken her to that alehouse. He definitely shouldn't have waited for her that evening by the stairwell.

There was a great list of things he *shouldn't* have done—and he'd ignored them all.

It wasn't surprising really that things had come to this. He'd fallen for a woman who was still in love with her dead husband. It was as if he'd *wanted* to come away from this bruised and battered.

28

BETWEEN HUSBAND AND WIFE

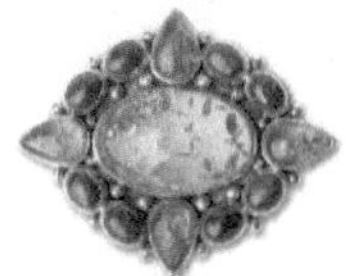

"YE ARE PALE this morning, Maggie. Does something ail ye?" Jaimee's inquiry roused Maggie from where she'd been listlessly weeding around the lavender bushes. She glanced up to see her sister-by-marriage sitting back on her heels, watching her.

"All is well," Maggie replied, forcing a smile. "I'm just a little tired."

Jaimee's brow furrowed. "I'm not surprised," she replied, her gaze never leaving Maggie's. "Ye've worked yer fingers to the bone since ye arrived here. Why don't ye take a few days off?" Her mouth curved then. "I'm sure Morgan would like to see more of ye."

Maggie swallowed hard. Usually, Maggie appreciated the lass's forthright manner—but not this morning. All she wanted was to be left alone. Forcing down her discomfort, Maggie favored Jaimee with a brittle smile. It was time to turn the conversation away from herself. "Would he? My husband is caught up with that petition to free Niel Mackay. He left again at dawn."

Jaimee sighed. "Of course, I'd forgotten ... after his success with the Sinclairs, he now plans to visit the Leslies. But I'm sure he'd be glad of yer company on his return."

Maggie straightened up and brushed the dirt off her hands. "He's certainly taken on Niel's cause. Are they really such good friends?"

"Not especially ... Connor and Niel have always been closer in age. However, Morgan has a strong sense of justice." Jaimee's green eyes clouded then. "I wish ye could have met our father ... Morgan takes after him. His loyalty to the Mackays was everything."

"I admire that in Morgan," Maggie admitted, her tone guarded. "He's passionate about the things he believes in."

She realized then that Jaimee was studying her intently. "Have ye quarreled?"

Maggie's mouth thinned, making her answer clear without uttering a word.

Jaimee huffed another sigh. "He can be aggravating."

Maggie dropped her gaze. Aye, he could be. But he hadn't been last night. Even now, she cringed at the memory of the words that had passed between them after their coupling.

How he'd confessed his love.

How she'd thrown it back in his face.

She felt ill whenever she thought of it. She didn't consider herself a cruel woman, the type to play with a man's affections. But Morgan would likely think of her so.

Stop worrying what he thinks of ye. She clenched her fingers around the wooden trowel she gripped.

In that way lay madness.

She glanced up once more to see Jaimee was still observing her with that piercing gaze both her brothers also possessed. Despite the cool morning and the shadowed courtyard garden in which they worked, Maggie's face flushed.

She didn't want to discuss her relationship with Morgan, especially not now when things were so raw.

"I'm not an expert on such things," Jaimee said after a pause, "but I think ye perfect for Morgan." Her mouth quirked then. "It takes a strong woman to tame my brother."

Maggie's belly twisted. Is that what she'd done? Tamed him?

Clack. Clack. Clack.

The sound of wooden blades colliding echoed over the landward bailey.

"Come on, Connor," Morgan goaded. "Ye can do better than that."

Sweat trickled down Morgan's back. It was the first hot afternoon of the spring, and so he'd stripped off his lèine to spar with his brother. Both of them were clad in nothing but braies. They'd even heeled off their boots to give them ease of movement.

Connor favored him with a hard smile. "Someone's in an ill mood today."

"Aye, ye'd be too if ye'd made a wasted trip." Morgan circled his brother, waiting for Connor to strike once more.

The two of them knew each other's fighting style well—which made it harder to best each other. Connor favored his left side when he feinted, while he insisted that Morgan often attacked too recklessly, leaving his guard open.

That was why Morgan had taken an injury the previous year during the journey back from visiting Keira's father. Maddoc Gunn and his men had come after them, attacking the Mackay party just before dawn one morning. Morgan had launched himself into the fray and cut down two of them before his haste earned him a deep cut across the flank.

"I warned ye the Leslies aren't interested in sticking their necks out for Niel Mackay," Connor replied. "They're worried about angering the king ... we all should be."

Morgan scowled. He didn't like being patronized. He danced away from his brother's swinging blade and brought his own up to parry—and felt the scar pull down one side.

It was a reminder of what happened when he didn't take care.

Ironic really that he now had another reminder. A wife.

Morgan clenched his jaw, pushing aside thoughts of Maggie. He'd been away for a week, gathering the support he needed. After returning late the night before, he slept in the stables rather than face his wife. He was avoiding her, but he wouldn't be able to do so forever.

Coward.

Teeth grinding, he leaped forward, striking hard at Connor's blade. "Aye, ye did," he grunted. "If I didn't know better, I'd think ye wished me to abandon this petition."

Clack. Clack.

Connor answered him with a scowl of his own. "I admire yer tenacity ... but King James has already ruled on Niel's future." He parried another vicious strike. "We did our best at the time to rectify the situation. If ye persist in this, ye do risk irritating the king further ... and then we could all be in trouble." Connor then landed a blow across Morgan's ribs. "Sometimes ye have to know when to let things go."

Snarling a curse, Morgan drove his brother back, knocking him off-balance slightly before he kicked out and tripped Connor up.

His brother fell heavily on his backside, letting out a curse as he did so. "Is that how ye win?" he growled. "By employing dirty tricks?"

Morgan flashed him a feral grin. "If it bests my opponent, so be it."

Connor's blond brows crashed together. "Sneaky bastard ... I won't let ye do that to me twice."

Morgan snorted. He spun his wooden blade, catching it by the hilt, and shook out his shoulders. "Ready to go again?"

Connor rolled to his feet, wincing as he tested the leg Morgan had kicked. "We've been at this for over an hour," he grumbled. "Aren't ye tired yet?"

"No."

Connor shook his head dismissively. He cast aside his wooden practice sword and strode across to the stone water trough that sat in the shade of the curtain wall. Leaning forward, he splashed water over his face and chest.

Glancing down at himself, Morgan realized that he too was slick with sweat. His muscles ached from exertion and his lungs burned, yet he hadn't noticed. He'd been too intent on the fight—on battering his brother into submission.

Connor turned to him, reaching for his lèine. "So … how are things with Maggie?"

Morgan ground his teeth. "Fine," he snapped.

Connor raised an eyebrow. "Ye slept in the stables last night. Why?"

Morgan scowled. Did nothing that went on within the walls of Farr Castle escape his brother's sharp eye? "It was late … I didn't want to wake her up," he lied.

"Ye didn't break yer fast with her this morning either," Connor continued, relentless. "And don't tell me yer grim mood is entirely to do with the appeal. I'm not a fool, Morgan. Something is amiss between ye and Maggie."

"Just leave it, Connor." Morgan tossed down his practice sword and turned on his heel, making for the keep. His throat was as dry as a herring left out too long in the sun. A cool tankard of ale was required. As he walked away, Morgan cast his brother a warning look over his shoulder. "Some things should remain between husband and wife."

Morgan and Maggie spoke little throughout supper. However, Maggie kept stealing glances at him.

He'd been away a week, yet it felt like months had passed since she'd seen her husband last—since he'd walked out of their bed-chamber without a backward glance. And Maggie had wrestled with her conscience ever since.

In truth, it hadn't given her a moment's peace.

She didn't take back what she'd said; she couldn't let Morgan shower her with love. Yet she wished she'd let him down more gently.

There was a hard edge to him this evening that she wagered had much to do with her treatment of him.

"How did it go with the Leslies, Morgan?" she asked finally. His silence was starting to bother her. "Did they agree to support yer petition?"

Morgan glanced her way, their gazes meeting properly for the first time all evening. His expression was veiled. "It could have gone better," he admitted. "Robbie Leslie has written a three-page letter extolling the strength of Niel's character and protesting the wrong done against him." He paused then, his features tightening. "But the rest of the Leslie chieftains wouldn't even sign their names to the petition."

"Don't worry, others will," Maggie replied, her tone firm. "Niel is fortunate indeed to have such a loyal friend as ye."

Their gazes held for a moment longer, and then Morgan frowned. "Aye," he murmured, before glancing away.

Maggie's supper churned in her belly; this was even more awkward than she'd feared. She didn't need to worry about rebuffing his attempts to converse with her any longer. The man clearly didn't want to be in her presence.

"So, what will ye do once ye have collected all the support ye need?" she asked, trying once more to engage him.

"I'll ride to Scone—alone if need be—and request another audience with the king." A harsh edge had crept into Morgan's voice. Glancing down the table, Maggie noted that Connor was scowling. She wondered if the brothers had argued.

"How did ye find King James, when the Mackay chieftains had their private audience with him?" she asked, intrigued now.

Morgan swung his gaze her way once more. "Bored … irritated."

"Did he give ye encouragement ... indicate he'd listen if ye prepared a proper petition?"

"Not really." Morgan sighed then, dragging a hand down his face. Maggie had noticed he did that when he was under stress. Their problems aside, this petition had him worried. "But I can't sit by while Niel rots in a cell."

Maggie's brow furrowed. Like everyone who'd witnessed the proceedings inside the great hall of Inverness castle, she'd seen that King James had a sharp mind and a ruthless streak that seemed at odds with his gentle manner. She just hoped for Morgan's sake the petition would be well received.

Glancing around, Maggie realized that their conversation wasn't being followed by any of the others at the table. Connor was discussing something with Kennan, while Jaimee and Keira laughed at a story Cait was recounting.

Maggie cleared her throat and leaned in closer to her husband. "Morgan ... I just wanted to say how sorry I am ... about w—what happened before ye left to visit the Leslies." She cursed her sudden stammer. "I didn't intend to wound ye, but I fear I have."

"I'm fine," he replied, his expression curt. "Don't worry yerself over me."

"Perhaps we could take a walk together ... tomorrow ... if ye are free?" She favored him with a weak smile.

"Perhaps," Morgan replied, his expression shuttered. "If there's time."

Maggie swallowed. Curse her to Hades, she'd actually missed him over the past days. Even though she'd done her best to limit their time together since her arrival at Farr Castle, she was used to Morgan teasing her at mealtimes, to feeling the mattress shift when he came to bed every night, and to waking up next to him in the mornings. She even missed that smelly hound of his. The hearth in their bed-chamber seemed bereft without Gritta curled up before it.

"Please," she said softly after a pause. "Don't hate me for this."

His mouth curved, although there was no humor in the expression. "I don't hate ye, Maggie." His voice was low, with a gravelly edge that pained her. "I doubt I ever could."

29

RESTLESS DAYS

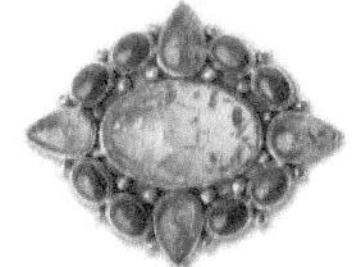

MAGGIE AWOKE EARLY and lay listening to the sound of her husband's breathing. Morgan usually rose before she did, but she'd slept fitfully the night before—her mind churning—and now found herself staring up at the rafters as the first grey glimmers of dawn peeked through the shutters.

Should I get up?

She was tempted, although she didn't want to wake Morgan. He'd made a bed for himself before the hearth—upon a thick sheepskin. After her rejection of him, he hadn't returned to share her bed.

She wondered if he ever would.

Ignoring the strange hollow sensation in her chest, Maggie gritted her teeth, threw back the covers, and swung her legs over the side of the bed.

It was no good. She couldn't stay abed.

She stood up and padded barefoot across to the screen in the corner of the room. Of late, she'd gotten in the habit of sleeping in a night-rail. It felt prim and spinsterish to do so, yet things had grown so awkward with Morgan she wouldn't feel comfortable going to bed naked.

Pouring cold water into the washbowl, Maggie stripped off her night-rail and went through her ablutions. She then reached for a fresh, ankle-length lèine and pulled it on. Usually, Aileana visited her just after dawn, to help her dress and fix her hair. Yet this morning, Maggie was filled with restlessness.

She couldn't remain in this chamber a moment longer. She needed to find something to occupy her unruly mind. The cooks would be up shortly—she would join them in the kitchens.

Maggie pulled a woolen kirtle over her head, yanked on her leather boots, and reached for a cloak. Her hair was still twisted into a messy braid from sleeping, but Aileana could untangle it later.

Morgan listened to the soft sounds of his wife's footsteps as she tip-toed across the bed-chamber and the gentle thud of the door opening and closing.

Then he opened his eyes.

Next to him, Gritta stirred. The hound's ears pricked, her gaze going to the doorway. "Aye, lass," Morgan mumbled. "There she goes."

Sitting up, he glanced over at the rumpled bed, where his wife had spent the night tossing and turning.

Aye, he'd heard her, for he too hadn't slept well.

Many times during the night, he'd wanted to call out to her, to ask what ailed her. But each time, he'd stilled his tongue.

As preoccupied as he was with this damn petition— for begging their allies for support was starting to feel just a little demeaning—he couldn't fail to note Maggie's disquiet.

He'd been brusque with her the evening before, when she'd tried to converse with him. It was hard to be natural around his wife these days, especially after *that* night. His pride had been more than dented—it had been smashed to pieces.

Bitterness filled Morgan's mouth, and he tore his gaze from the bed—from the place he longed to spend each night. Maggie wasn't the only one who was restless. It was just as well he had the petition to keep him occupied, he realized, or he'd go mad.

"The smell of herbs always reminds me of my Ma," Maggie admitted as she poured ground herbs into a pot. "My grandmother was a healer, and she taught Ma much about herbs. We used to make poultices together."

Cullodina glanced up from where she was sorting through a basket of moss she'd collected that morning. "A healer, eh? So, herbs are in yer blood."

Maggie nodded, smiling back. However, the expression felt strained. She didn't smile often these days. Even so, she enjoyed her afternoons with Cullodina.

Morgan had been gone for nearly two weeks on another trip, this time to visit the MacLeods and the Munros. During his absence, Maggie sometimes helped Cullodina collect herbs for her healing tinctures, powders, and unguents. After foraging, the two women worked together in the healer's small cottage, hanging up herbs to dry, bashing those that had already dried in a pestle and mortar, and steeping fresh herbs to make potions.

"Did ye ever meet yer grandmother?" Cullodina asked.

Maggie shook her head. "She died a year before my birth ... a pity, for she sounded like an interesting woman."

"Healers are *always* interesting women," Cullodina replied, a smile stretching her round face. "In many ways, we are the only women with real power."

Maggie considered these words. "More than a laird's wife?"

"Aye, for even if her husband is kind, she must always defer to him."

Maggie frowned. "Morgan's never expected me to defer to him," she murmured, voicing her thoughts aloud without realizing.

The healer cocked her head, eyes crinkling at the corners as her smile widened. "Morgan's always been a bit wild … but he's a good lad. And if he sees ye as his equal, ye are fortunate indeed."

Maggie nodded, although a sudden pressure behind her eyes made her hurriedly look away. She reached for a stopper and sealed the pot of ground herbs.

"Maggie?" Cullodina's voice was gentle with concern. "For such a fortunate woman, ye often wear a hunted look. Are ye and Morgan not happy together?"

Steeling herself, Maggie straightened her spine and glanced over at Cullodina. The healer was watching her intently. "Our marriage was one of convenience," Maggie replied, inwardly cursing as her voice caught. "I'm sure ye will have heard what happened in Inverness?"

Cullodina nodded.

Maggie fought the urge to cringe. She wouldn't be surprised if every last villager had heard the tale. "So, ye know I was widowed?"

"Aye, lass … when did ye lose yer first husband?"

"Just over two years ago."

"It's not long." Cullodina reached out and placed a work-worn hand over Maggie's forearm, squeezing gently. "Grief is a strange beast. It ebbs and flows like the tide. Some days the future looks a little brighter, while others it's as if a stone lies in yer heart. Just give yerself time."

Something in the healer's voice made Maggie grow still. "Ye sound as if ye too know something about loss," she murmured.

Cullodina favored her with another smile, although this one was wistful. "Aye, I was wed to a fine man once … but he left me a widow just two years and five months after our wedding."

Maggie placed a hand over Cullodina's. "I'm sorry."

"Och, lass … it was a long time ago."

"And ye never thought to wed again?" The question struck Maggie as ironic, for after she lost Campbell, she'd tired of folk asking her that.

However, Cullodina didn't appear bothered by the question. She merely shrugged. "I never found another man who was right for me." Her gaze speared Maggie's then, before she favored her with an impish grin. "But if the likes of Morgan Mackay had wished to make me his wife, I might have reconsidered my decision."

Deep in thought, Maggie made her way back toward the castle. She was around twenty yards distant when the thunder of approaching hoofbeats made her glance up.

A large grey horse approached from the south. A lean hound raced at its side.

Maggie halted. *Morgan.*

The sight of him made her belly pitch, her heart lurch.

Morgan had been gone longer this time, and she'd found herself wondering every day when he might return. The keep seemed empty without him, despite that she was surrounded by people. His unoccupied place at the chieftain's table grew more noticeable with each passing day. She even found herself missing not being able to throw Gritta some scraps.

"Good afternoon, Maggie," Morgan drew up Archer next to her. The gelding was breathing hard, his nostrils flaring as Morgan leaned forward and stroked the beast's sweaty neck. Not for the first time, Maggie considered how good this man was with animals, and how well they responded to him in turn. "All is well with ye?"

Gritta rushed up to Maggie, tongue lolling, before flopping down at her feet. Bending over, Maggie patted the dog's back. She then glanced up at her husband. "Very well, thank ye." Morgan wore a warm, if slightly wary smile. She was relieved to see that his mood had improved. "I take it this visit went better than the last?"

"It did ... I've now got a ledger full of signatures and letters to bring to the king." He patted the saddlebag strapped on behind him. "It seems that Niel has more friends among the MacLeods and the Munros than I realized."

Supper that evening was merrier than usual. Morgan was animated, describing his visit south in great detail as his kin listened.

"Douglas MacLeod insisted on signing his letter with his own blood," Morgan concluded. "To ensure that the king takes his word seriously."

Maggie winced at this—the gesture sounded a bit extreme to her.

Connor, who'd been listening to his brother intently, leaned back in his carven chair, a smile stretching his lips. "Well done, Morgan," he murmured. "Hopefully, King James will be persuaded to change his mind. This must be handled carefully though ... we don't want to vex him."

The brothers' gazes met and held, a silent look passing between them.

"We all know how persuasive ye can be," Kennan spoke up, raising his horn of mead to Morgan in a toast. "Well done, cousin."

"So, when do ye ride for Scone?" Jaimee asked, her green eyes gleaming with excitement.

"The day after tomorrow," Morgan answered.

Maggie's breathing caught. "So soon." The words were out before she could check them, and when Morgan's gaze swung her way, she cursed herself. What was she saying? He'd wonder what had come over her.

"Aye," he replied, his attention never straying from her face. "It's best I move quickly ... before the parliament at Inverness fades from the king's memory. The sooner Niel is released, the better."

Connor frowned. "Ye shouldn't go before him alone. I shall come with ye."

Morgan shook his head. "Ye are needed here. Tax collection is coming up and—" Morgan's attention shifted then to where Keira sat next to her husband "— yer wife won't thank me for dragging ye away."

Connor's frown deepened, and he opened his mouth to argue. However, Kennan interceded. "Morgan's right. The king won't look favorably on us if we're late delivering his levies.” He paused there. “I’ll go with Morgan to Scone.”

Connor scowled. “Still … it doesn’t—”

“Kennan’s coming with me,” Morgan cut him off, before favoring his brother with a rueful smile. “Don’t worry … he’ll make sure I mind my tongue before the king.”

30

AN AUDIENCE

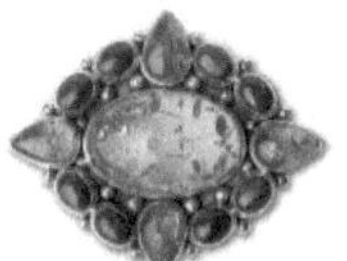

Scone Abbey
Perthshire, Scotland

MORGAN PACED THE hallway, his boots whispering on the flagstone floor. "How long is he going to make us wait?" The question was muttered, although it echoed off the surrounding stone.

A few yards away, Kennan shifted uncomfortably before resuming his position, leaning up against the wall. "As long as he wants to ... he is the king, after all."

Morgan halted, swiveling to face his cousin. Kennan looked as bored as he felt. The pair of them had been standing in this hallway since just after the noon meal. At the end of the corridor, Morgan could see that, beyond the arched window framing an overcast sky, the afternoon was waning.

Meeting Kennan's eye, Morgan frowned. "Ye don't think he's forgotten about us, do ye? Maybe I should go fetch a servant."

Kennan's mouth pursed. "He hasn't forgotten us."

Morgan ground his jaw. He wore a leather satchel slung across his front, weighed down with the ledger of signatures and letters he would set before the king. "So, he's playing with us then?"

Kennan cocked an auburn eyebrow, making his answer clear.

They were Highlanders, men who followed their clan-chief before the king. James likely intended to teach them both some manners. He wished to remind them who ruled their corner of the Highlands. Not Angus-Dow Mackay but King James of Scotland.

The lesson chafed.

Drawing in a deep breath, Morgan joined Kennan. He leaned up against the wall, folding his arms across his chest.

"We should have brought a pouch of knucklebones," Kennan said after a pause. "It would have helped to pass the time."

Morgan snorted. "Or a skin or two of ale."

"Best not to go before the king in yer cups," his cousin replied with a rueful smile. "We want to have our wits about us."

Morgan rolled his eyes. "It doesn't matter if I'm pickled, I won't forget the speech I've prepared." It was true. On the journey south, he'd repeatedly gone over the plea he'd make to the king. The words were so familiar to him now that he felt he could have repeated the speech in his sleep.

Silence fell between the cousins then. It was so quiet in this wing of the abbey that it was easy to imagine the king had overlooked them. However, Morgan knew Kennan was right.

The king would see them when he was ready, and not a moment before.

After a spell, Morgan glanced right at Kennan's profile once more. "How's Cait faring these days?" he asked. "I noticed before we left that her belly has started to swell."

Kennan's mouth curved. "Cait's well. Cullodina predicts the bairn will be born just before Samhuinn."

Morgan's gaze rested upon his cousin. "I used to tease ye when we were younger … about how shy ye were around women. Do ye remember?"

Kennan pulled a face. "How could I forget? Ye never had my problem though … ye made it look so easy."

Morgan gave a pained expression. He had once, but not anymore. "There was only ever one woman for ye, Ken, wasn't there?"

Kennan nodded, a little embarrassed now. The pair never spoke of such things. "I've never wanted anyone other than Cait," he admitted gruffly. "And if I lost her, I doubt I'd ever wed again."

His cousin's declaration made Morgan tense. He thought of Maggie, and of the loyalty she bore Campbell Munro. Love could be like that. If he had lived, Morgan's father likely wouldn't have taken another wife. Rose had been Rory Mackay's world.

Everyone says I'm like him. Morgan's lips thinned. *But if that's the case, I'm done for.* It didn't matter how much time had passed since the night in which he'd laid his heart bare to Maggie—his feelings hadn't changed.

If anything, he was even more certain of them. The realization was a stone in his belly.

The creak of a door opening roused Morgan from his brooding. A liveried servant appeared—a tall, thin man who bore a harassed expression. His gaze swept over the two Mackays, his mouth pursing in silent disapproval. "The king will see ye now," he announced stiffly.

Morgan pushed off the wall and cast his cousin a hard smile. In response, Kennan winked. "See ... he hasn't forgotten us."

"Maggie! Yer husband has returned."

Glancing up from where she was sorting through jars of lard on the stone shelf inside the spence, Maggie met Aileana's gaze. Her maid stood in the doorway, her face flushed. The lass had clearly rushed into the keep to deliver the news.

Mastering the strange fluttering in her belly, Maggie turned from the shelf and drew herself up, squaring her shoulders. "Thank ye, Aileana. Where is he?"

"In the landward bailey … the others have all gone out to see him."

"Then I shall join them," Maggie replied briskly. She left the spence and made her way through the crowded kitchen toward the main entrance hall and the doors that would take her outside.

The kitchen was busy at this hour, for the noon meal approached. Elsa was bellowing orders at the servants setting up platters to be carried into the great hall. The aroma of baking meat pie wafted through the air.

Maggie left the keep, picking up her skirts as she hurried down the steps to the landward bailey.

Anticipation quickened her breath. Had Morgan succeeded? Was Niel Mackay now a free man?

She spied her husband at a distance. He and Kennan had drawn up their horses and dismounted. Connor, Jaimee, Cait—and even Keira—stood with them. The latter must have struggled to get down the stairs, for her belly was huge these days.

As she neared the group, Maggie's gaze went to Morgan's face.

But when her attention settled upon him, she knew that the appeal had failed.

Morgan's expression was strained, weary. He was talking to his brother, a deep furrow between his eyes. Next to him, Kennan was scowling.

As she drew closer, Maggie caught his words. "He barely listened to a word I said."

"But ye showed him all the letters?" Connor pressed. "Surely—"

"I showed him *everything*. I read out all the missives detailing the Gunn's constant acts of aggression toward us. I recited all the character references." A nerve flickered under Morgan's eye. Maggie's chest constricted. The man looked exhausted. "But he just sat there completely unmoved."

"He didn't ask ye any questions?" Jaimee asked, frowning.

"Not one. When I finished speaking, the king poured himself a goblet of wine. We stood there watching him drink half of it before he thanked me for my time, and told me that he'd send someone with his answer the following day." Morgan's voice roughened. "One of his servants knocked on my door the following dawn to tell me my appeal for Niel's release had been denied."

Silence fell then, before Connor stepped up close to Morgan. "Ye did yer best," he murmured, placing a hand on his brother's shoulder. "Ye couldn't do any more than that."

Morgan looked Maggie's way then. His tall, lean frame grew still, every muscle suddenly taut. He hadn't seen her approach, and her arrival seemed to unbalance him.

"Hello Morgan," Maggie called out to him, raising a hand in greeting.

In response, her husband merely favored her with a tight smile.

Maggie waited until Morgan was alone before she approached him again. He'd led his gelding into the stables and was rubbing the beast down.

Maggie hovered at the entrance to the stall. She didn't want to disturb him, especially since he was clearly fatigued from his journey. And yet, she wanted to speak with him directly. "I'm sorry to hear that yer petition failed, Morgan," she said softly.

Morgan halted his work and turned to face her. "So am I," he replied, bitterness lacing his voice. "What a waste of time."

She took a step closer. "No, it wasn't. Ye tried yer best."

His mouth twisted. "Aye, and I failed. Niel's going to rot at Bass Rock for the rest of his life, while the Gunns are probably planning their next campaign against us. The Mackay clan has been weakened ... and our enemies know it. And now we're turning against each other."

The bleakness of his words made her frown. Part of her thought he was overreacting. Connor had ignored Robert Mackay's attempt to stir things up, and he would likely do so again. All the same, she didn't like to see Morgan like this—so defeated.

Maggie drew closer still, raising her chin to maintain eye contact. "They might, but while warriors like ye and Connor live, yer clan isn't forsaken. Don't despair."

He held her gaze, before his mouth lifted at the corners. "Aye ... I'll try not to."

Tension unknotted within Maggie. That was better. A little of the Morgan she recognized had returned.

A pause stretched out then, before Morgan eventually broke it. "How have ye been?" he asked, his gaze roaming her face.

"Busy. Keira's going to be confined to her bed soon, so I'm taking over all her duties."

He frowned. "I hope ye haven't been exhausting yerself?"

She shook her head. "Keira insists I sit with her every afternoon and embroider. Fear not, I won't wear myself out doing that."

His mouth curved into a proper smile. "Good."

Maggie stepped back from him. She'd done what she'd intended and welcomed him back properly. It was time to let the man be. "I shall see ye at the noon meal then?"

He nodded. "I'll be up shortly."

Maggie moved toward the doorway to the stall. However, instead of leaving, she paused on the threshold. She turned back to see that her husband had resumed rubbing down Archer. The gelding had his nose in a net of hay, while Gritta had flopped down in a corner of the stall, panting.

"Morgan," she said, drawing his attention once more.

He glanced over his shoulder. "Aye?"

"I'm pleased ye are home."

31

A BROKEN VOW

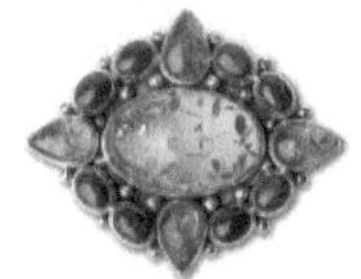

"I TIRE OF sitting around all day like an overstuffed cushion," Keira grumbled, glancing longingly toward the open window. Outdoors it was a bright and breezy morning. "Can't I go out for a short walk at least?"

"Ye went out this morning, mo ghràdh," Connor replied, with a shake of his head. "Cullodina will have my head if ye tire yerself out. Plus, ye have company, which should help pass the time quickly enough." The laird cast a smile at Maggie and Cait, who both sat near the window of the women's solar, and rose to his feet. "I've got a mob of angry tenants awaiting me in the great hall. I'd better get down there before Morgan says something to vex them further."

Keira frowned. "What's the problem this time?"

Connor pulled a face. "Cattle. They insist they've had some go missing ... and are blaming the Gunns."

Keira's full lips thinned. "Surely, George Gunn wouldn't be so foolish ... not so soon after Inverness?"

The irony of Keira's words wasn't lost on Maggie. The laird's wife was a Gunn after all. Watching the way her friend's gaze shadowed, Maggie wondered what Keira thought of all of this. Did she, like Maggie, still bear loyalty to the clan of her birth? Such things were hard to give up.

Connor's brow furrowed. "Ye would think not ... but the Gunns escaped the king's wrath. I wouldn't be surprised if it's made them bold." He leaned down and kissed Keira. "I'll see ye at noon, my love."

Watching the chieftain leave the women's solar, Maggie realized that she was also frowning. A week had passed since Morgan and Kennan's return from Scone, since the king had denied his appeal—it was worrying to hear that the Gunns were up to their old tricks already.

Her attention then shifted to Keira. Leaning back in her high-backed chair, the laird's wife looked in the full-bloom of health, despite her swollen belly, which rose like a hillock under her voluminous kirtle. Her cheeks had a healthy rouge, and her eyes were bright. Maggie could understand why she hated being confined to the keep. Maggie had felt the same way, although exhaustion had dogged her throughout her pregnancy.

Keira looked well enough to take numerous strolls. However, despite that low-born women worked until their bairns came, a laird's wife was expected to take care of herself. Keira's 'lying in' would begin within days—a period of confinement to bed that she wasn't looking forward to.

Keira sighed and glanced down at the embroidery she had balanced upon her knees. She then placed her hand on her belly, a smile flowering across her face. "I felt a kick."

Cait let out an excited squeal. "Ye did?" The woman, whose own belly was now becoming increasingly evident, rose to her feet and hurried across to Keira. Cait then leaned down and placed a hand over her belly. "Ye are right ... I just felt it too."

Maggie watched them, her throat constricting. She had felt too few of those during her own pregnancy, a sign there was something amiss with the bairn she carried.

She hadn't mentioned her inability to bear bairns to any of the Mackays save Morgan, and she held her tongue now. Keira and Cait would mean well, yet she couldn't bear to see pity for her in their eyes. And she certainly didn't want them to start fussing over her.

"Do ye think it will be a lass or lad?" Cait asked.

"I have no idea," Keira replied with a smile, "although Cullodina tells me I am carrying the bairn high … so it is likely a girl." Keira's expression grew soft then. "I would like a daughter." She then turned her attention to their silent companion seated by the window. "What do ye think, Maggie?"

Maggie smiled, even if the expression felt a little fragile. She had a basket of wool upon her lap and was winding it onto a spindle, a mindless task that relaxed her. "I agree with the healer," she replied. "It sounds like a lass to me."

"Have ye thought of names?" Cait asked, taking her seat by the window once more and returning to her loom.

"Rose if it's a lass," Keira replied, her mouth curving once more. "And Rory if it's a lad … after Connor's parents."

"They are fine names," Maggie answered. It wasn't unusual for lairds to use parental names for their offspring.

Keira picked up her embroidery. "I like them too … I certainly wasn't going to use my parents' names."

Maggie took in the way Keira's gaze shadowed when she spoke of her kin. In the past weeks, the pair of them had started spending more time together. Keira had told her of her unhappy childhood, of her shrewish sisters and cruel parents. It made Maggie's early years seem charmed in comparison.

And as the two women had gotten to know each other, Maggie began to understand why Keira had agreed to swap places with Rhianna. It hadn't just been self-sacrifice to aid a friend in need, but a desperate bid to claim a place for herself in the world, to find some happiness.

Maggie had never told Keira that she'd met Rhianna in Inverness. She couldn't do that to her. Keira wanted to believe that her friend had forged a bright future for herself with the man she loved. The reality would only disappoint her, and so Maggie carried the secret close to her breast.

"It's such a fine day out," Keira said wistfully, glancing out of the window once more. She was right. The sky was a deep, unblemished blue. The sweet scent of approaching summer was in the air. "Ye two mustn't spend it trapped indoors with me."

Maggie's mouth curved. "Jaimee suggested she and I go out for a ride this afternoon. Walnut needs to stretch his legs." It was true, she'd neglected her garron since arriving here. He was starting to resemble an overstuffed sack of barley.

"There's a bonny vale around two hours' ride east of here … ask her to take ye there," Keira told Maggie with a smile. "Heather carpets the hillsides. Ye can see kites wheeling overhead, and a bubbling burn cuts through the heart of it." She paused then, her cheeks growing pink. "It's where Connor and I mended things between us."

"Really?" Cait inclined her head, her gaze bright with curiosity. "Ye never told me that."

"Ye must have worried things could never be resolved between ye?" Maggie ventured when silence fell in the solar once more. "When Connor brought ye back to Farr."

"Aye," Keira replied softly, her midnight-blue eyes darkening. "They were difficult days … the first period after our return. I thought he'd brought me back out of a sense of obligation but secretly hated me. I was relieved to discover that wasn't the case."

Maggie nodded. She was glad the two of them had worked out their differences.

Her mood shadowed then, as she pondered the state of her own marriage.

Since Morgan's return, they'd settled into a routine of sorts. They were painfully polite and respectful with each other, and although Morgan slept in their bed-chamber, they still didn't share the bed. Instead, he continued to sleep upon a sheepskin before the hearth, Gritta curled up next to him.

And with each passing day, Maggie grew steadily unhappier.

She didn't understand it. This was what she'd wanted: a marriage of convenience, one where her heart wouldn't be in peril.

Why then, did her pulse skip every time Morgan entered the room?

Why did she lie abed listening for the sound of his footfalls approaching their chamber?

Why did she keep glancing his way at mealtimes, hoping to catch his eye?

I've even grown envious of his hound.

Maggie swallowed hard, her fingers clenching around the spindle she held.

The devil take her—she'd done what she promised herself she never would. She'd fallen for the man.

Despair swept over Maggie, and her eyes blurred with unshed tears.

She couldn't believe it—despite her best efforts to the contrary, she'd let Campbell down. Again.

In the end, Jaimee couldn't join Maggie on their planned ride. She twisted her ankle on the stairs shortly after the noon meal, and so would have to spend the afternoon in the solar with her bandaged leg upon a settle.

Maggie suggested that she keep her company, but Jaimee, infuriated by her own 'foolish clumsiness' waved her off. "Go on. Give that portly pony of yers a run. I have Keira to chat to."

Maggie needed little convincing. Leaving the keep, she decided she'd indeed ride out to the valley Keira had mentioned. Truthfully, she desperately needed some time alone.

Walnut was in high spirits. The pony had been cooped up indoors for too long, and Maggie whispered an apology to him as she tightened his girth and led him out of the stables into the landward bailey.

Morgan was out there, overseeing the farrier as he lanced an abscess on one of the horse's feet. Hearing the 'clip-clop' of hooves, Morgan straightened up, his gaze alighting upon Maggie.

And as always, the impact of their gazes meeting made Maggie catch her breath.

The moment drew out.

Maggie swallowed hard, straightening her shoulders. That look had the power to undo her. How many nights had she lain awake, listening to the gentle rhythm of his breathing a few feet away, and fought the urge to call out to him? She'd longed for him to join her in the bed, for him to tumble her passionately, to chase away the thoughts that tormented her.

But in the end, she'd remained silent.

Murmuring something to the farrier, Morgan moved toward her. "Off for a ride?" His voice was pleasant, although with the reserve she'd come to expect from him of late.

"Aye … Walnut needs some exercise."

Morgan ran his eye over the sturdy garron. "He certainly does … the beast is running to fat."

Despite herself, Maggie smiled. "I've noticed … it was a struggle to tighten his girth."

Silence fell between them then, and Maggie's smile faded. There was a seriousness to the man these days that put her on edge. She wondered if the disappointment of his failed petition had yet to fade.

Things had gotten so awkward between them over the past weeks. She'd half-expected him to find another woman to warm his bed—for rumors of him swiving servants to reach her ears. But Morgan spent each night before the hearth, and at mealtimes, he barely looked the way of the comely lasses who served them in the great hall. His apparent loyalty just made her feel worse.

"Are ye going on yer own?" he asked after an awkward pause.

"Aye … now Jaimee's laid up with a sprained ankle." She paused then. "Keira tells me of a wide vale a couple of hours east of here ... I thought I'd head there. Is it easy to find?"

His mouth curved, although his gaze remained solemn. He stepped back then. "Aye, it's a bonny spot. Just head over the hills behind the kirk, and ride east. Ye'll come upon it soon enough."

Maggie smiled back. "Thank ye."

The moment drew out, and Morgan's lips parted once more, as if he was about to say something else. However, he didn't. A pained look then flitted across his face.

Maggie's smile faded. "What is it?"

"Nothing," he said, turning away. "Enjoy yer ride. Take care though, the terrain can be rough in places."

32

RIDING OUT ALONE

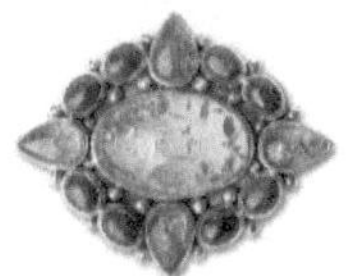

MAGGIE RODE WALNUT out the gates and urged the fat pony into a trot, taking the path that would lead them through the village. She could feel the sun on her back. They'd had a spell of good weather, although a gusty wind had picked up this afternoon.

After the few words she'd shared with Morgan, Maggie was relieved to leave Farr Castle behind. That was how it had been between them of late. Awkward. She'd have almost preferred it if he'd taken to ignoring her, but he didn't. Morgan was civil, often inquiring how her day had gone. But their conversations never went beyond that.

He'd erected a shield between them now, and she couldn't exactly blame him.

And of course, after the truth of her feelings for him had slapped her across the face that morning as she sat in the women's solar with Keira and Cait, Maggie felt even more uncomfortable in his presence.

She was going to have to speak to the man—she just lacked the courage to do so today.

Kicking Walnut into a jolting canter, Maggie struck out east across the hills. Keira had said that the vale lay about two hours east from Farr. Luckily, since night fell late in the evening this far north this time of year, she had plenty of time to enjoy her ride.

Maggie had donned a light woolen cloak to ward off the wind. Nonetheless, with the sun on her back, she started to sweat. She'd braided her hair into a long plait down her back, but tendrils came free as she rode, tickling her cheeks. And despite her brittle nerves and churning belly, Maggie began to enjoy herself.

It was a relief to be outdoors with the breeze on her face. She'd make sure she took Walnut out more often. She'd forgotten the exhilaration of cantering free across windswept hills.

Life wasn't that bad.

The people she lived amongst, the Mackays, were so different to her own clan, and to the Munros. It was ironic, but she'd never felt so welcome anywhere.

Even though she'd told Morgan otherwise, she loved Farr Castle's wild setting, upon the lofty cliffs looking out to sea. It was treeless and windy, and no doubt could be viciously cold in winter, but she adored its remoteness and the warm way the folk of this tight-knit community interacted with each other.

She enjoyed the added responsibilities she'd shouldered of late as well. Initially, she'd taken them on as a way to stay focused, to keep her mind off what she'd done. But these days, when she went down to oversee the servants in the mornings, she felt a sense of usefulness. At the Munro holding, she'd always been forced to defer to Campbell's mother. The woman had refused to give up her role as lady of the castle, and so Maggie had been rendered largely redundant.

But the best thing about living at Farr Castle was that everyone just let her be. There was no nagging uncle who watched her with gimlet eyes, demanding to know why she couldn't stop grieving and find herself another husband.

She was trusted here; she could go for walks and rides unescorted. Maggie had never thought she'd find freedom in this place, but she had.

Ye will never have any peace until ye make things right with Morgan, her conscience needled. *Ye must speak to him.*

Maggie's mouth thinned. God's teeth, couldn't her mind let her have a moment's peace?

Walnut stumbled then, and Maggie winced before shifting in the saddle. Her mount's gait was jarring. Now that he'd gotten fat, Walnut wasn't a comfortable ride. It was like trying to sit astride a barrel. Even so, she urged him on, her gaze fixed upon the eastern horizon.

Eventually, they reached the vale.

Maggie's gaze swept over the wide valley before her. She took in the winding burn at the bottom and the kites that hunted on the wind above. The heather was in bloom, carpeting the rocky sides of the vale in purple. Maggie smiled, her worries about Morgan fading once more. It truly was a beautiful spot.

She'd slowed Walnut to walk, but she now urged the pony into a brisk trot, heading toward the glittering burn. It was such a bonny afternoon, and she wanted to make the most of it. She'd dismount on the banks for a spell, take off her boots, and paddle in the cool water.

Morgan couldn't concentrate.

After over-seeing the farrier, he'd gone back indoors and taken the stairs up to the chieftain's solar.

Connor had asked him to go over the accounts with him this afternoon. It was tedious work, but his brother preferred two pairs of eyes on the numbers—just to make sure Connor hadn't miscalculated anything.

Entering the large chamber, Morgan found his brother at a desk in the corner of the solar, surrounded by piles of parchment, with a large leather-bound ledger open before him. Connor's fingers were stained with black ink, his brow furrowed in concentration.

"Do ye really need my help?" Morgan asked, ambling across to the desk. "It looks like ye've got everything under control here."

Connor snorted. "Pull up a seat. Ye aren't getting out of things so easily."

Morgan did as bid, grabbing a chair and hauling it up next to his brother before lowering himself into it. "Any word yet from Robert Mackay?" he asked casually. Thoughts of the Mackay chieftain and the unrest that simmered amongst their own clan distracted him from more personal worries.

Connor shook his head. "The man's gone suspiciously silent."

"Do ye think he's plotting something?"

Connor shrugged, although his gaze was wary. "Who knows ... although maybe it's time I paid Balnakeil broch a visit, just to make sure he's not stirring the other chieftains up."

Morgan nodded, his mouth thinning. "Good idea. I'll come with ye."

The brothers worked together on the accounts for a while, with Morgan reading off the various chits and demands, and Connor cross-referencing them with the numbers he'd written in the ledger.

But Morgan found it increasingly difficult to focus.

All he could think about was Maggie.

All he had been able to think about over the past moon was Maggie.

The woman behaved as if nothing had happened between them. In the past weeks, she'd thawed toward him. These days, Maggie was pleasant, yet gratingly self-contained.

It was torture—sleeping in the same chamber every night. It wasn't that comfortable on the fur before the fire, and Gritta smelled like a wet sheep. He often woke up to hear the dog's snoring in his ear. He'd lie awake, longing to join his wife abed.

He was being a fool, for she'd told him she wouldn't deny him his rights as a husband. But after being spurned, he didn't feel like making any advances.

Aye, he still longed for her—with an intensity that grew with each passing day. But it wasn't just a longing of the body, but of the soul. Unfortunately, Maggie had made it clear she didn't feel the same way and never would.

He'd been surprised to see her riding out alone that afternoon. Maggie usually kept herself busy inside the castle. He was pleased to see she was taking time for herself at least.

He'd cautioned her to take care, but he still didn't like her riding out unescorted.

I should have gone with her, he thought, frowning as Connor asked him to repeat himself. He'd been about to suggest he joined her, but the words had stuck in his throat. This corner of their territory was reasonably safe these days, for it was far enough away from the Gunn borders, yet he hoped she wouldn't stray too far from the vale.

Eventually, the accounts were all checked. Connor went off to see his wife, leaving Morgan alone in the solar.

Gritta sat at Morgan's feet, tail thumping on the flagstone floor.

The dog was full of energy and wanted a walk.

Morgan glanced over at the open window, frowning as he realized it was much later in the day than he'd thought. A sunny afternoon had slipped into a golden evening.

Morgan went downstairs, Gritta trailing at his heel. He checked the landward bailey and the stables, but there was no sign of his wife or her garron, and an uneasy sensation settled over Morgan—an intuition that something was amiss.

He hadn't been able to stop thinking about Maggie all afternoon, but part of him now worried that something had happened to her.

Striding back into the stables, he saddled Archer. Leading the horse out into the bailey, Morgan then whistled to his hound and cantered through the gates, heading east in the direction his wife had gone.

Beyond the castle, the stone cottages of Farr cast long shadows, warning Morgan that indeed it was growing late in the day.

Maggie should have been well home by now, and fussing over her pony in the stables.

He knew the vale she'd headed out to; it was a popular hunting ground. No harm should have befallen her there, but the uneasy sensation in his belly refused to settle.

The farther east Morgan traveled, the more on edge he became.

Where is she? The vale was only a few furlongs away; he should have encountered her on her way back by now. *Maybe she hasn't come this way after all?*

But then, on the horizon, he spotted something.

A fat pony, limping heavily, appeared upon the brow of a hill, led by a small dark-haired figure.

Maggie. He'd found her.

Urging Archer into a swift canter, Morgan headed toward them.

Maggie saw his approach and raised a hand in greeting. However, as he drew near, Morgan observed that her expression was pained.

Morgan frowned. "What happened?"

"Walnut stepped in a hole," she replied, casting a worried glance at her garron. "At first I thought he'd broken his leg, but he can still walk, so that mustn't be the case."

"Let me have a look." Morgan swung down from Archer, letting Gritta go to Maggie. His wife stroked the dog's neck, murmuring words of endearment.

Jealousy spiked through Morgan at the sight. She had tenderness for his dog, but not for him.

Pushing aside his churlish response, Morgan hunkered down to the foreleg that Walnut favored.

Running practiced fingers down the tendon and the bone, Morgan checked for injury. "Aye, ye are right … nothing's broken," he said after a moment. "However, it's a sprain … a bad one. The beast shouldn't walk much farther this evening." Slapping the garron on the shoulder, Morgan rose to his feet and turned to Maggie. "Are ye hurt?"

Maggie pulled a face, before raising her right arm. "I twisted my wrist," she admitted sheepishly. "It aches a little."

Morgan stepped close to her. "Can I have a look?"

She nodded, her gaze never leaving his face before she offered her hand to him.

Morgan took it gently, aware that this was the first time they'd touched since that fateful evening.

The feel of her smooth, warm skin under his fingertips made Morgan's breathing constrict. He pushed the sensation aside, focusing on checking for injury instead.

Maggie had delicate, slender wrists, and although there was a little swelling, and a faint bruise coming up, he was relieved to see that she hadn't broken anything.

"At least Gritta isn't responsible for this fall," he murmured, his gaze shifting back up to meet hers.

Maggie pulled a face. "No, the fault is mine. I should have watched where I was going. I was so mesmerized by the vale's beauty that I didn't pay any attention to where I was leading my pony."

"I shouldn't have let ye ride out alone," he said after a pause.

She snorted. "I told ye I was careless."

"All the same, I should have accompanied ye."

Their gazes held. "I'm surprised ye'd want to spend any time with me, Morgan," Maggie murmured. "After everything."

"Ye are my wife," he replied, unsmiling. "I'm supposed to protect ye." He realized then that he still had hold of her wrist. He released it. Her proximity unsettled him. He could smell her warm, sweet skin and the scent of fresh sweat. An ache rose in his chest, a longing that clawed at him night and day.

An awkward silence fell between them then. Eventually, Maggie cleared her throat. "So, Walnut should rest his leg?" she asked, her brow furrowing.

Morgan nodded. "I'll splint it, but he won't make the journey home in the state he's in. We need to find somewhere to shelter overnight."

33

MENDING MISTAKES

MAGGIE FOLLOWED MORGAN south, across the gently curving hills. Walnut was limping badly, which made it slow-going. Gritta, tired after a long run, was happy to lope at Maggie's side, tongue lolling.

As they walked, Maggie found her gaze drawn constantly to her husband. Now that he wasn't looking her way, she drank him in. She admired the breadth of his shoulders, his long, easy stride, and the way his wavy hair stirred in the breeze.

Maggie cursed herself for being so careless today. She'd risked Walnut's life. A broken leg would have been the end of him, and she certainly didn't need anything else to feel guilty about.

Maggie's attention returned to Morgan then.

He came looking for me.

Of course he had. She'd been away for far longer than she promised. He was only being protective, and yet she hadn't missed the concern that shadowed his pine-green eyes as he'd approached her. Despite everything, Morgan still cared for her.

Yet she'd wounded him all the same. He hid his hurt well, but it was still there, smoldering just beneath the surface.

A squat stone hut hove into view in the distance. The shieling was a simple structure with a turf roof.

Morgan cast a look over his shoulder then and favored Maggie with a tight smile. "Yer castle awaits, My Lady."

Maggie attempted to smile back, although the expression was forced.

Until she spoke frankly with him, she wouldn't be able to relax in this man's presence.

They hobbled their mounts outside the shieling, and as he'd promised, Morgan splinted Walnut's injured foreleg, using a branch from a solitary broom bush growing nearby. Maggie tore off a strip of linen from the hem of her lèine, so that he could bind the splint. It was a shame to rip such a fine garment, but there was nothing else available.

Once Archer and Walnut were happily cropping grass nearby, Morgan and Maggie settled down, both taking a seat in front of the hut. Leaning her back against the sun-warmed stone, her gaze traveling west to where the last rays of sun stained the sky, Maggie felt uneasiness steal over her once more.

His presence made tension coil in her gut. *Talk to him.*

"I appreciate ye coming to look for me, Morgan," she said when the silence drew out.

Morgan glanced her way. "I couldn't leave ye out here alone." His gaze searched her face then. "Ye appear to have settled in well, Maggie. Do ye think ye could one day be happy at Farr?"

Maggie's mouth quirked. "I love this place," she admitted. "And I thank ye for bringing me to live here. For the first time in a long while, I feel myself."

He arched an eyebrow. "I thought ye found Farr too barren, isolated … and small?"

Maggie's smile turned sheepish. "I must apologize for the things I said," she murmured. "None of them were true." Her smile faded then, her pulse quickening. This was it—the time had come for her to be honest with him. "And I'm sorry for the way I treated ye … I was trying to make ye dislike me."

Morgan went still. "Why would ye wish to do that?"

Maggie heaved in a deep breath and tore her gaze from his. Why indeed? It was such a simple question, and yet she wasn't sure how to begin her answer.

Her attention settled upon Gritta then. The wolfhound sat a few feet away and was gnawing upon a dry stick, oblivious to them. There wasn't any point in delaying. The dog wasn't going to be any help. Only she could bridge the gulf between her and Morgan. And to do that, she'd have to tell him everything.

Clearing her throat, she swiveled around to face Morgan properly. Like her, he sat with his back against the stone wall, his long legs stretched out before him and crossed at the ankle. He was watching her, patiently awaiting her answer.

"Morgan ... there is something ye must know about me," she said softly.

He inclined his head toward her, his gaze questioning. "Aye?"

Maggie held his gaze. "Since Campbell died ... guilt has been my constant companion."

Morgan's gaze widened. "Guilt?"

"Aye."

It was difficult to speak: her throat felt unnaturally tight, and her mind screamed at her to stop. But she had to say this. Keeping all of this inside was tearing her up. Eventually, it would make her ill. And Morgan deserved to hear the truth, she realized that now. She should have been open with him from the start.

"Ye remember how I told ye back in Inverness that I had lost my bairn and was pronounced barren?"

Morgan nodded, his gaze shadowing in concern.

"Well, initially I took the news badly." Lord, speaking of this was an effort. "I denied the healer's words, and then I became very angry. Campbell weathered the brunt of my fury."

Morgan said nothing, only waiting for her to continue.

Hauling in a deep, fortifying breath, Maggie forced herself on. "He just wanted to take care of me, but I wouldn't let him." A hot lump rose in her throat, but she swallowed it down. "I thought he was just being kind. What use was I to him, if I couldn't give him children?" Maggie could hear her voice rise, heard the tremor in it as the memories clawed at her. "And so … I turned my back on him. I entered a bleak world … where I wished to see and speak to no one." Maggie shut her eyes. Even now, memories of those grim days made her break out in a cold sweat. "I closed the shutters to my bed-chamber and spent days abed."

She broke off then as painful memories swamped her. She hadn't thought it was possible to feel such desolation, such a lack of hope, as she had in those days. Even the love she shared with her husband hadn't been enough to weather it.

Drawing in a shaky breath, Maggie opened her eyes. "Eventually, Campbell had had enough of my obstinacy," she continued, her voice husky. "He forced me to get dressed and go outdoors with him to take in the fresh air. He was worried that I would sicken … for I was still weak after losing so much blood." Maggie raised a hand to her breastbone and rubbed the ache that had risen in her chest. "I fought him the entire way … but he was only trying to help."

"He sounds like a good man," Morgan observed gently.

"Aye, he was," she admitted with a sad smile. "Campbell tried to draw me out of my rage and sadness … and he would have succeeded eventually, but then one day he rode out with the other warriors on a patrol." She swallowed hard. "And he never returned."

Silence fell, and eventually, Morgan broke it. "And yer guilt … it's because ye never got a chance to mend things between ye?"

"Aye." Her voice cracked. "When they brought back his body, I was inconsolable. I wanted to tell him I was sorry—to take back all my angry words. But it was too late. I'd been so selfish. I looked down at his bloodless face, and I vowed there and then that I'd never take another husband." She drew in a shaky breath. "After what I did to him, I—I deserved to spend the rest of my life alone."

Heart pounding against her ribs, Maggie tilted her head back against the stone wall of the shieling. It was too much. Her heart ached.

Morgan would surely see her differently now.

She was a woman who broke her promises.

After a brief pause, Morgan spoke. "So, by pushing me away, ye have been trying to put things right?"

Maggie nodded.

"Ye do realize ye gave yerself an impossible task?"

She huffed a bitter laugh. "Aye."

"If only we could go back and mend our mistakes." There was a pensive edge to his voice. "But we can't."

She opened her eyes and shifted her attention back to him. "But I was determined."

His mouth lifted at the corners. "I thought I was stubborn ... but ye are the most single-minded person I've ever met. Still ... ye shouldered too much blame. Ye realize that now, don't ye?"

Maggie's shoulders sagged. His words made her feel as if a great weight had just been lifted from her. She then nodded.

"Few of us are strangers to regret," Morgan continued, his voice lowering. "On the morning my father died, before we went into battle against the Gunns, I snapped at him over something trivial. I can't even remember what the disagreement was about." His gaze guttered then. "But those were the last words that ever passed between us."

Maggie's throat constricted. His revelation was a brutal reminder of how little control any of them had over life. He was right. She couldn't change the past, and nor could she martyr herself any longer.

Morgan cleared his throat then, before plucking a blade of grass next to him and rolling it between his fingers. "Ye can't live in the past, Maggie. Yer husband died tragically. If he had lived, ye two would most likely have reconciled and enjoyed a happy life together." He paused a few moments, his throat bobbing. "But fate intervened ... and brought us together instead. I wasn't lying when I said I love ye. My feelings haven't changed. Can ye never find it within ye to feel the same way?"

Maggie stilled. Her heart was beating so fast now that it pounded in her ears. And in that moment, the last of her restraint, the last barrier between them, crumbled.

"I already do, Morgan," she whispered. "I've loved ye for a while ... I just didn't want to admit it."

Morgan cast aside the blade of grass and moved across so that he was kneeling before her. Wordlessly, he reached out then and took her hands in his. The warmth of the skin, the strength of his fingers, made Maggie's breathing hitch.

"I want ye ... as my lover and my life's companion, mo chridhe," he said, his gaze spearing hers. Will ye let the past go and walk into the unknown with me?"

34

NO MORE SECRETS

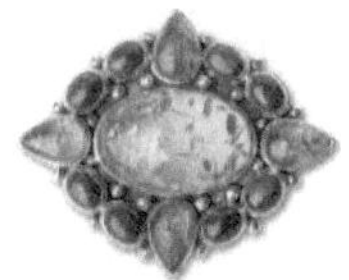

MO CHRIDHE. MY love.

Tears welled, trickling down Maggie's face. "Aye, Morgan," she gasped. "I am yers."

She blinked, in an attempt to clear her vision of tears, but there was no stemming them. An instant later, he pulled her into his arms, enveloping her in a hard hug.

Maggie buried her face in the hollow of his neck and wept.

They were tears of sorrow, of loss, and of relief. She didn't have to fight anymore.

And eventually, as the tears abated, she heaved a deep, steadying breath. "Apologies ... I've left a huge wet patch on yer lèine again," she sniffed. "I seem to be making a habit of this."

Morgan smiled, his gaze never leaving hers. "It will dry."

Warmth suffused Maggie as their stare drew out. Without thinking, she reached out, tracing her fingertips down the strong line of his jaw, and along his firm chin, before exploring the sensual lines of his mouth. Leaning in, she brushed his lips with hers.

Morgan didn't move. His smile faded. He didn't pull her into his arms as he had in their past encounters. Instead, he stilled. She heard his breathing slow, sensed the tension that now vibrated off his body. He wanted her, but he wasn't going to make the first move. She had

to do that. She had to make the nature of their
relationship clear.

Maggie favored him with a tremulous smile. "My
heart is truly yers, Morgan." And with that, she leaned in
once more and gave him a lingering kiss this time. Her
tongue slid along the seam of his lips, teasing them
apart.

With a soft moan, Morgan surrendered to her.

The kiss deepened, while Maggie reached up,
wrapping her arms around his neck, pulling him close.
She wanted to get closer to him, to crawl inside his skin.
The need to connect, to let her body show him just how
madly she loved him, was overwhelming. She breathed
him in, her tongue caressing his.

With a groan, Morgan hauled her against him. He
then swiveled around, pulling her with him so that he
was sitting with his back to the wall.

Maggie perched astride him. The heat of his body
drew her in, and need burned deep in the cradle of her
belly. It made her restless, daring.

Breathing hard, she broke off the kiss. She then
leaned back slightly, reaching for the hem of his lèine
and yanking it up. He raised his arms, allowing her to
pull it over his head.

She bent her head, letting her lips trail across the
hard planes of his chest. She'd been aching to touch him
like this for weeks now; she couldn't believe this was
actually happening. Heart racing, Maggie reached down
and let her hands explore, sliding down to his belly and
the waistband of his braies. And although the trews were
loose, there was no mistaking his arousal that tented the
material.

Maggie unlaced his braies, pushing them down.

Her breathing caught when her hand molded the
hard heat of his shaft. She stared down at its curved
length, her fingers exploring the velvet hardness.

She took him in hand firmly, slowly sliding down the
length of his rod, and thrilling when he groaned loudly.
Maggie glanced up, to see that he was watching her
under hooded lids, a languid, sensual expression upon

his face. A thrill shivered through her. She loved seeing him like this, loved knowing that she could give him this much pleasure.

They were indeed equals, a match of two strong-minded people, and their story had only just begun.

Maggie continued to stroke him, marveling at how his rod grew harder and hotter still under her touch. The tender flesh between her thighs throbbed as her yearning for him grew fiercer still.

"Come here, love," Morgan said huskily. He drew her up and pushed her skirts high around her hips. The cool breeze feathered against Maggie's naked skin, heightening her aroused state. "I want to be inside ye," he continued, his gaze ensnaring hers. "I need to lose myself in ye."

Maggie's breathing hitched. How his words inflamed her. "And I ache for ye, Morgan," she breathed. Trembling, she lowered herself down upon him, guiding his shaft between her thighs. She let him fill her completely as she took him in to the hilt.

Morgan's hands gripped her hips. He guided her, lifting her up so that she slid up the length of his engorged shaft, and then down again. The movement was achingly slow, almost unbearably so. And yet he was relentless.

Maggie arched back, exquisite pleasure trembling through her. She let out a low, sensual groan, rolling her hips against him. Wildness arched within her. Finally, she let herself go. She'd been desperately clinging to the illusion of control for too long, but now she gave in. The past couldn't be changed—this moment was all she had, and she offered herself up to it.

Morgan murmured a low curse. "God's teeth, Maggie."

Maggie gasped. Passion quickened within her like dry tinder to a flame. Already, she was lost. She wanted him to plow her mindlessly, but he held her hips steady, continuing the sensual slide, up and down his rod.

Maggie cried out, her voice hoarse. She bucked against him, delightful shivers convulsing her body, radiating out from her lower belly. A keening, sobbing cry broke forth from her. If he hadn't been holding her fast, she would have collapsed.

Morgan stared up at her, and their gazes locked. "Ye are so lovely, Maggie," he gasped out. "Ye are everything to me."

A wave of tenderness, of fierce love, swept over Maggie. And then, lowering her head, she kissed him.

Breathing hard, Morgan rolled over onto his back, taking Maggie with him. For a while, he was unable to speak. The storm that had broken over them both had completely robbed him of words. In its aftermath, he could do nothing but hold the woman he loved close, so that she could feel the thunder of his heart against her cheek.

He wasn't just reeling from the passion that had caught them up in its grip, but from all the things she'd told him. Maggie had taken on responsibility for things that were beyond her control. He hated to think how she must have tortured herself over the past years.

They lay like that for a while, the rasp of their breathing mingling with the sigh of the breeze. The wind had eased off a little with the coming of the dusk. The light was fading in earnest now, darkness settling over the hills in a heavy grey cloak.

Eventually, Morgan stirred, his hand tracing lazy strokes down Maggie's back. "I should see if there are any lumps of peat and kindling inside," he murmured. "Before it gets too dark for me to light a fire."

"It's not cold," she murmured, "and we have our cloaks. Let's sleep out here."

Morgan's mouth curved. It was tempting, for they lay upon a grassy spot, surrounded by the sweet smell of thyme growing up against the shieling's wall.

"Sleeping outdoors is a romantic notion," he replied, brushing his lips over her forehead. "But don't berate me in the morning when yer back has seized up."

She laughed, a musical, soft sound that carried in the quietness of the gloaming. A few feet away, Gritta looked up. She was still gnawing her stick, ignoring the lovers.

"Well then, I shall have to use ye, husband, as my mattress and pillow."

Morgan snorted, although warmth spread through him. He'd enjoyed the teasing between them in Inverness before events spiraled out of control. Now he could be natural with her once more.

Maggie had a way of viewing the world that was utterly unique. He was looking forward to bantering with her for many more years. However, the tenderness of this scene meant that he didn't tease her back.

Instead, he wrapped his arms around Maggie and buried his face in her rosemary-scented hair. "I will gladly be yer mattress and pillow, wife," he murmured.

Maggie stirred, raising her chin from his chest to meet his eye. "I'm sorry ye've been forced to sleep on the floor for so long. I felt bad about that."

"There's no need to ... the fur was comfortable enough ... and Gritta couldn't believe her good fortune."

Maggie smiled, and despite that the light was nearly gone now, Morgan could see the love gleaming in her eyes. "I wanted to call to ye," she whispered, "to tell ye why I spurned ye so ..."

He lifted his hand, cupping her cheek. "It's all right ... I understand."

Her expression sobered, a nerve flickering in her cheek. "And the fact I can't bear ye bairns ... are ye sure it doesn't bother ye?"

Their gazes held for a long moment. "It doesn't," he answered honestly. "I'm the second son ... it's not a tragedy if I don't sire offspring. That's Connor's role, not mine." His face grew serious then. "Will I have to compete with Campbell Munro's ghost, Maggie?"

It pained him to ask this, yet he had to. He wasn't sure he could live up to the man's memory.

Maggie's gaze widened, before realization dawned. "Ye think I still grieve for him?"

"Don't ye?"

Shaking her head, Maggie placed her palm upon his chest, over his heart. "I loved Campbell very much ... and I always will, but I was holding onto him out of guilt." She paused. "I'd be a fool to let my past come between us ... to let it ruin our happiness."

Relief washed over Morgan. "So I can stop feeling jealous?" He offered her a weak smile.

Maggie's mouth curved in response, although her sea-blue eyes shadowed. "Aye ... but ye may have to be patient with me, Morgan," she said softly.

The moment drew out, before Morgan stroked the curve of her jaw. "I will give ye all the space ye need ... so long as there are no more secrets between us. I vow never to hide anything from ye, if ye can promise me the same." His gaze held hers. "Will ye?"

A heartbeat passed, and then her mouth stretched into a winsome smile. "Aye," she whispered. "I promise."

They lay wrapped up in their woolen cloaks, side-by-side upon the ground. A wide swathe of stars spanned the sky overhead, and when the moon rose, it bathed them in its silvery glow.

Maggie had her back pressed into Morgan's chest and belly, spooned against him. The heat of his body enveloped her, causing any lingering tension to drain away.

Gritta joined them presently, wriggling in close next to Maggie.

And although the dog stank, she didn't have the heart to push her away. The wolfhound liked to remain close to her master and mistress.

Maggie fell asleep with a smile upon her face and awoke in the early dawn to a loud rumbling noise.

Gritta.

"Yer dog snores, Mackay," she muttered.

"I apologize for the hound, my love. Indeed, it wheezes like a veritable banshee at times."

Giggling, Maggie swiveled around to face him. The morning light bathed the handsome lines of Morgan's face and the fine dark-blond stubble upon his jaw. His eyes were sleepy, his face relaxed.

Maggie's chest constricted. She'd promised him in earnest the night before. There would be no more secrets between them. This morning she felt as if a yoke had been lifted from her shoulders. Everything seemed brighter, more hopeful.

Campbell's ghost had finally been laid to rest. She'd loved her first husband, and if she was honest with herself, she knew he'd never doubted that. She'd always regret not telling him so that last morning, but the opportunity was long past.

Just like she'd done with her uncle and sister, she had to let him go.

Her belly rumbled then, reminding her that she'd missed supper the evening before. They both had.

Morgan's mouth quirked. "Sorry, I didn't bring any food with me. Just a skin of ale."

Maggie nodded, realizing that she was indeed thirsty. She stretched her body, covering her mouth as she yawned. "It's still early," she murmured. "If we set off now, we might just make it back before the last of the bannocks are gone."

He arched an eyebrow. "Ye clearly haven't seen my cousin eat?"

Laughter bubbled up within Maggie. Aye, she'd seen Kennan wolf down an entire round of bannock at one sitting. Cait was always teasing him over his great appetite. "Well then, we'd better see if Walnut has it in him to hobble home," she replied with a grin. "Before Kennan stuffs himself silly."

EPILOGUE

WELCOME TO THE WORLD, LASS

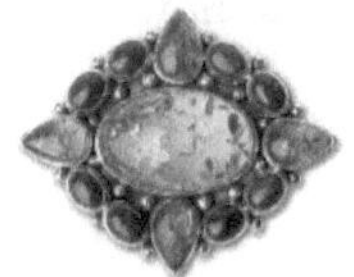

ROSE ADAIR MACKAY was born at first light on a balmy late July morning. She came into the world with such a squall that Cullodina declared she had the strongest lungs of any bairn she'd helped birth.

"Ye have a feisty one there, My Lady," the healer pronounced with a wide smile as she swaddled the tiny red babe in linen and passed her over to Keira.

Favoring the healer with an exhausted smile, Keira took the bairn in her arms. "And I'm pleased to hear it," she replied, her gaze riveted upon the tiny face. "The world is cruel to the meek."

Cullodina bent down then and gently extracted one of the babe's hands from her swaddling. She placed a silver coin in Rose's palm—a custom that was supposed to ensure a life of wealth and prosperity. All gazes remained on wee Rose, as her tiny fingers closed tightly over the coin.

The healer grinned. "It looks like she will be a frugal one too."

Laughter echoed off the walls at this comment.

"She is bonny, Keira." Seated next to the bed, Connor Mackay's eyes glittered with tears. "Just like ye."

Keira's smile widened, her gaze locking with her husband's.

Watching them, a lump rose in Maggie's throat.

Of course she was delighted that the birth had been an easy one and that the laird and lady of Farr now had a bonny baby daughter, but this was the first birth she'd attended since her own traumatic one.

She'd recently confided in Keira, Cait, and Jaimee that she'd never be able to have children of her own. She'd braced herself for their pity, yet Jaimee had merely enfolded her in a hug, while Keira and Cait assured her that she would be godmother to their bairns. Maggie wondered if they worried about how Morgan had taken the news that he would never father a child with his wife, yet if so, all of them were too polite to ask. Their kindness had reduced her to tears all the same.

A warm breeze filtered into the chamber. A mild spring had slid into a balmy summer, the warmest in years. Locals were saying that it would be an excellent harvest. Life was good, and the sound of a newborn's lusty wail brought a smile to Maggie's face.

Next to her, Morgan placed an arm around his wife's shoulders, squeezing gently. He didn't need to say anything, for he understood how she felt today. Glancing up at his face, she saw a smile curving his mouth.

"I hope Rose knows what an overbearing Da she's got," Morgan quipped, winking at his brother. "Just wait till the day a strapping warrior asks ye for her hand."

Connor cut him a frown. "I'll chase the bastard off," he growled.

This comment brought a snort from the doorway. Jaimee stood there, leaning against the doorframe, her gaze riveted upon the cooing bundle in Keira's arms. "That's rich, brother … since ye continue to harp on about finding me a husband."

The laird's attention swiveled to his sister. Their gazes locked in a duel that Maggie was coming to know well of late.

A month earlier, Connor had invited a handful of his clansmen from the other Mackay holdings to Farr for a few days, in the hope that Jaimee would find one of them to be a suitable husband.

She hadn't.

"Ye are two and twenty, Jaimee," Connor reminded her, unnecessarily, Maggie thought. "It is time ye wed."

Jaimee's mouth thinned. "Or no man will want me, is that yer point?"

"No ... but ye—"

"Jaimee," a soft yet insistent female voice interrupted. "Come over and meet yer wee niece." Keira cast her husband a quelling look and beckoned to Jaimee with her free hand. "She will be as lovely as her auntie, I'd say."

Jaimee's expression softened, and she pushed herself off the door-frame, venturing forward.

"Come closer," Keira encouraged her. "Pull up a stool at my side, and ye may hold Rose."

Jaimee's face tensed. "I don't want to hurt her."

"Ye won't ... here."

Warmth spread through Maggie as she watched the scene before her. Jaimee's cheeks flushed with pleasure when she took the swaddled bairn from Keira, holding her reverently in the crook of her arm.

"Hello, Rose Mackay," Jaimee murmured, her gaze gleaming. "Welcome to the world, lass."

The afternoon sun slanted across the walled garden, causing heat to radiate off the surrounding stone. Sweating, Maggie sat back on her heels and pushed a damp lock of hair off her face.

She rose to her feet then, wincing as she shook out her cramped legs and back. She'd been working in the garden, weeding in amongst the flower-beds, for most of the afternoon, and her limbs now protested.

Surveying her work, Maggie's lips curved in satisfaction. This garden was Keira's pride and joy, although her friend hadn't been able to do any work here for a while. She'd surely be pleased to see it looking so beautiful.

"There ye are." A man's low voice intruded upon her solitude. "I thought ye might be out riding Walnut … it's too fine an afternoon to be pulling up weeds."

Maggie turned to see her husband striding toward her. "Someone has to," she replied. "I want Keira to be impressed when she ventures down here again." She paused there, glancing up at the keep above. The faint cry of a bairn drifted down from one of the open windows. "How is she faring?"

"Connor assures me Keira's recovering well … she keeps pestering Cullodina to let her get out of bed." He grinned then. "She'll be back in the garden sooner than ye think."

Maggie smiled at this news, relief weakening her limbs. The hours after giving birth were a dangerous time for women.

Sensing her shift in mood, Morgan drew close, his expression growing serious. "Is all well, Maggie?" he asked gently. "I know today would've been hard for ye."

Maggie's smile faded. However, seeing the worry clouding his eyes, she sought to allay his fears. "It's an emotional time," she admitted, for she didn't hold back what she felt these days—she'd made him a promise that she intended to keep. "But the joy of the day overshadows everything else, and I'm happy for that." She stepped close to him. "Soon Connor and Keira will have a noisy brood of bairns … and I'll be so busy helping to look after them that I won't have time to dwell on my own childless state." She paused there, tensing as worry wreathed up inside her. "And ye, Morgan. Did seeing Rose this morning make ye wish for bairns of yer own?"

It pained her to ask the question again. But he wanted her to be open with him, and so she would. This afternoon, she needed her husband's reassurance.

His eyes met hers, surprise shadowing their green depths. "No, my love," he murmured. "I've made peace with how things are … although I know it's easier for a man to say such things." He favored her with a slow, tender smile. "Yet I already have everything I need, standing right here before me."

Maggie's throat thickened. Morgan had no idea what his words meant to her.

Her husband's smile turned wicked then. "Plus, I've always preferred dogs to bairns. The keep's huntsman tells me Gritta is in whelp … we can expect a brood of excitable pups by the end of the harvest."

Maggie laughed. "So she did get in with the dogs when she was last in heat, after all?" Gritta had disappeared for an entire afternoon a couple of weeks previous and had returned to their bed-chamber looking decidedly smug.

"Aye, it appears so."

Maggie studied his face. "And what of ye and the situation with Niel? I know ye were worried about the safety of the clan. Ye haven't spoken much about it recently."

Her husband released a sigh, before giving her a rueful grin. "Like ye, I have to learn when to let things go—to accept that some things are just bigger than me. The Gunns are likely to cause the Mackays problems again at some point, but we'll all just have to deal with that when the day comes." Morgan stepped close then, his smile fading. "But enough about such things. That's not why I sought ye out this afternoon."

Maggie realized then he was carrying something in his right hand. She hadn't even noticed.

"I have a gift for ye," he said, holding out his hand. Soft velvet encased the offering.

Maggie cast her husband an enquiring look. "But my birthday isn't till December."

"I know that," he answered with a snort. "This is a belated wedding gift, mo chridhe. Our ceremony in Inverness was hardly romantic. I can never relive that day, but I'd like to make amends for it."

Smiling, Maggie took the parcel and unwrapped it. A beautiful amber brooch lay within, framed by tiny garnets of obsidian. "Oh, Morgan," she breathed. "It's lovely."

"Ye like it then?" He smiled down at her, his face hopeful. "Here, let me pin it to yer kirtle." Morgan took the brooch and fastened it, just above the curve of her left breast, against her heart. "I had a jeweler in Tongue fashion it," he admitted. "I wanted something truly special for ye."

Maggie lifted a hand to her chest, her fingers curving over the brooch. "It's the bonniest thing anyone has ever given me," she replied, her voice catching. "Thank ye, mo ghràdh. I will treasure it always." She paused then and raised her face to look at him. The tenderness and love in his eyes made her chest ache.

"I'm glad it pleases ye," he said softly.

Maggie's vision misted. Reaching up, she cupped his cheek. "Aye, it's beautiful," she replied huskily. "But, like ye, I already have everything I will ever need before me. Ye are the greatest gift of all, Morgan Mackay."

The End

FROM THE AUTHOR

Wow, I absolutely adored writing this emotional story ... but it was also a lot of work to get 'just right'. Maggie and Morgan were such a fun couple to bring together. However, their story is a complex, multi-layered one. They're both mature and a little 'world-weary'—my favorite characters to write about. I also enjoyed being able to split this novel between Inverness and Farr Castle, with a little side trip to Scone.

HIGHLANDER ENTANGLED has some meaty themes: dealing with grief, guilt, fear of love, and the inability to have children. My heroine had to face her fears to get her happy ending, but fortunately, she had Morgan. Sigh—I loved writing that guy!

Get ready for Jaimee and Alexander's exciting story. Up next!

Jayne x

HISTORICAL NOTES

Like Book One, HIGHLANDER ENTANGLED is a character-driven story. But, as with all my novels, I base it around real historical figures and events.

The story starts in 1427, in the aftermath of the Battle of Harpsdale the year before. This battle was where Connor, Morgan, and Jaimee lost their father. It was a Scottish clan battle fought at Achardale, about 8 miles (13 km) south of Thurso in the Highlands. The Clan Mackay had invaded Caithness from the west, and Harpsdale was where the local Clan Gunn chose to make a stand. Despite 'great slaughter' on both sides, the battle appears to have been inconclusive.

King James's parliament in Inverness did take place in the spring of 1427. The purpose was to restore order in the Highlands. Many Highland chiefs were arrested and punished including Alexander MacDonald, 'Lord of the Isles', and his mother, Mary, the Countess of Ross. Some of the arrested clan-chiefs were imprisoned and a small number were beheaded.

Angus-Dow Mackay and his son, Niel (the historical sources spell his name as both 'Niel' and 'Neil'—I've opted for the former use), were real historical figures (full character glossary on the next page), as is George Gunn, the Gunn clan-chief.

In my story, Niel Mackay is sentenced to imprisonment at Bass Rock in the Firth of Forth—this did happen. Henceforth, he was known as Niel-Bass-Mackay. Angus Mackay really did offer up his son as a pledge of obedience to the king, although the telling of this incident is entirely mine!

I've tried to stay accurate to the historical records of King James I of Scotland. Of the House of Stewart, James was a highly cultured man and a popular king. His popularity was due to improvements he made in the administration of justice for the common people. At the time of my story, King James would have been 33 years old. Before that, he'd spent many years in England, after being taken prisoner at the age of 11, as an uncrowned king. It was only with his marriage to Joan Beaufort in 1424 that he was able to return to Scotland and take the throne. King James was murdered on 20 February, 1437, in his chambers in the Greyfrairs monastery in Perth, by men acting for his uncle, Walter, Earl of Atholl.

The Mackays of Farr did reside at Farr Castle (also known as Borve Castle). These days only the ruined shell of Farr Castle remains. With a stunning position overlooking the sea, the castle was used in ancient times as an outpost for raiding other clans. It is said that a Norseman called Torquil may have built the castle.

The ruins of Farr Castle sit upon a precipitous promontory, joined to the mainland by a narrow neck, across which a high rampart with flanking ditches has been drawn. The site could also be approached from the north-east by sea. Only footings and the courtyard wall remain, but the outline of a range of rectangular buildings, with thick stone walls, can be traced on the west. The promontory slopes down towards the seaward end where there are circular and rectangular hollows, probably marking the site of the well and more foundations.

And of course, Inverness Castle did stand at the time of this novel. King James did hold his parliament there in the spring of 1427. However, the grand pink-hued castle we see today in Inverness bears little resemblance to the much smaller structure that would have stood in the early fifteenth century. When Morgan makes his trip to

Scone, he would have visited the abbey. Scone Palace wasn't constructed until later.

I also mention the feud between Clan Forbes and Clan Leslie in this novel. Just like the feuding between the Gunns and Mackays, it was a real one. The feud started in 1400 with a Leslie stealing and marrying the fiancée of a Forbes. Andrew Leslie, 3rd Baron of Balquhain (who just happened to have over 70 illegitimate children!), ran off with the 'Fair Maid of Kemnay' the betrothed of John 'of the Black Lip' Forbes of Druminor. This launched the pair into a long-running dispute that would span many generations.

I hope you have enjoyed my notes. I really enjoyed researching the history and landscape of this wild and beautiful corner of Scotland.

STOLEN HIGHLAND HEARTS CHARACTER GLOSSARY

The Mackay clan
Angus-Dow Mackay (clan-chief)
Estelle Mackay (Mackay clan-chief's wife)
Niel Mackay (Mackay clan-chief's son)
Rory Mackay (former chieftain of Farr—deceased)
Connor Mackay (current chieftain of Farr)
Morgan Mackay (Connor's brother)
Jaimee Mackay (Connor's sister)
Kennan Mackay (Connor, Morgan, and Jaimee's cousin)
Cait Mackay (Kennan's wife)
Domhnall Mackay (Connor's uncle)
Chrissa (servant at Farr Castle)
Robert Mackay (chieftain of Balnakeil broch)
Duncan Mackay (Robert Mackay's brother)

The Gunn clan
Maddoc Gunn (sheep farmer and wool merchant)
Moira Gunn (Maddoc's wife)
Keira Gunn (the youngest of Maddoc and Morag's six daughters)
George Gunn (clan-chief)
Alexander Gunn (Gunn clan-chief's eldest son)

The Ross clan
Graeme Ross (Ross chieftain)
Rhianna Ross (Graeme Ross's niece—eloped with a warrior named Callum)
Maggie Ross (Rhianna's elder sister—widowed)
Athol Ross (the chieftain's manservant)

Other characters
Mother Jean (Prioress of Iona nunnery)
Father Lachlan (chaplain at Farr Castle)
Cullodina (healer at Farr Castle)
Aileana Munro (Maggie's maid)
Campbell Munro (Maggie's first husband—deceased)
Elsa (head cook at Farr Castle)

ABOUT THE AUTHOR

Award-winning author Jayne Castel writes epic Historical and Fantasy Romance. Her vibrant characters, richly researched historical settings and action-packed adventure romance transport readers to forgotten times and imaginary worlds.

Jayne is the author of the Amazon bestselling BRIDES OF SKYE series—a Medieval Scottish Romance trilogy about three strong-willed sisters and the men who love them. An exciting new series about three lost Roman centurions and the brave-hearted Scottish women who love them, THE IMMORTAL HIGHLAND CENTURIONS is now available as well. In love with all things Scottish, Jayne also writes romances set in Dark Ages Scotland ... sexy Pict warriors anyone?

When she's not writing, Jayne is reading (and re-reading) her favorite authors, cooking Italian feasts, and taking her dog, Juno, for walks. She lives in New Zealand's beautiful South Island.

Connect with Jayne online:
www.jaynecastel.com
www.facebook.com/JayneCastelRomance/
www.instagram.com/jaynecastelromance/
Email: contact@jaynecastel.com